THE DUKE'S VIRGIN

FILTHY RICH ROYALS

M. S. PARKER

D1506325

BELMONTE PUBLISHING, LLC

Copyright © 2019 Belmonte Publishing LLC

Published by Belmonte Publishing LLC

ONE

STACIA

If my phone rang one more time, I might rip my hair out.

And honestly, considering how hot it was proving to be, that might be a good idea. It was only May, and the temperature in New York City already had me sweltering.

I eyed the number on my screen, then shoved it into my purse, deciding I'd much rather find a ponytail holder than answer the phone.

I'd have to take the call sooner or later, though.

It was my mother, and if I didn't answer, she'd send one of her people around to *collect* me.

That was how it was always phrased.

Like I was some lost bauble.

If I proved to be hard to *collect*, my father would be reeled into the game, and that would make it so much more fun. The entire thing was enough to give me a headache, and I'd only dodged two calls from her in the past few days.

Two.

It might as well have been twenty, because I already knew what she wanted.

Come join me for tea, Stacia. We haven't caught up in some time. Or dinner. We should chat.

Her lightly accented Italian voice would be bright and warm, offering no insight as to what lay ahead, but as soon as I appeared on her doorstep, the ax would fall.

The marital ax.

Ever since I completed my Master's degree a few months earlier, she'd been on me about *finding a good man*. Well, before that really. The subtle suggestions had started a year into my studies at Oxford, but I'd brushed them aside. Each year, they'd grown more and more direct, and now, *nobody* could consider the questions *subtle*. Frankly, they bordered on obnoxious, in my opinion, but I doubted Mom would listen if I tried to tell her.

I finally found a hairband in the bottom of the Gucci purse I'd bought myself as a graduation present. It was ridiculously impractical—bonus. Also, it was in no way subtle or discreet—another bonus. It was a soft, demure pink, but that was the only *subtle* thing about the purse.

On the front was a giant bee, wings spread out, and the glitzy little insect with its red crystal stones caught the light in a delightfully frivolous fashion. My mother hated it. It was juvenile, but that had been my goal when I bought it, although I *had* loved the purse itself.

After securing the purse and settling the long, crossbody strap over my shoulder, I gathered the heavy weight of my dark hair into my hands and twisted it up, securing it with the ponytail holder. Immediately, I felt the relief of a breeze kissing my bare nape, and I breathed a little easier.

"That's more like it," I murmured.

As I started down the wide path that wound through Central Park, I tried to push away the lingering irritation caused by my mother's phone call, despite having not answered.

It wouldn't get any easier to dodge her. She'd called once already today.

Dad had called earlier, and I wouldn't be able to put them off much longer.

I hadn't seen either of them since my graduation party nearly three weeks earlier, and each time I *did* talk to one of them, the message became less and less subtle.

Especially on my mother's part.

You graduated. That's what you said you wanted. Now what, darling?

"Now what, *what?*" That was what I *wanted* to say. That was what the rebellious part of me *demanded* I say. That rebellious streak was wide and deep, although very well hidden. Sure, it managed to gain control and nudge me into the store where I'd seen the silly pink purse with its silly bumblebee decoration. But that rebellious streak wasn't so wide as to tell my *mother* what I really wanted to tell her.

Fuck off.

Even the idea struck me as so absurd, I had to swallow back a wild laugh.

Abruptly, I realized people were looking at me, and I glanced around. I'd made it all the way to Belvedere Castle in Central Park. Blowing out a breath, I peered at the structure, using my hand to shade my eyes from the sun while all around me, kids played and voices rose in the air.

"Screw it," I said in a final tone. I'd come out here to get away from her phone calls—*and* my father's—and that was exactly what I was going to do.

Not giving myself a second to think about it, I turned off my phone, then looked around, centering myself.

I'd head toward Broadway, I decided. It was early yet, but I'd grab dinner and see a play. Tomorrow, I'd figure out just what my parents wanted, although it might not be anything specific.

And if it was?

"I'll deal with it," I told myself.

After all, what else could I do?

Avoiding them forever might sound appealing on rare occasion—okay, maybe it was more than *rare*—but it wasn't practical. My parents were cool and distant, but I loved them. Besides, it wasn't like they could force me to settle down, and that was what Mom was after these days.

She could nag, nudge, and try to negotiate all she wanted, but in the end, it was my choice.

THE ITALIAN BISTRO I selected for dinner had a shaded area out front, with fans overhead that kept the area cool in the unseasonable heat, and I thanked the hostess as she put a menu in front of me.

I had time to kill before the seven o'clock showing I'd selected. It was only five, and the theater was less than a ten-minute walk from the bistro, so I was going to indulge in a lengthy meal. While working on my master's, time to indulge hadn't always been available, even during the breaks. In order to avoid my mother's meddling, I'd spent summers volunteering, doing everything from volunteering down in Puerto Rico after Hurricane Maria, to spending a month with Habitat for Humanity after a hurricane hit Florida, to traveling to South Dakota to spend a few weeks at a Lakota reservation for more volunteer work.

Mom loved to talk up the volunteer work, although she always got digs in about how little time it left me to spend with her and my father. She never seemed to get that was a small part of why I did it. A small part. Not all. Nowhere near all.

There was too much outside the pampered and polished world that existed for my parents, and I didn't want to be so isolated that I was ignorant of it.

But that was something neither of them would ever understand.

Sitting at the table, I flipped open the menu. As I started to skim the appetizers, a server approached, carrying a carafe of water.

My phone started ringing as she poured, and I ignored it, figuring it was my mom. Again. "Can I get you something other than water?"

"Oh, yes..."

She laughed at the fervent reply. "Do you have something in mind or would you like a suggestion?"

"I'm always open to suggestions."

She grinned and listed the current house specialties as

the phone went silent. I went with the house version of a Manhattan, and after she left, I picked up my water and grudgingly looked at my phone.

To my surprise, it wasn't my mother or my father.

Actually, the missed call was from the *one* relative I didn't hate hearing from.

My cousin Aeric. With a grin, I hit the phone icon as I pulled my Bluetooth device from my purse. I hadn't even had time to connect it before he answered, his richly accented voice booming out of my phone's speaker.

"Cousin!"

"Hello, Your Royal Highness." I grinned, tapping the icon to switch over to video as the Bluetooth finally connected. His lean, handsome face filled my phone's screen.

"Don't start," he said in a warning tone, although he smiled back.

"If I can't razz my royal cousin, then who can?" I shrugged and took a sip of my water.

He peered at the screen with a frown. "You're out. Are you busy? Am I interrupting?"

"No. Just having dinner."

"Alone or with a friend?"

Rolling my eyes, I said, "Don't start."

"I'm just asking." His lashes swept low, all but concealing his pale gray eyes, although not the mischievous sparkle. "I'm always on the search for my princess, you know. Maybe she's eating dinner with you now."

"Ha, ha." I made a face at him. "I take it your mother is after you to settle down and get married too?"

Our mothers were sisters, and one more thing we had in

common was our mothers' obsession with seeing us settled down and married, producing offspring one after the other. In his mother's defense, it was a familial obligation. A prince needed an heir and all that shit.

"It's what they do, right?" He shrugged, some of the humor slipping from his eyes. "But I didn't call to talk about our annoying parents. Listen...are you doing anything this weekend?"

"Ah..." I blinked, scanning my mental schedule, although I shouldn't have bothered. It was blank. "Nope. Other than the usual. Sleeping in, taking care of groceries, that sort of thing."

He cocked his head thoughtfully. "I've never had to take care of the usual. I've had a more normal life than some people in my position, I know, but I'd be lost in a grocery store. Where do you even start?"

"With a list." I grinned at him. "I figured it out. You could too."

He gave me a look that was a mix of speculation and panic, and I had a sudden image of him wandering around one of the mega-sized grocery stores here in the United States. Granted, those weren't predominant over in Europe, but the image of my royal cousin getting lost in the aisles of Walmart or a Super Target was mildly entertaining, and I wondered what his parents would think.

"If you decide to go on such an adventure, let me know so I can record it for posterity," I told him.

"Your drink, ma'am."

I looked up at the sound of the server's voice. "Thank

you." I tapped an item on the appetizer menu. "Can I get an order, please?"

She nodded and disappeared as quickly as she'd appeared, leaving me alone to my conversation. Picking up the Manhattan, I took a sip and smiled at Aeric. "It's past midnight there. What has you calling me?"

"You know me. I'm a night owl." He faked a big yawn. "Up at all hours, partying."

I cocked a brow at him, grinning. "That is so *not* you."

He laughed. "True, true. Well, if you'd look at your phone's call history, you'd notice I've called a couple of times today...I'd almost swear you've been avoiding me."

"You...I..." Scowling, I checked the call log. Blood rushed to my cheeks as I saw that I had, indeed, missed a few calls from him. "Sorry, Aeric. I've been dodging most calls the past two days. Mom is at it again. Last week, she was all set on fixing me up with the son of a banker she knows." I made a face at him. "The guy is a total douche. He went to Oxford, graduated a year before I did and has an awful reputation, but when I pointed that out to my mother, I got the standard line...'boys will be boys.'"

"Shall I point out to her that you shouldn't settle for a *boy*, but a man?" Aeric offered a polite smile, but there was a glint in his eyes.

The protectiveness he felt toward me warmed me.

The two of us had a closer relationship than I had with my own parents, a fact that saddened me even as it comforted. At least I *had* a good relationship with somebody I was related to, but at the same time, it was pathetic that I relied on somebody besides my parents to be there when I needed someone to lean on.

"I already told her that I'd rather not get involved with somebody who was still falling back on the '*boys will be boys*' line to excuses shitty behavior in his twenties." Taking a sip of my drink, I added, "She didn't have much of a response to that. Bonus, she left me alone for a few days."

"Then you didn't just win, you scored extra points." He tipped an imaginary hat. "But we've digressed. I was actually calling to see if you wanted to join me for the weekend. I've got an engagement party to attend, and I need a companion."

In the middle of taking another sip of the cocktail, I paused, then lowered the glass. "Are you hard up for company, Aeric?"

"No." He snorted. "But you know as well as I do that things can get...sticky for a man in my position."

"Poor prince." I gave him a faux pout.

"Poor little rich girl," he retorted. "And don't act like you don't know what I mean. I don't have an excess of casual female acquaintances. You understand the reason. If I ask some woman I hardly know, the press will have a field day, and it could set that woman up for rampant speculation. But with you..."

Rolling my eyes, I finished his sentence for him, "We don't have to worry. I'm not that recognizable in European society, or even among American society since I prefer to hide away and cultivate my *Ice Princess* reputation. If I go with you, I'm in and out, and people can just speculate away. Do I have it right?"

"You're a smart one. Have I ever told you how much I

admire your intelligence, Stacia?" Aeric flashed a brilliant, blinding smile at me.

"Whatever." I couldn't help but laugh a little. "So...an engagement...who is getting engaged?"

"A friend. You might know him. He went to Oxford. Geraint Hahn from Luxembourg. I'm friends with his brother."

Frowning, I riffled through my mental files. I'd met far too many people at Oxford. "I think...wait a second. Isn't he a member of one of the royal families over there?"

"One and the same. Were you friends?"

"Not so much. He wasn't in any of my classes, but we might have seen each other in passing a few times. That's it. He wasn't opposed to parties, and you know me."

"You were opposed to anything resembling fun," he teased with a light laugh.

"Fuck you," I said with little heat. I had no problem with *fun*, but the wild parties of college life had always left me unsettled, and since I was several years younger than my classmates, it made things that much more awkward. Aeric was well aware of this too. Because he knew, because he didn't judge me about any of this, I didn't resent his teasing. "So, Geraint is getting married. Who is his fiancée?"

"The Princess of Liechtenstein," he replied in a deadpan voice.

"Wow." Having a cousin with a royal title—and knowing he'd one day be the reigning monarch—had given me a much more down-to-earth viewpoint of royals. But the casual way he'd just dropped the news of what would probably be one of *the* royal wedding events had my eyes going wide. "That will be quite an event."

"Yes...and I need a companion for the engagement party. Will you come? Then there's a Formula One racing event I thought we could attend while you're here." Voice cajoling now, he added, "You'd have a week away from your mother's meddling, at least. What do you say?"

He hadn't even had to add the last part, really.

"Okay. I'm in. I'll look at flights once I'm off the phone."

"Brilliant...and no need. I've already got my people taking care of it." His satisfaction was unmistakable.

"That sure of me, huh?"

"Well." Humor laced his words. "I do know my cousin."

TWO

LUKA

Life would be a lot easier if I could move through it wearing a mask.

It was a crazy idea and would never come to pass, but I decided it was acceptable to indulge in the fantasy as I moved through halls discreetly lit, while doorways to the areas closed off were manned by black-garbed security staff wearing simple black domino masks that did little to hide their features.

I recognized each of them, and they, in turn, recognized me, dipping their heads in polite recognition while their gazes remained ever watchful, wire-thin communication devices running from ear to jaw so they could conduct their routine perimeter checks.

Near the end of the hall just before the grand staircase, I paused and checked the decorative mirror on the far left wall. My face was half-hidden by a mask, from mid-cheek upward. People who knew me well would recognize me, but of everyone attending the ball, I could only think of a handful who might fit that description, and most were family. My parents, my brother. Maybe a friend or two.

The one clear indicator that would have given me away was clothing and the unique accoutrements that went with formal garb worn by royalty at such an event.

But the plain black velvet coat displayed none of those, not the order nor the badge. I felt lighter for it and decided it was a welcome change. It likely wasn't one I'd enjoy again either.

The masquerade ball taking place in the palace's grand ballroom was the only reason it was happening now, and I had a feeling Geraint was behind the suggestion that we forgo tradition for the night.

Our mother had resisted, but the Grand Duke, our father, had laughed at Geraint's suggestion and waved a hand. "Why not? Enjoy it for the night."

I'd have to thank them both, I decided, appreciating the relative anonymity more than I'd expected as I walked down the hall through the ever-thickening crowds.

There were no lulls in conversation as I approached, and crowds didn't part like the Red Sea.

Save for the staff who took care to pay me little interest, it seemed nobody really noticed me.

It was fucking fantastic, a freedom I'd never known before, not growing up as the heir to the Grand Duchy of Luxembourg. Even traveling throughout Europe, I couldn't go too often without being recognized. It wasn't as incessant for me as it was for the British royal family—there were entire web pages devoted to tracking them as they traveled and vacationed, tips to watch for them when they tried to quietly leave home. All in all, that would have been enough to drive me mad, so I should appreciate my somewhat lesser notoriety.

Royal-spotting had become a modern-day hobby, though.

A trip to Paris could become a pain in the ass when I wanted to simply go about my business, and some tour group leader spotted me and pointed me out, making me the focus of a pack of Instagram-snapping tourists, all of them staring at me as if my trousers were around my ankles.

Tension crept through me as I pushed through the crowd near the grand arched doorways leading to the ballroom. Taking a deep breath, I slowly let the air escape. I had no idea that much frustration had been building inside me.

"I should probably keep this short," I muttered to myself, staring out over the throng of bodies already filling the dance floor.

My younger brother's engagement ball. I was still having a hard time believing that he would be married soon.

He had always been the more social one, so it shouldn't be such a surprise, but I had been so busy over the past few years that time had slipped away from me. How had he matured so quickly? When had it even started to happen?

I knew the answer, though.

I'd seen the change, practically overnight.

It had been just over two years ago at a funeral for one of my close friends. Brooding, I rested my hands on the balustrade and stared hard into the crowd without seeing a single soul. The death of the Heredity Prince of Liechtenstein had hit my brother harder than it had hit me.

Marcel and I had been friends. Geraint, though...well,

he'd idolized Marcel. We were close, my brother and me, but there was something akin to hero worship about the way he'd always looked at Marcel.

Then just like that, Marcel was gone.

Maturity had come on my younger brother hard and fast after that. Of course, so had love.

He'd met Katrina Von Brandt before. The younger sister of the two Von Brandt brothers, the girl was bright, sweet, and cheerful, and had half of Europe eating out of her palm.

She hadn't realized it, but within a few short hours, she'd had my little brother doing the same thing.

He'd waited nearly a year before approaching her, out of respect for her loss, but since then, the two of them had been all but attached at the hip.

Now, they were getting married.

I went to push away from the banister but stopped as an idea occurred to me. My brother as a father. I started to laugh, but the sound faded before it fully formed, and an odd, hollow ache settled in my chest instead.

Gazing down in the mass of bodies, I searched for him. It wasn't hard to pick my brother out of the crowd, even with the mask. It helped that I had seen him leaving his quarters earlier and knew what he wore. Plus, his bride-to-be had a head of pale, almost white-gold hair that was unmistakable.

They swung by almost directly below me only seconds after I'd spotted them, her full, wide skirt swirling out around her.

As they moved away from me, lost to the rhythm of the music and each other, it was impossible to miss how ridiculously happy they looked together.

Watching them, I was certain of one thing. They'd want to make a happy little family, sooner rather than later. It seemed like every royal on the continent was required to produce a baby within a year of marriage.

My parents were no doubt looking at me discreetly and wondering when I would get with the program. Not that I was old. I hadn't hit thirty yet, but I had no doubt they were starting to wonder.

At least if Geraint and Katrina got down to business, my parents would have a grandbaby to fuss over soon, there'd be another potential heir, and I would be off the hook for a while.

But they'd go back to it.

Back to wondering.

For the first time, I found myself doing the same thing.

"Stop it," I muttered.

Sooner or later, I'd have to find a wife and produce an heir myself, unless I wanted to let Geraint's future offspring become the next to inherit. Not that I minded the idea, but a country tended to look upon their leadership more securely if the current monarch had a direct heir.

Well, at least those few countries that still had monarchs.

Like mine. And even though I wasn't in a hurry, sooner was probably better.

For now, though, I wanted to enjoy spending time wandering around, having a drink, and having not a fucking soul realize who in the hell I was.

THREE

STACIA

"Wow."

My cousin looked over at me. Deadpan, he echoed my voice, right down to the flat American accent. *"Wow."*

Suppressing a smile, I nodded and looked around, taking in the lighting, the overall feel of age and wealth and elegance. Overhead, the ceiling was painted, and I wanted to spend time studying it. I even considered it, thinking about how much it would exasperate Aeric, but decided against it.

"Exactly what has you so *wowed*, cousin Stacia?" he asked.

"This." I waved a hand at the palace and shot another discreet look at the lovely ceiling overhead. "It's kind of amazing, isn't it?"

"It's okay," he said, tone bored. "You've seen where *I* live, Stacia. It's pretty amazing too."

I let the grin spill free as I met his eyes. "You don't have to be jealous, Aeric. Your palace is very special too. In its own way."

"In its..." He stopped and shook his head. "There are times when I wonder why I put up with you."

"Because I'm the only person on earth who will actually tease you. You live for it," I said as we followed the line winding through the elegant home.

It truly *was* a palace, and it did rival the Prince's Palace of Monaco, where Aeric lived with his family, although both were distinctly unique. I darted another look at the ceiling just as we moved into another room. Aeric leaned in. "If you like, I can ask if they have a divan so you can lay back and gawk at the ceiling like a typical American tourist."

"Be nice," I said, jabbing him in the ribs.

He flinched and muffled a laugh. "That's not playing very nice."

I ignored him and resisted the urge to crane my neck so I could see around the couple in front of us. We were almost to the doors. The music swelled, filling the air like a bubble waiting to burst, but it just...lingered, poignant and beautiful and bright.

When it finally ended, I let out a breath. "Wow."

"You keep saying that," he teased.

"The music is phenomenal." I squeezed his arm lightly with my fingers. "I think I'm glad you talked me into coming."

"I hardly had to twist your arm," he said with a light laugh. "You were more than ready to get away from your parents for a while. Have you thought more about just staying the summer here? Longer if you wanted."

"I don't know." He'd mentioned it earlier, but part of me felt like it was time I start looking for a job. I hadn't gotten my economics degree to *not* put it to use, had I?

"We do have a need for economists in Monaco, Stacia," he said.

Startled, I went to look at him.

But I never quite finished the movement.

The ballroom caught my gaze and my mouth parted.

"If you say *wow* again," Aeric murmured, leaning in, "my feelings will be hurt. The Prince's Palace in Monaco has a ballroom every bit as wonderful as this."

He could be right.

But I'd never seen the ballroom fully outfitted for its intended use.

Chandeliers glittered overhead, golden with light, while shards of crystal sent fractals of that gold glistening in ten thousand directions. The ceiling, again, was painted, but this depicted a midnight sky and the light from the chandeliers picked out what looked like pinpoint pricks of starlight and set them to gleaming. More crystal and gold sconces gleamed on the walls, and painted panels depicting celestial scenes were interspersed with mirrors that reflected gleaming light back into infinity.

"Come, Stacia. We're holding up the masses," Aeric said in my ear.

I followed his lead and let him guide me down the steps, still staring and trying to take everything in. I was grateful for the golden lace mask covering my face, giving me some obscurity because I had no doubt I was gawking.

"There's my friend, Geraint," Aeric said, leaning in and pointing out a man just as he danced by with a slim, petite blonde. They wore masks as well, but nothing could hide the glowing smiles on their faces. "And his fiancée, Princess Katrina Von Brandt of Lichtenstein."

"They look insanely happy." I smiled, not quite sure what to make of the hitch I felt in my chest. The marriage between my parents had given me a somewhat cynical view of romance and love.

Had they *ever* once looked at each other the way those two just had?

I doubted it.

Just like that, I was irritated with myself because now I was thinking of them again, and I'd come here to get away from all of that, to get away from my mother's incessant nagging and the annoyed looks I'd get from my father, as if he expected me to do something just to silence her. And I just might, for that very reason.

It was a terrible reason to marry anybody.

"You've got that face again."

Glancing over at Aeric, I frowned. "What face?"

"The one that tells me you're thinking of your parents." He flagged down a passing server and took two flutes of champagne. "What's the point of coming here so you could *not* think about them if you're *still* going to think about them?"

I sipped the bubbly, pausing to appreciate it before meeting Aeric's gaze. "She's been on me to *get serious about life* ever since Christmas, Aeric. It's like...I don't know. She finally got it in her head that I was determined to get my master's and she let it go for the time being, but once she saw the end was near? She's practically been lining up guys to launch at me."

"Launch them back." He shrugged dismissively. "It's not like you have to produce a fucking heir to the throne."

I made a face at him. "No. Just one for my father's business interests and preferably another for my mother to turn into another little society doll."

"Because she did so well with you." He gave me an amused glance and squeezed my arm to soften the words. "Stop worrying about Aunt Willa and Uncle Wade so much, darling. They can't *force* you to marry, and although you don't show it very often, you've got the spine to put your foot down. They know it, too."

I scowled at him.

"It's probably why she's giving you so much grief," he added. "She *knows* her only chance is to wear you down, and even that chance is slim. You're tougher than she is. You always have been."

"I know." I sighed and looked out over the whirl of bodies. "I guess. I just...shit. It's hard to date anyone in the city when most everyone knows who my father is. They either want to schmooze with him, or they're worried he'll get wind of their interest in me and swoop in like some financial hawk to make sure the man isn't a pauper."

"Well, he is a bit of a bastard in that field." Aeric shrugged and finished his champagne. A server was there to take the glass only seconds after he'd lowered it.

I finished mine in a rush and let her take that flute as well. Clutching Aeric's arm, I tugged him along. "Come on. You're right. I don't want to think about my mother, my father...any of that. Distract me, cousin."

Aeric grinned wide and gave me a regal bow. "As you

wish."

I laughed as he swept me around with a grand flourish, then onto the dance floor. "I bet you're hoping I don't step on your toes," I said, laughing as we fell into step with those around us. Aeric had told me earlier that the ball would be less *stuffy*—his term, not mine—than most, but for the first hours, there would be traditions like waltzes that must be observed.

"You dance very well." He gazed at me somberly. "Wherever did you learn?"

Rolling my eyes, I went along with the joke. "On the wild streets of New York City."

"They teach waltzing there as well as criminal mischief. Excellent. You're a well-rounded individual."

The glimmer in his eyes had me laughing. "Be careful. Somebody will hear you and believe it."

He lifted a shoulder. "Anyone with a brain knows that crime infestation is a problem, especially in large cities. The way my mother talks about it—"

I gave a very undignified snort. "Mine doesn't help. Half the time, I wonder why she doesn't talk my father into moving upstate to get *away from the bad elements.*"

He rolled his eyes. "The closest your mother comes to any 'bad element' is if a tourist stumbles across her path on her way into Goldman Sachs."

"That happened." I gave him a look of mock concern. "It was horrifying. I really don't know how she recovered from the trauma of seeing some average-class citizen standing there on the sidewalk just...*breathing.*"

Aeric laughed, the sound booming out over the crowd,

catching the attention of others near us. "Appalling, Stacia. Absolutely appalling."

My cheeks heated even though the gazes drifted away quickly. Glaring at him through the eyeholes of the mask, I said, "Don't be so dramatic. You're an attention hound, but I'm not."

"I'm not an attention hound." His smile faded, and he lifted an elegant shoulder. "It just...comes with the life. This is nice, though. I don't get to enjoy the relative anonymity of a masked ball often. I should make a practice of them at home... then sneak out to enjoy some solitude."

"Your mother wouldn't like that."

"I know." He sighed pragmatically. "We are our mothers' children."

A couple drifted by, and he nodded at them. "The happily engaged couple. Geraint, with the Princess Katrina of Lichtenstein. Geraint's father is the Grand Duke of Luxembourg."

"I'm in the presence of such royalty," I said, teasing him. "How did they meet? *The Bachelor: European Royals* edition?"

"Don't go saying that out loud," he muttered. "You'll give somebody ideas. And...no. I think they've vaguely known each other off and on for years, but not long ago, Princess Katrina's oldest brother was killed in an accident." He hesitated a moment, and I saw a flicker in his eyes that told me he'd been friendly, at least, with the young woman's brother.

"I'm sorry." I touched his arm.

He covered my hand with his and nodded. "Thank you. We were friends. Not close, but friends nonetheless. Geraint briefly spoke with her at the funeral and has been starry-eyed ever since, from what I've heard. Not that he'd admit to that. He waited about a year for the sake of propriety, then asked her out."

"Propriety?"

"Her brother was next in line to rule Lichtenstein. Since then, that's fallen to the next oldest, her brother, Prince Bastian."

"So many titles."

"Oh, that's just the start...come on." He gave me another quick smile, then took my hand, giving a quick tug.

Thirty minutes later, my head full of names and titles and quick little snatches of background information, I stood on the sideline, sipping water while Aeric spoke to an acquaintance. He'd tried to draw me into the conversation, but I wanted a few minutes to just breathe, and he'd gotten the point, chatting softly while I waited a few steps away.

That put me in the perfect position to witness a terribly intimate moment. A couple had their heads close together, murmuring softly as they came to a stop at the edge of the dance floor. He lifted his hand and stroked it down her neck. She shivered in response. I could see it from several feet away.

That was all that happened. Nothing improper or vulgar. But standing there watching, it hit me hard that I'd never had that sort of connection. Even a brief one.

Thinking of my decidedly lonely social life back home, all the pressure I was facing from my mother, none of that helped the odd ache suddenly weighing me down.

A loneliness that wouldn't be getting better any time

soon.

That was just a grim reality. The men at home who showed any interest usually fell into one of two categories. They were pushed toward me by my mother or people in her circle. Or they knew enough about me on their own and decided to 'try their luck,' as one arrogant douchebag had informed me after I declined several invitations to dinner. "You really are an ice princess, aren't you?" he'd said. "I thought I'd try my luck...nobody can be that icy, but I guess you proved me wrong.

It was enough to make just about any woman leery.

Melancholy, I watched the couple from under my lashes until they broke apart. A moment later, they were gone. I swung my gaze away only to find myself staring at another couple, these two engaged in a light flirtation.

Something else I hadn't experienced.

Was I the only one?

I wasn't. Logically, I knew that.

Just like logically, I knew my intentional isolation didn't help me much on the social front. I'd earned my *Ice Princess* reputation all on my own, and the social circle I moved in—when forced—was decidedly small. They all knew I was somewhat withdrawn, although they assumed it was just because I was stand-offish, uptight, and as snooty as my parents.

That wasn't the problem. It just took me a while to open up to people. A bit of shyness mixed in was all it took to convince others my age that I was just cold.

Having that rep—and having a father who could buy any given block in New York City at the drop of a whim—didn't exactly make me *approachable*. Besides, I had to worry about gossip back home, because I definitely didn't want to feed my mother's obsession, nor did I want to start up a relationship with someone intent on garnering my family connections—and the money.

Or somebody who might be working with my mother in some miserable match making attempt.

But nobody here knows.

The idea hit me then.

Suddenly, like a bolt of lightning.

Nobody here knows...

Nobody knew about my Ice Princess rep. Nobody knew about my parents' money or their social standing or anything else about me.

I didn't have to worry about that stuff popping up and becoming a barrier, did I?

Sure, I couldn't find some magical cure to my loneliness, but I wasn't expecting that. My parents' business-like, tidy marriage had opened my eyes to the idea of a *romance*. But there was more to relationships than romance, right?

I was also a virgin at twenty-three. I didn't even know *how* to approach a guy and that got in the way of things too. If I couldn't figure out how to approach a man, how was I supposed to get past this awkward thing on my end? I could always be the initiator back home, which would help when it came to circumventing parental hookups, but first I needed to figure all of that out.

If I fumbled things here, it wouldn't matter. Nobody knew me, and I'd never see this hypothetical someone again.

My mind started to race.

FOUR

LUKA

I'd stayed only as late as was polite at the party, ready to retire to my quarters so I could be alone.

Turning in early, I got a relatively decent night's sleep and woke fully rested and ready to go when the alarm went off.

My parents had off-handedly mentioned breakfast plans but didn't give me any details on said plans. That had been my personal assistant, Stuart. He'd asked what I planned on wearing for the breakfast with the Hereditary Prince, which clued me in. My parents were subtly nudging more and more responsibility onto me, and that often came with having meals or meetings worked into my schedule.

Our country was friendly with Lichtenstein. Luxembourg was friendly with most every country in Europe, but there were some with which we shared a closer relationship.

Lichtenstein was one of them, and I was already friends with the Hereditary Prince, Sebastian Von Brandt. I'd known his older brother, Marcel, better than the younger Von

Brandt, but we got along well. We'd spoken briefly at his wedding a little more than a year ago, and once or twice since then.

Now as I finished reviewing the file Stuart had put together, I was grateful of one thing more than any other. At least I wouldn't be bored senseless during the meal. Bastian and I were close in age and had similar interests, plus his wife was wonderful.

Stuart waited in the hall as I left, his round, faintly flushed face folded into an affable smile. "Do you need anything before your breakfast, Your Highness?"

"No." I gestured down the hall. "I told you it wasn't necessary to be here today. I'm heading to Monaco later."

"The race." His eyes lit. "Are you driving this time or working on the car?"

"Don't mention the driving," I warned, shaking my head. My parents would never let me hear the end of it if they knew I'd taken a few turns around the track in a Formula One race car.

They weren't overly protective, but they were acutely aware of familial responsibilities. I tried to be, but that didn't mean I wasn't determined to live my own life as much as I could.

They understood that better than some, but the accident that had killed Marcel had shaken many of the older families in Europe, mine included.

Stuart's face sobered, although his eyes still reflected amusement. "Of course. But you should know they're out on a walk with Princess Katrina's parents, showing them the grounds."

"Discussing the wedding, I'd bet." I was glad I hadn't gotten dragged into that mess.

Stuart gave a quick nod. "I'll be off if you're certain you don't need me. I've checked your transportation plans. Everything is set."

I checked the time as I jogged down the stairs to the formal dining room. We didn't always use the large one, but with guests in residence—and many of them people like Bastian Von Brandt—everything was formal.

Bastian and his wife were already there, sitting and drinking coffee. Spying me, he went to rise, but I waved him back toward his seat. "Please, don't." With a grin, I said, "We know each other well enough not to bother with such etiquette when it's just us, don't we?"

"I have no problem with it." He gestured to Regan as she lowered herself back to her seat. "You remember my wife."

"Of course."

She flashed me a smile. "It was a lovely party last night. Katrina was delighted."

"I'm glad. Your German is improving."

"Slowly." She made a face. "Almost everybody in Vaduz speaks English, which makes it easy to be lazy."

"You've got enough on your..." Frowning, I paused, trying to remember the expression.

"Plate?" she suggested. "It sounds odd in German, but I get the point."

"It does sound better in English. But the point is the same. You've enough to learn, enough to adjust to, moving from New York City to Vaduz, going from a Broadway star to the life you now live."

"I wouldn't give it up for anything." She sipped her coffee and rolled her eyes. "Although it was nice to sleep in this morning. I adore those rotten babies, but not hearing *Mama* at the crack of dawn for once is nice."

"That wasn't what you said earlier." Bastian stroked his fingers down her arm. "You were talking about how odd it was, how quiet it was, not having them around."

"Well. It is." She wrinkled her nose and went to add something else, but the arrival of breakfast had her breaking off.

She chatted with the staff and Bastian looked at me, a faint smile on his lips. "Regan makes friends with everybody she meets."

I couldn't tell if it was an explanation or a warning.

I knew there were those who'd be bothered by her friendliness toward the house staff. I wasn't, although I rarely said more than hello. I found myself smiling as she chatted with them, teasing out answering smiles and responses in just a few minutes.

Once we were alone, I looked at Bastian. "You've got a diplomatic weapon there. She just smiles and people melt."

Regan blushed. "What?"

"Nothing." Bastian leaned over and stroked his hand down her hair before kissing her temple. "Absolutely nothing."

"WHEN DO you plan to head back to Lichtenstein?"

Bastian glanced back at me while Regan continued ahead, lingering in front of a painting in the gallery.

"We leave later today." He nodded toward his wife. "She doesn't like being away from the babies too long. I don't either."

"It sounds like being a father agrees with you." Together, we walked over to study a wall that held old weapons, some of them more than a century old. "It's odd how well it suits you. I never would have imagined saying that."

Bastian laughed. "Neither would I." He rocked back on his heels, studying an ancient broadsword with admiring eyes. "I reviewed the information your assistant sent me about the software company. I've got a man in mind who would work well, if you're interested."

"Just send the names to Stuart. We'll talk again later." Ruefully, I smiled. "We're about to be family, after all. We have time. Which reminds me..." I checked my watch, a Blancpain Le Brassus Geraint had given me for my twenty-fifth birthday. "I need to leave. I have plans in Monaco, and if I don't leave now, I'll be late. Sorry."

I tried to actually sound that way, although I wasn't. I liked Bastian, but my plans for today had been set for months. The ball hadn't been planned until eight weeks ago.

To my surprise, Bastian gave me a quicksilver smile. "The Formula One race?"

"Excuse me?"

"Marcel and I used to watch. You've been seen on the track a few times. There's speculation, but he knows...he *knew* you." A shadow flicked across his face. "He mentioned you were friends with the driver."

"I...yes. We are friends."

"Have you ever driven one of the cars?" Bastian asked, a somewhat wistful note in his voice.

I glanced around, then leaned in. "Tell nobody. My parents have this terrible idea that I'm always responsible. It's easier if they keep thinking so."

"I understand." Humor glinting in his eyes, he held out a hand. "Enjoy your trip. I think I'll take Regan out to find my parents. It won't be long before we need to leave as well."

FIVE

STACIA

GIDDY WASN'T A FEELING I WAS OVERLY FAMILIAR WITH.
I had a passing acquaintance with it, sure. Like when I *finally*
escaped my parents' overwhelming presence by attending
Oxford, a university on the other side of the Atlantic Ocean.

Of course, my *giddy* glee at being away from their ever-
watchful presence hadn't lasted too long because, within a
few days, a *family friend* had dropped by to check on me,
setting up a pattern that had followed for years.

But I felt giddy now.

In an effort not to point at everything and everybody, I
had my hands shoved into my front pockets as Aeric led me
through yet another security checkpoint.

He was clearly a familiar figure here, and after a few
seconds to look me over and check the pass he'd arranged for
me, we were waved on through.

In moments, we were in the thick of things, surrounded
by people rushing around, dressed in everything from suits to
dressy casual to colorful jumpers...although I doubted the

guys in the jumpers would appreciate the term *jumper.* Coveralls, maybe? Uniform?

Uniform seemed apt, I decided as Aeric led me deeper into the midst, and I started seeing matching ones here and there.

"If I'd known you'd be this gleeful, I would have brought you to a Formula One race years ago."

Looking over at my cousin, I grinned. "I wish you would have. This is going to be *fun.*"

Somebody caught Aeric's attention, and I lapsed into silence, crossing my arms over my mid-section as I tried to fade away into the background. It wasn't hard. Nobody knew me here, and Aeric was Monaco's Crown Prince. His security guards were roaming around in a loose grid, and as the man who'd haled Aeric approached, I could see the bodyguards drawing in closer, but in such a subtle way, nobody was likely to notice unless they knew to look.

Aeric dismissed them with a casual wave of his hand, and they all fell back.

"Felix. Good to see you." Aeric half-turned to me and gestured. "May I introduce you to Stacia? She's visiting from America. An old family friend."

I'd asked him to keep quiet on the family connection, and after some teasing, Aeric had agreed.

Felix's eyes slid my way, a glint of speculation in them. "An old friend?"

"I've known her since she was in diapers," Aeric added dryly.

The speculative glint died, which pleased me, and Felix

went back to talking to my cousin. "Once you both get settled, maybe I could steal you for a few minutes and..."

I tuned him out and wandered a few feet away, peering through the crowd and trying to see through the packed bodies. I thought that might be one of the cars.

I was about to move closer when Aeric said, "We don't cheer for that one."

"We don't?" Confused, I blinked up at him, then glanced around. "Where's Felix?"

"Off looking for another patron." He waved a hand. "I told him I was at your disposal for the day, and he seemed to think his...project needed immediate attention so I told him I couldn't help."

"What kind of project?"

Aeric rolled his eyes and leaned in before answering. "Who knows? He's a friend of my father's, but Felix is getting more eccentric. Father's finally figured that out and has his staff fielding the more ridiculous requests. I'm not going to become the stand-in. I do know that one of his pet projects had something to do with..." He paused, a line forming between his brows as he thought. "Oh, yes. He wanted funding for the Association for the Preservation of Old French."

"Old French."

"Yes."

I blinked. "Nobody speaks Old French anymore. Nobody writes it. Anything *written* in Old French will be old enough that it must be preserved, so it's not like you can just flip open an old copy of..." I searched my brain, trying to think of something. I couldn't.

"Precisely." Aeric took my hand and tucked it into the crook of his arm. "Old French was all but gone by the fourteen hundreds and anything written in the ancient language would have been handwritten. Certainly, there are some documents, but they're all in museums or private collections. I'm not opposed to anybody wanting to start up a private association for the purposes of keeping the heritage alive, but it certainly won't be a national endeavor sponsored by the royal house on the purposes of educating the people of Monaco."

We'd started walking, and I noted the ever-growing crowds and couldn't ignore the occasional look being cast my way. I was glad I'd pulled on an oversized pair of sunglasses and had weaved my hair into a braid. The large-brimmed hat doubled as both protection from the sun and to shield my face, but still, I felt exposed, and all the attention made me nervous. "Are we going to end up on the front page of a newspaper, Aeric?"

He didn't answer right away, and I looked up to see him looking around, a pensive frown on his face. "I hadn't even considered it. It's a possibility. Does it bother you?"

"I..." Blowing out a sigh, I shrugged. "Not really. It's not like anybody here knows me, and it's unlikely they'll be connecting me to American financing magnate Wade Harden III...unless you go dropping my full name."

"I told you I wouldn't." He sounded annoyed but had a smile on his face. "You know, sooner or later, you'll have to stop worrying about the shadow cast by your parents and live your own life."

"Ha." I poked him in the ribs, earning a smothered yelp and a hard look.

And around us, more than a few people stared.

"If you don't want to attract attention, Stacia, you probably shouldn't poke the Crown Prince of Monaco in the ribs in front of so many people." His voice was filled with a mix of annoyance and amusement. His gaze slid off to the left, and I glanced over just in time to see one of his security team smoothly block what was clearly a member of the press.

"Great," I muttered.

He patted my hand. "Relax. If they start speculating about our upcoming marriage, I'll just have my assistant issue a statement addressing the fact that we're cousins."

"Which will just point more attention my way." Rolling my eyes, I adjusted my sunglasses and squared my shoulders, mentally and physically. "Get me through this pack, Your Highness. Surely the press isn't allowed everywhere."

He laughed, and after settling my hand in the crook of his elbow, picked up his pace. "You need to learn to brazen your way through this shit, darling. Fix that very look on your face, pull your shoulders back like you just did, and stride right through the fray. Learn the attitude, Stacia, and you can brazen your way through most things. It could even help you deal with your parents, make *that* nightmare easier."

"Nothing would make that nightmare easier unless they suddenly have a rapid personality adjustment." Sighing, I squeezed his arm. "Okay, so tell me about who we're to see."

"Some friends of mine." He gestured ahead at the next gate where several uniformed officers waited. "One of them sponsors a team. I'm friends with the driver too. And *that* team, by the way, is the one we want to win."

"Okay." Curiosity stirred inside me, warranting enough interest that it brushed aside the concern about the press and any possible interest Aeric and I might have piqued. "Do you sponsor a team?"

"No." He shot me an abashed look. "Part of me wants to, but with it being so popular here, it doesn't seem fair to favor one team over another."

"But we're rooting for this team, the one with a couple of friends to win? Are they from Monaco?"

"No." He gave me a wide grin. "That's what makes it safe. The driver is from America. If I'm not avidly pushing for one of the Monaco drivers to win, then I don't feel guilty if one wins and the others don't."

I rolled my eyes. "Please. It's not like they *all* expect to win."

"No. But you'd be amazed at how petty some people can be. Not necessarily the drivers, but the sponsors, the well-financed companies that support the drivers." He hitched up a shoulder in a Gallic shrug. "If I don't pick a personal favorite from among them, then I don't have to listen to petty squabbles later on."

"Ah...staying distant right off the bat. I like it. I use that technique myself."

With a snort, he said, "It's called diplomacy when I do it, darling. You aren't being *diplomatic*. You just stay cut off from society as much as possible because you don't want to risk getting involved with...well..." He paused for so long that I looked up at him, wondering what had him hedging.

Finally, he stopped and looked at me, his expression wistful. "With anything. You're letting life pass you by, Stacia, all because of the shitty way your family raised you, and the shitty example they set for you. If they want to stand by and sneer down their noses at everything, let them. You don't have to do the same."

Words trapped in my throat, and I wanted to argue.

The problem was...I couldn't. I couldn't even force a smile. "It's..."

That was all I got out.

Somebody shouted Aeric's name in a distinctly American voice. There was none of the typical royal address, and I saw more than a few people around me wince. Aeric just grinned and bent down to murmur in my ear. "Another friend. Come on."

Soon, I was swept into a chaotic whirl of names and handshakes.

Aeric kept me to his side for most of it, but bit by bit, the noise and the curiosity took its toll, and I broke away, squeezing his arm and smiling at him, then nodding to the side to let him know where I'd be.

He gave me a concerned look, and I patted his shoulder, hoping he'd understand.

I didn't want him to feel like he had to hover around me. He was obviously enjoying himself, and I just needed a break away from all the questions and the people and the noise and the...socializing.

Everybody did so well at it.

Except for me.

"Are you well, Miss Stacia?"

I looked up into the cocoa-brown eyes of Paulo, one of Aeric's bodyguards. Forcing a smile, I nodded. "I'm fine. Just more people than I'm used to. I wanted a break."

"Of course." He offered a polite nod. "Would you care for a drink? There is wine, a mini bar? Or I can fetch you a bite to eat?"

"Ah...wine." Maybe it would take the edge off my nerves.

As Paulo strode away, I eased a bit farther from the crowd and looked around, taking in more now that I wasn't surrounded. There was a *lot* going on. A few yards ahead, men wore colorful uniforms—green, black, and white. Most of them moved back and forth rapidly or were talking, the energy about them frenetic. A few gathered around a car, and my curiosity stirred again. I'd never seen a race car up close before.

"Miss Stacia."

Paulo, quiet as a whisper, reappeared by my side.

"Wow. That was quick. Thank you." I smiled at him and accepted the glass, gesturing toward the car. "Ah...would it be okay if I took a closer look?"

"Of course." He checked his watch. "They won't be moving onto the grid for another forty-five minutes. You have plenty of time to go look. Would you like me to come along and introduce you?"

"No. I don't want to interfere or anything. I just want to get a closer look at the car. But thank you."

He nodded and retreated. After taking a sip of wine, I made my way through the clutch of people until only ten or fifteen feet separated me from the car. There was excitement here, too, but it was muted, more focused on the machine and the race.

Adrenaline all but pulsed in the air as I studied everybody, taking them all in and deciding that most of the men were part of the crew. I'd seen a few races before on TV. Some of the people I'd been friendly with at Oxford had loved the Formula One series, and I'd seen enough to know that the pit crews were crazy fast with their hands and the drivers were crazy fast with the cars.

At the very edge of the throng, close to the fence, I watched two of the men in uniform as they stood near the car. One was bent in front of it, checking on something, while the other gestured off in the distance.

He'd be the driver, I decided. He wore the same colors as everybody else, but the design was markedly different.

The man bent over the car glanced up at him and nodded, then resumed his study.

My gaze went to him—or more specifically, to his ass.

Blood heated my cheeks even as I made a deliberate effort to redirect my focus, but ten seconds later, my eyes drifted back down. He straightened a moment later and half turned, looking at the driver, his hands braced on his hips.

My heart gave a hard bump against my ribs as I got a full look at his profile. If his tight, perfect butt had been a thing worth a few seconds of consideration, the full body look was worth much, much more. His hair was a warm, dark brown, but the sun picked up hints of red and gold, the kind of highlights and lowlights some of us women—and men, too, I guessed—paid pretty pennies for. Something about *this* man made me think he wasn't the sort to pay for highlights or anything more than a basic haircut, though.

A heavy growth of shadow darkened his chin. As I watched, he reached up to scratch at his jaw, and I found myself biting my lip, wishing I could do the same.

Since when had I *ever* thought about doing something like dragging my nails down some guy's stubbled jaw?

We'll go with never for a thousand, Alex, I thought as an unfamiliar heat wound lazily through me.

He nodded at the man in front of him, then gestured to the car as he spoke, pausing to listen.

The other guy, the one I'd pegged as the driver, answered with a wide grin, hands moving animatedly.

Both of them laughed.

And the odd heat in my chest burst to spread throughout my entire body as the two of them turned toward the crowd.

Mr. Delicious glanced my way, and his gaze landed on me, then slid past as if I wasn't even there.

I wasn't surprised. Actually, I was *grateful*. As they walked by, I lifted the wine to my lips and guzzled half of it.

It wouldn't do a damn thing to slow the rapid beat of my heart, but I was too hot and flustered to care.

Hell.

What had just happened?

SIX

LUKA

When she came walking in with my friend Aeric, I noticed her. It was hard *not* to take notice, if I was being honest.

Slimly built, her peaches-and-cream complexion was protected with a wide-brimmed hat while a long, flowing overshirt of some sort of sheer material dotted with a chaotic bloom of tropical flowers brushed loosely over a pair of white jeans, cropped at the knee. Strappy sandals did amazing things for her legs...especially her calves.

As she shifted to listen to somebody Aeric was talking to, I got a better look at her legs, the wind catching the flowery overshirt and tangling it around her figure, then blowing it away. Very, very nice legs, the calves sleekly muscled as if she spent a great deal of time walking.

I didn't have much more time than that to appreciate her because Emmett directed my attention back to the car, and I leaned forward to study the engine. I was the top sponsor, although the fact wasn't well known. A popular sporting outfitter in Luxembourg took top billing while I continued to handle the bulk of the financing, but I also enjoyed working with the engineering and mechanical team when I had time.

It wasn't as often as I'd like, and as time went on, I knew that I'd been spending even fewer weekends here in Monaco with my American friend, but I had every intention of enjoying it while I could.

"What do you think of the changes?" Emmett asked.

"I think they'll help," sliding him a look from the corner of my eye, I said pointedly, "but I'm not driving the car. The question is what do *you* think?"

"Hey, if I wasn't on board with them, I wouldn't have said yes. I've got a great sponsor who gives me a *lot* of control when it comes to shit like this." He winked at me.

"Lucky bastard."

We talked a few more minutes, and he pointed out some other minor changes. I'd noticed two of them, but the others were so minute, I wouldn't have seen them without his direction. "Why take that route?"

Emmett went into a complicated explanation that I mostly followed, but Formula One racing regulations changed so frequently, staying on top of them all but required one's attention on a regular basis, which was something I couldn't give.

I wasn't bitter. As much as I'd prefer to spend my days getting my hands black and messy with grease as I tinkered with a prime machine like this with the express intent to make it go *faster* when it was already one of the fastest machines on earth, it wasn't my reality. But I had parents who'd encouraged me to spend free time on my hobbies when I could, so I'd had the chance to pursue this passion freely.

There were others in my position who couldn't say the same.

"You've got a new admirer."

I frowned at him.

"Hey, at least she's not rushing at you with her tits hanging out." Emmett grinned, his eyes straying only briefly over my shoulder.

I didn't follow his gaze, but my attention went on red alert. "Slim? Wearing a hat and some sort of floral overshirt?"

"It's called a duster." His lips twitched in a smile. "You already noticed her. Can't say I blame you. She's pretty. And, like I said...she's not trying to hang all over you with her tits out. That puts her over some of the other...admirers you've picked up."

"I haven't picked them up," I said irritably. "I can't help if women stare. They stare at you too."

Emmett shrug. "Because I win races and get my face plastered on TV and the internet. If I start losing, they won't pay me any attention. That's not the case with you."

"You're right." Crossing my arms over my chest, I said, "They stare at me because I have a title and money."

Emmett ran his tongue across his teeth. "We should give ourselves more credit. We're both good looking bastards, Luka. And I don't know about you, but I'm hung like a fucking horse."

I burst out laughing. Emmett had that effect on me. He always had, from the time we'd met as teenagers. There were some Americans who had a fascination with my title, but most were like Emmett. It didn't mean shit to them.

That bothered some people in my station.

I liked it.

It was...freeing to be taken for who you were instead of where you came from.

A booming sound came over the speaker system. Next to me, Emmett smacked his hands together before clapping one over my shoulder. "Almost time, man. We're going to win this one, I know it."

His excitement was contagious, but I responded only with a smile. "A bonus, then, if you make it happen."

"Hot damn." His southern American accent thickened when he was excited, and the words came out like *hhawwt day-yum.* "Another reason for me to win. I keep telling my mom I'm going to redo their back yard and give them a swimming pool setup like you see on one of the crazy TV shows. A bonus would take care of that just fine."

At his obvious glee, I couldn't help but laugh, and I returned his hug. As we broke apart, I caught sight of her again, the slim, pretty woman.

She'd removed her hat and held a glass of wine in a ringless hand, her nails unpainted, oddly alluring. Without the hat, I could see her features more clearly, although she hadn't removed her oversized sunglasses. Her hair was a warm shade, caught between golden and brown, and the sun plucked out paler shades that seemed too natural to have been forced at a salon. A few strands escaped and curled around her face, making me think that when she didn't pull it back, her hair might be a crazy mass of ringlets and waves. I found it an appealing picture.

"Go talk to her," Emmett suggested.

I scowled at him, then gestured to the team as they bore down on us. "You've got other things to worry about, ace. Let's see about securing that bonus for you."

THE ENTIRE ATMOSPHERE was charged with excitement. I felt it vibrating in the air even before I cleared the security set up outside the Prince's Palace, home to Monaco's Royal Family. Aeric, the Crown Prince and a friend of mine, was a fan of Formula One, like many others in the small city-state. His parents were casual fans, but Aeric lived and breathed it, and it wasn't uncommon for him to throw parties to celebrate the winner.

He was friendly with Emmett, so I hadn't been surprised at the invitation to a party in his wing at the palace.

Emmett and the rest of the crew were already there, but I'd had business matters to take care of before heading over, so the party was already well underway.

Security recognized me as well as the men from my security team who had accompanied me. We were waved through without pause, and I squinted as lights assailed my eyes and the deep, rhythmic pulse of music filled my ears.

Once inside, my small security team fell back to a discreet distance.

Aeric had excellent security himself, a veritable army roving the grounds, and the friendship between his family and mine was solid. There were other state heads in attendance, and I wouldn't be surprised to see a few other familiar faces from the small pool of European royalty, possibly even some figures from one of the royal houses in the Middle East or Africa. The world loved sporting events. It was one of the few things we could all still agree on.

Although the crowd was thick, I'd been to enough of Aeric's events to know where I'd likely find him and his guests of honor, so I headed in that direction, pausing at a freestanding bar to grab a tall pilsner of a craft beer from Belgium I enjoyed.

A few familiar faces popped out as I wound through the crowd, but I didn't slow down, set on finding Emmett and the team. A couple of times, a determined individual started to approach, and I caught sight of security—either mine or Aeric's—moving to intervene. Part of me felt shitty for not stopping to just talk, but on the other hand, if I did, I might never make it to where Emmett was waiting for me.

It took maybe fifteen minutes to get through the masses and reach the sunken sitting area that accommodated roughly thirty people. It was barricaded by guards and a velvet rope.

As I approached, one started to step in front, only to pause, then offer a polite nod as he recognized me. His partner, a woman who stood a solid six feet, freed the rope and cleared my path, greeting me as I crossed. "Good evening, Your Highness. I hope you are enjoying yourself."

"Thank you, Blanche. Good evening to you as well."

Her smile widened a fraction at my reply. "If there's anything you need, please let me or one of my men know. We'll see right to you."

"Thank you again." As I descended the three stairs, I looked around for Aeric. Emmett was easy to locate. He stood a little off-center, holding court almost, next to the fireplace that had been covered and turned into a makeshift table holding various canapes and little pastries. As I drew closer, Emmett bent down and plucked something from a tray, revealing the person in front of him.

Aeric.

Both of them saw me and grinned.

Emmett shoved the food into his mouth and wiped his fingers on a napkin before waving. I had to give him credit. A few years ago, he would have just wiped his hands on his jeans. Cocking a brow at him, I mouthed, "Good job."

He flipped me off good naturedly and finished chewing his food.

Aeric had already risen from his seat.

It wasn't until I was halfway across the floor that I saw who'd been sitting with him.

Her.

The woman who'd been with him earlier.

Were they dating?

The idea left me more than a little unsettled for reasons I couldn't put my finger on. Shrugging the idea aside, I focused on Aeric and Emmett. Emmett's hug was so enthusiastic I had to brace myself or risk toppling over.

"Fuck, man," I said, pushing him back lightly. "Easy there, or security might think you're trying to smother me."

Emmett laughed, his overbright eyes and flushed face leading me to think he'd already partaken of more than a glass or two of champagne. "Nah, they know me by now. I'm a crazy son of a bitch, but harmless. I called my mom earlier, told her she's getting the backyard makeover of her dreams, man."

"The bonus." I nodded. "It's already taken care of. You did well. Congratulations."

"Congratulations to us." He slung an arm around my neck and planted a smacking kiss on my cheek before looking at Aeric. "That rookie from Monaco *almost* caught me, you know."

Aeric rolled his eyes. "Yes, Emmett. You've mentioned it once or twice. Or a dozen times."

Emmett laughed and let me go. "I need some food. Real food, or I'm going to be sick as a dog in the morning."

"I'll have Blanche get someone to escort you," Aeric said.

Emmett went to argue, but he was ignored. A few minutes later, Aeric and I were crossing over to the long, plush couch. People scooted or rose to make room, and Aeric grinned at me as he picked up a crystal high-ball. "You won me a fair amount of money on that race today. I had a feeling Emmett would win. I made a substantial bet, and he came through, several times over."

"Then Emmett won you a fair amount of money, not me." I glanced past him with studied casualness at the woman. "Hello."

She'd been staring at her drink, but at my greeting, her eyes came up, brows raising a fraction. "Ah...hi."

I'd spoken in French, a language common in both Luxembourg and Monaco.

She'd replied in the same language but with an accent that was distinctly American.

Curiosity piqued even more, I said, "I'm Luka, a...friend of Emmett's." Aeric's attention shifted to me, but I ignored him. Neither of us went around dropping our title everywhere we went, so he couldn't exactly say anything, could he?

I half expected him to interject and introduce her as a friend. A girlfriend perhaps, maybe some fashion designer or perhaps a statesman's daughter he'd met while traveling.

But Aeric remained silent, and I assumed that while she might be friendly with him, they weren't particularly close.

Her eyes, a soft, winsome blue, held mine for a long moment before she finally answered. "Stacia. I'm visiting from New York."

"I saw you at the race earlier."

"Yes." She sipped her wine before answering. "Aeric thought I'd enjoy it."

"I was right." Aeric tossed back the rest of his whiskey and waved over a server. "Would you like another drink, Stacia?"

She declined and leaned in to whisper something, her voice too low for me to hear.

A moment later, she rose, and I focused on my drink instead of watching her walk away as I wanted to.

I started to ask Aeric about her, but before I could, Emmett reappeared and dropped down in the seat she'd vacated. A woman was close behind, and she bent over, placing a plate of food on his lap and offering a bottle of water.

"Thank you, honey." He gave her the same smile that charmed the media the world over, and I shook my head at the blush that tinted the woman's cheeks as she walked away.

"Aeric, you've got people on hand who've waited on some of the richest, most charming pricks in the world and that loudmouth American over there can reduce them to blushing with just a smile. How do you explain that?"

Aeric laughed.

Emmett straightened, cradling the plate carefully. "That's easy, Luka. Rich and charming doesn't necessarily mean shit if you're not authentic. And there's one thing about me...I'm about as real as they come." He winked before digging into his food.

"Full of authentic bullshit."

He laughed. "That, too."

SHE RETURNED MAYBE thirty minutes later, loitering on the far end of the seating pit, watching everything as she sipped champagne, her expression smooth and serene...aloof, I decided. I'd noticed that earlier, and it was hard not to notice now.

But even as I thought that, Blanche, the head of Aeric's personal security descended into the sitting area and spoke to her. Stacia smiled at Blanche, a smile I recognized easily. *No, no, I'm fine...*

From my vantage point, I could see Blanche's expression, how she frowned and shook her head. She pointed to the floor as she spoke. I could almost imagine what she was saying. *Stay right here.*

Then the tall, trim woman turned and came over to where we sat, walking past me, only to stop a meter or so away. She bent down and spoke to one of the men there. He was one of the pit crew. I recognized him and wondered what was being said. He frowned, then abruptly nodded and rose, tugging the hands of the women who'd been cuddling against him. They pouted, and he laughed, clearly intent on teasing them into smiles.

A few moments later, Emmett was situated at my side, and Stacia was back in her position by Aeric, her expression slightly flustered even as something akin to gratitude flashed through her eyes when she nodded at Blanche.

Aeric, talking to one of the pit crew members in front of him, seemed completely unaware, but as I watched, he reached over and took Stacia's hand, squeezing it companionably. He glanced over at her, then up at Blanche, and the two of them spoke briefly before the security guard disappeared.

Stacia settled more comfortably into the cushions and resumed her study of everything going on.

As I watched, an odd tension fell away from her, and I realized I'd pegged her wrong.

She wasn't aloof at all.

She was just...shy.

She hid it well, but she was shy.

SEVEN

STACIA

THE CHAOTIC WHIRL OF THE PARTY HAD MY HEAD spinning. Making my way down the hall in search of a restroom and a few minutes of privacy, I tried to decide if I was enjoying it.

"It's definitely not one of Mom's little soirees," I told myself.

"*Excusez-moi?*"

The sound of the voice had me jumping.

Abashed, the security guard came closer, holding out a hand. "*Pour s'excuser,*" he said, smiling reassuringly.

"No, *I'm* the one who's sorry. Wandering around here, talking to myself," I said, responding to him in French. "I wasn't paying attention. I just wanted to get away from the party for a few minutes."

He nodded in understanding. "Of course."

I could tell he recognized me, but as he went to offer assistance, I waved him off. "I'm fine. I just wanted some quiet."

Two more turns led me to a private restroom in a hall deeper in the residential wing occupied by Aeric, one that had been cordoned off, keeping the partygoers away. One thing about being Aeric's cousin, I didn't have to worry about that. I wasn't likely to be granted entrance to his personal office, but shy of that, none of the staff worried much if I went wandering around the palace.

Slipping inside the opulent restroom, I leaned back and closed my eyes. Just being someplace nobody would see me was a welcome respite. Giving myself thirty seconds to appreciate it, I focused on smoothing out nerves left raw by the stress of being social. It was something my mother had never understood—and never would. *Social anxiety* was a made-up concept in her mind, and she claimed I was being overly theatrical when I tried to explain how much it stressed me out to attend all the functions she tried to foist on me. The coping mechanisms I'd developed to deal with her world had saved my sanity more than once.

Aeric's party was nowhere near as bad, the people far less rigid, and none of them seemed to be intent on watching my every move, although that was because I was *definitely* one of the least interesting people here. I had no doubt of that.

I'd seen K-pop stars, social media icons, a couple of fashion designers that I knew mostly because of my mother's influence, no less than *ten* movie and TV stars in attendance. I knew there were several others who were royalty, ranging from the UK to the Middle East.

If I could have seen Meghan and Prince Harry, I would have been ecstatic, and I would have demanded an introduction from my cousin, but it hadn't happened.

Pushing off the door, I checked to make sure it was locked before taking a look around. I'd been in five-star spas in New York that weren't as luxurious as this restroom, with the plush aubergine carpet and the divan, several shades deeper, tucked against the wall, in case a guest had need of it. The walls were decorated with a design that was clearly hand-painted, and closer inspection made me think the golden coloring used wasn't just *golden colored*, but *real gold*, and not the gold leaf that just mimicked the effects of the metal.

Amused, I shook my head and wandered deeper into the bathroom. There were various toiletries and high dollar makeup in more shades than I'd seen offered in some New York boutiques, all of them brand new and untouched. In case a guest needed to touch up her makeup, of course.

Curious, I pulled out the tray of lipsticks and studied the shades, selecting a deep rose, caught between pink and red. Trying it on, I studied the effect, then slid it into the small, cross-body purse.

The color looked good, I decided on a lengthier study. Better than good, really. It was a bolder shade than I normally wore, which made me like it even more.

Reaching for a wide-toothed comb left on a silver tray, I tidied my hair, then selected one of the products displayed on a shelf, smoothing down the frizzies that inevitably happened to curly hair after a long day.

"Well, you're not going to compete with a Kardashian," I told my reflection. "But you look good."

I felt calmer, too, just getting away from the noise for a few minutes.

Getting away from the curious eyes.

And getting a few minutes away from...*him*.

That thought alone had my calmed belly *uncalming*, although the jumping inside was for entirely different reasons now. I'd seen him approach the recessed seating area where I'd been sitting with Aeric, and as unobtrusively as I could, I'd watched.

He must be a regular at Aeric's house because Blanche had let him in without pause, and I'd been paying attention to how things operated at the party. Most of the guests were briefly questioned by either the head of Aeric's security team or one of her men.

Not the tall, lean man with his dark brown hair and sculpted face and a mouth that looked like Michelangelo might have played a part in its creation.

He'd strolled right in and came up to Aeric as if they'd been friends for years.

His eyes had flicked to mine, and he'd greeted me, given me his name.

Luka.

My belly flipped again, just thinking about how close he'd been to me.

"You're acting like a girl who just saw a guy naked for the first time," I muttered, disgusted with myself.

And wasn't *that* a stupid thought to allow into my head? Because now I was thinking about Luka naked.

I SHOULD JUST ASK HIM, I decided on my walk back to the party.

Not even twenty seconds later, I changed my mind. I *shouldn't* ask him. What I needed to do was mingle—I knew how to do it, even if I wasn't always comfortable. Nobody ever realized just how *uncomfortable* I was with the socializing thing because I'd gotten good at faking my comfort level.

I'd make my way through the party, find a guy who seemed to click and put the proposal before him.

It was simple.

Women did this thing *all* the time, didn't they?

Yes. They did.

So just ask him.

The internal argument circled over and over again in my head. In an effort to quell it, I grabbed a glass of champagne from a passing server. It tasted like liquid gold and pure luxury, the bubbles dancing down my throat and going straight to my head. After the first reckless, deep drink, I slowed down. I had to pace myself, or I'd end up too drunk to proposition *anybody*—or I'd do it in the worst possible way and humiliate myself and Aeric.

That image was enough to bring me back down to earth, and I got myself under control as I made my way back toward where I'd been sitting with my cousin. *Aeric*, I reminded myself firmly. *Not* to the sexy mechanic I'd noticed earlier.

He probably wouldn't even still be there.

Most of the others had drifted off to mingle or dance, save for Emmett and a couple members of his pit crew.

And damn it, Mr. Delicious, the sexy, sexy mechanic.

For a second, I saw only him, despite the throng of people still gathered there, like acolytes paying homage to their perceived god. I ignored it, having seen it all before, but I also forced myself to ignore Mr. D. as I circled around the seating area and settled in one of the few vacant areas. My seat by Aeric had been taken, which I'd expected, but that was fine. I liked observing, and the vantage point from here made for a better view.

"Miss Stacia."

I recognized the voice, even over the dull roar of music and laughter.

Blanche Pietro, the tall, athletic blonde who'd handled Aeric's security team for years, stood just a foot away, smiling at me.

"Hi, Blanche."

"You don't need to stand here," she said, her English beautifully accented with both Italian and French. Her mother had been born in Paris, but her father had been with the *Servizio per le Informazioni e la Sicurezza Democratica*, the Intelligence and Democratic Security Service, Italy's primary intelligence agency of the time. He'd been killed in the line of duty when she was younger.

I'd been around her enough to know that smile she gave me was more open than it was with most. I could also tell that she was miffed that I was standing there instead of relaxing with my cousin.

"I'm fine, Blanche."

She shook her head and gestured to me. "You wait right here, Miss Stacia."

I started to argue, but she had already turned away, moving over to the stretch of couch where several people from Emmett's pit crew still sat.

Moments later, my face hot with a blush, Blanche led me to Aeric's side. "There." She beamed at me, satisfied. "Would you like more champagne? Something to eat?"

"I'm fine, Blanche."

Aeric glanced over and took my hand. He shot Blanche a teasing smile. "You're such a protective, nurturing sort, Blanche." He frowned and added, "With everyone but me."

"Your Highness, you hardly need *nurturing*." She gave him a wicked smile, then gave both of us an abbreviated nod before disappearing back into the crowd.

Aeric gave my hand another squeeze. Picking up on his unspoken message, I squeezed back. *I'm fine.*

He let go and resumed his discussion with the man at his side as I settled more comfortably into the cushions. The people who'd been watching the interaction between Blanche and me lost interest, and I relaxed.

Sipping my champagne, I regrouped.

I was going to finish my bubbly, I decided, then go do that mingling thing. I wanted to go home back properly divested of my virginity, without worrying that I'd run into my newly acquired lover at some party thrown by some friend of my parents—or worse, *by* my parents.

The man next to me got up, and unconsciously, I shifted position, turning more toward Aeric even though he was engaged in a discussion with a short, portly man I couldn't place.

I needed to get up and start doing my mingling.

After I finish my champagne, I promised.

The flute was almost empty. I had every intention of keeping that promise to myself. I just needed a little more time to mentally prepare. And plan. I'd go to the dance floor. It was the best bet. I'd been at enough parties, even those hosted by friends of my parents, to know that a young, fairly attractive woman tended to find a partner easily enough on a dance floor. I'd had luck in the aspect before.

If I didn't have any luck at first, then I'd just keep trying.

Mind made up, I finished the champagne and put the glass on the space behind the couch where others had placed their own used drinkware. Leaning in, I tapped Aeric's shoulder. "I'm going to mingle," I said after he turned to me.

His brows shot up, his surprise clear. "All right. Would you like company?"

"No. I'm fine." I rose slowly, taking my time so I could make sure the wine hadn't hit any harder than I thought.

"Stacia, right?"

The sound of that low voice, edged with an accent I couldn't place, had my skin prickling with awareness.

Slowly, I lifted my head and met warm amber eyes. Amber, like aged bourbon, I decided, and just as intoxicating. My mouth had gone dry, and already, I wished I had another drink in my hand.

"Yes," I said, managing to squeeze the word out. "And you're Luka."

A slow, charming smile spread across his face. "I am. Were you leaving?"

"What? Oh. No, I'm not leaving. I was just going to..." I waved my hand toward the mass of bodies on the dance floor. "I thought I'd go..."

My brain blanked out.

"Dance?"

"Yes." My face heated, and I had to clear my throat before I could continue. "I'm sorry. It's warm in here, and I'm really thirsty."

He offered his arm. "Why don't we take care of that?"

My plan fell apart on me, and nervously, I looked back at Aeric. He sensed it and gave me an easy smile before going back to his discussion, but the smile settled me. He'd seen the man with me—I knew that.

More, as we started out of the area, Blanche smiled at me. If this man was some sort of twisted bastard, neither of them would be letting him escort me out to the dance floor.

"You said you were thirsty?"

"I did, yes." I caught myself before it could form into a question and gave him a smile. "Yes. As I said, it's warm in here."

"The palace is old. With this many people in here, it's hard to keep the temperature moderated."

"I'd imagine." I wanted to kick myself. What a boring response. "Have you...ah...you work with Emmett. On the car, I mean. Have you done that long?"

We reached one of the servers holding a tray of drinks. There was a variety, from champagne to wine to tall pilsners of beer. I was tempted by the champagne but didn't want to risk it and selected a bottle of sparkling water. Luka took one of the pilsners and gestured to the dance floor. "Shall we?"

"I should drink this first," I said warily. "Otherwise, I'll spill it. *And* I'll knock your beer all over you."

He blinked, then laughed, a slow, low rumble that was entirely too appealing. "Well, we can't have that." He offered his arm again. "How about a wall along the balcony? It overlooks the prince's gardens, and they're lovely. Have you seen them?"

I used to play in them, but I didn't want to tell him that. "Why don't you show me?"

"THE STAFF SEEMS COMFORTABLE WITH YOU," Luka noted.

I glanced at the bottle of wine that had just been left, along with a plate of fruit, cheese, and crackers. Blanche had strolled along the balcony earlier and given me a quizzical look, which I'd responded to with a smile. The arrival of the bottle of wine, glasses, and food twenty minutes later hadn't surprised me at all.

Blanche really did enjoy taking care of people.

"I've spent time here before," I said vaguely, shrugging as I selected a wedge of cheese. It was pale yellow, and I suspected gouda. The first bite confirmed my guess, and I sampled another before taking a sip of my wine.

"Friends with Aeric? Or with his sister?"

I heard the speculation in his eyes and kept my attention on the glass in my hand as I pondered my answer. We sat on a low stone wall down in the garden, a breeze that bordered on cool toying with my hair, but I was enjoying myself too much to go inside.

Luka sat close. Very close. So close I felt the heat of him on my skin. When he shifted, his knee brushed against mine, something that should have been innocent and simple, but it really, really wasn't.

He moved again, and I sensed him leaning closer. With the movement, his knee wasn't brushing mine but pressing into it. My heart bumped hard, and I lifted my eyes to his.

"Stacia?"

There seemed to be a world of unasked questions hidden inside the syllables of my name, made poetic by his enigmatic accent and unbelievably sexy voice.

"Friends with them both, I guess you could say. We're cousins, so I come to visit from time to time."

Luka's brows arched slightly, then lowered. His lids drooped and his eyes fell, focusing on my mouth.

My breathing hitched, and I tore my gaze away, lifting my wine to my lips.

The moment shattered, and when I looked back, he had lifted a slice of apple to his lips.

Just ask him, that sly, annoying voice in my mind nudged again.

And this time, I didn't try to silence it. I didn't ask.

But I would.

Soon.

Maybe thirty minutes later, we started up the stairs leading away from the garden. Lights and music still pulsed from inside. Luka slid his gaze over to me, a faint smile on his lips.

"You still haven't had your dance. Shall we?"

Heart hammering against my ribs, I looked through the windows to all the people inside. I thought of the noise in there, the chaos. Then I thought of going back home, dealing with my mother's meddling, the match making, me wondering if I'd ever even feel a *spark* with somebody.

I wasn't looking for romance, or even for a man who'd completely blow me away the first time.

But I did want that first time to be...*mine*. Something I chose, not something that just came about after I got tired of her meddling and gave in, started dating some guy she threw at me just to shut her up. More, I wanted it to be with somebody who had no idea who I was, who my parents were... somebody outside their sphere of influence, somebody who'd *stay* that way. So whatever happened would *stay* mine.

More, I wouldn't have to listen to anything from them about it.

I doubted my parents would be shocked at the idea of me having sex. I wasn't a child, but my mother, in particular, had no idea what boundaries were, and I could already imagine the commentary I'd get from her.

He's attractive, Stacia, but he's beneath you. Get it out of your system, then move on. That would sum up her reaction nicely.

I shoved thoughts of her out of my head and focused on Luka.

Just ask him.

So I did.

"Would you think I was crazy if I said I'd rather we go to my room instead?"

His lids flickered once more, and I could see that I'd surprised him, but I didn't say anything else. Neither did he.

If he said no, I'd just calmly go back to my room and pretend I wasn't embarrassed. I'd never have to see him again, right?

The silence was thick and heavy, and just when I thought

he wasn't going to answer, he lifted his hand and cupped my chin, angling my head back.

I caught my breath as his mouth came down on mine. He tasted sweet like the oranges, apples, and strawberries we'd snacked on, tart and rich, like the wine. And...unique. Like the man he was.

My breath hitched and caught as he pushed his fingers into my hair and caught a fistful of curls, twisting, then tangling.

His tongue slid over my lower lip, then pushed inside. My knees wobbled, and I reached for him, clenching my fingers in the soft, fine weave of his shirt.

A moment later, the kiss was over.

"I'd love to go to your room, Stacia. But are you sure that's what you want?" He studied me in the glow of light cast from the moon and through palace windows.

Still gripping his shirt in my hands, I stared at him and nodded. "Yes."

You better tell him, the voice of reason urged.

His eyes darkened, and intrinsically, I knew I was staring into the face of raw, blatant lust. My belly tightened, and my nipples started to throb just holding his gaze.

I'll tell him, I promised. *In a couple of minutes.*

A couple of minutes turned into five, then ten, because we had to go through the ballroom to get to my room, and the ever-moving wall of people didn't make for a quick retreat.

Luka held my hand the entire time, his thumb sweeping over skin I'd never realized was so sensitive.

By the time we broke free of the crowd, my heart was racing like I'd run five miles. It made it hard to project a calm smile to the security men who held position at the hall leading to the suites set aside for personal guests or visiting family.

They looked from me to Luka, but even as the shorter, stubby man on the right went to speak, I smiled and sailed right past them.

Luka tightened his hand on mine.

"Afraid they'll stop and subject you to a round of Twenty Questions?"

My face heated. "Maybe you're the one who should worry about that. But...no. That's not my concern."

It might have been a tiny part of it. Okay, all of it, but I had enough issues with all my nerves at play. I didn't need anything else.

We passed another set of guards, turned a corner, and abruptly, Luka stopped. Since I still held his hand, I came to a halt as well. Looking up at him, I went to speak, but before I could, he cupped my face with his free hand, fingers splaying over my jaw. I whimpered, but the sound was lost against his lips as he kissed me.

His tongue stroked over mine while he released my hand, reaching up to grip my hip and tug me closer to him.

Something thick and heavy pulsed against me, and I felt an answering pulse deep inside my core, but it took several seconds and him guiding my hip as I started to rock back and forth, for me to figure out just *what* I was feeling.

Blood, molten hot, pooled low inside me while simultaneously rushing to heat my face.

He broke away and looked down at me, a faint smile on

his face. "We better get to your room before I decide to just push open the next door I see."

"Um. Okay." That sounded *so* sophisticated. With a slight shake of my head, I eased back and resumed my walk down the hall. He caught up with me, sliding his arm around my waist, his fingers curling over my hip once more as he tugged me close against him.

My nipples, tight and hard, stabbed into my bra, the padded silk suddenly torturous.

"My suite's here." We rounded the hall, and I gestured to the doors, suddenly feeling awkward.

Luka either didn't notice or decided to ignore it as he led me into the suite. The light from the sitting room directly in front of us came to life, a gentle golden glow that spilled over a wide, soft couch with a back that looked like a clamshell. The entire suite had a design that evoked a mermaid's playground, although elegantly done.

He didn't even look around as he caught me up against him. Sinking back against the door, he pulled me in closer and fisted a hand in my hair, urging my mouth back to his. "You're the sexiest woman I've ever seen," he murmured against my lips before delivering yet another deep, drugging kiss.

I clung to him, one hand fisting in his shirt while curling my free arm around his neck. My legs were weak. I'd read books where the heroine claimed such, had seen it referenced in movies and had overheard girls in school gossiping about kisses that did such things.

But I'd never experienced it.

Just the stroke of his tongue, the brush of his hand over my side, that was all it took to turn my bones to water.

He broke the kiss and murmured against my mouth.

It took a few seconds for the words to process, then I blinked and nodded. "Yes...I...I've got a couple of condoms in my purse."

I'd found them in the bathroom drawer here in my suite. Probably standard for the guest rooms, because I doubted my aunt and uncle's household staff was actively involved in making sure I had prophylactics on hand. And none of that mattered because I had a beautiful man in the room with me, and I had condoms, and I was going to have sex for the very first time.

"Good." A slow smile curled his lips, and he tugged me against him. Sliding his fingers under the strap that ran between my breasts, holding the purse securely in place, he said, "And the purse is so handy right now. I have half a mind to push your skirt up and fuck you right here for the first time. You've been seducing me from the moment I laid eyes on you. Do you know that?"

My breath skittered out of my lungs. "I have?"

Luka bent down and nuzzled my neck right below my ear. "Yes. You have. Tell me, Stacia. Should I have you right here the first time, rough and fast? Or would you rather me take you to bed and draw things out? Either way works for me, as long as I have you wrapped around my cock by the time we're done."

My heart lunged and leaped in my chest, hard enough to leave me breathless. "I...um..." Twisting my fingers in his shirt, I shoved him back a few inches and met his eyes. "I should tell you something."

He'd been smiling, but now the smile faded. "Tell me what?"

"I'm a virgin."

A blank expression followed after I blurted it out, his smile gone and brows furrowing over his eyes as if he wasn't sure he'd understood me.

Damn it. Had I screwed this up?

"It's not a big deal, Luka." I feigned indifference, giving a careless shrug as I continued, "I graduated high school young. I was always ahead of everybody my age and that doesn't make for the easiest social life. When I was in college, it was the same thing. I was awkward while everybody else was comfortable with who they were, or it seemed that way. I might have had two or three guys ask me out by the time I was twenty. And..."

"Why me? Why now?" He caught a lock of my hair and twisted it around his finger.

His question wasn't a surprise. I mean, I would have wanted to know myself if I had been in his place. But I couldn't find the right way to explain that wouldn't sound awkward.

Just how did you go about telling somebody you wanted to have sex with them because they were super-hot and because you appreciated the fact you wouldn't have to worry about seeing them once you left the country?

The super-hot part would be easy. But the rest of it? *That* would be awkward. I licked my lower lip and mentally squared my shoulders. If I could ask a near stranger to my room, then I could answer this simple question. Or part of it.

"I'm just tired of wondering and waiting, and you...well, I noticed you earlier today too. You kind of turned my belly inside out. If that makes sense."

He trailed his hand down my side, then smoothed his fingers over my belly. "Right here?" A smile teased his lips. "I don't know if that's a good thing. It almost sounds unpleasant."

Sparks of heat went through me at his touch, leaving me shivering. "No. Not unpleasant. Not at all."

He slid his hand higher, tracing it in a meandering path across my mid-section so that his thumb brushed the underside of my breast before his hand curved over my side. I shivered again and inadvertently arched closer.

But he didn't deepen the touch. He just leaned in and murmured, "Are you certain, Stacia? This isn't something you can do over once it's done. Your first time only happens once."

I inched closer and wrapped my arms around his neck. Rising on my toes, I pressed my mouth to his. Echoing the way he'd kissed me, I traced my tongue across his lower lip and then teased my way inside. His chest rumbled against mine, and when I pulled back, he caught my hips and pulled me back. "I'm certain, Luka."

His arms came around me. I hitched out a breath as he hauled me up against him, fully straightening so that my toes left the ground. We were pressed together from chest all the way down to my knees, and my heart banged hard at the contact.

"I guess we've settled on the where and the how."

"What?" Dazed, I stared at him, not certain what he was talking about.

He rubbed his mouth over mine before answering, "Remember? I couldn't make up my mind if I wanted to shove your skirt up and fuck you right up against the door or take you to bed and seduce you slowly."

My face heated as he stared down at me. "Um..."

"I'll be taking you to bed. A virgin's first time shouldn't be a quick fuck against a door."

My breath caught yet again as he laid me down. He'd carried me through the suite into the bedroom, and I'd never noticed.

The mattress was soft yet firm underneath me, and I curled my fingers into the silk comforter as he went to his knees in front of me and tugged my shoes off.

Had my skin ever been this sensitive? The brush of his fingers sent electricity coursing through me, and all he'd done was wrap his fingers around my ankles, thumbs soothing the marks left by my strappy sandals.

His gaze slid lazily up over my legs to meet my eyes as he dragged the flats of his palms along the outsides of my legs, and even more sparks of electricity jolted through me. By the time he reached the hem of my skirt, a bright, poppy red that ended a few inches above my knees, I was kneading the silk comforter and squirming restlessly.

If this was seduction, I wasn't sure I could stand it.

Luka bent down and pressed his lips to my right knee.

"You have the prettiest, sexiest legs. And your skin is so, so soft," he murmured, his lips feathering over my flesh before he lifted and transferred his attention to my other leg. He tugged me to my feet, and I shivered as he reached around and freed the hidden zipper.

He tugged the stretchy, narrow-fitting skirt down, leaving me clad in my panties, bra, and blouse. Then it was just the bra and panties, both a shimmery red that echoed the shade of my skirt. I had to fight the instinctive urge to cross my arms over my chest.

Luka straightened in front of me, that hungry look darkening his eyes again while his lids drooped low and his mouth parted. He took a step back, staring at me, tongue stroking over his lower lip.

"I don't think I've done you credit. You're not just the sexiest woman I've ever seen. I think you may well be the sexiest woman ever created." Under his heavy lids, his eyes glittered as he slowly shifted his gaze back to mine.

A nervous giggle bubbled up in my throat, but I managed to swallow it down. It would be silly to argue when he was complimenting me, wouldn't it? Even if it was just in-the-moment flattery, it made me feel good.

The thought was still forming when he closed the distance between us and caught my face in his hands. My breath hitched as he tunneled his fingers into my hair and used his hold to arch my head back, angling me for the possession of his mouth. His lips crashed into mine, the kiss hungry and devouring. All-consuming.

In the back of my mind, I found myself wondering if maybe his words were a little bit more than just flattery.

I moaned and pushed more fully against him. Luka muttered against my mouth, and one hand slid from my scalp to my neck, then lower, seeking out the strapless bra. I felt it give way but was so caught up in his kiss, I didn't give it more than a second's thought, even when he stroked his fingers down my naked spine.

He broke the kiss and started on a path down my neck, his lips marking his progress. His arm, now at my waist, banded me against him, and I whimpered at the feel of his cock pressed into me.

His mouth closed around one nipple, and I jerked in reaction, the feel sending startling jolts of pleasure all the way to where that empty, aching void between my thighs had started to pulse.

His teeth scraped over me.

I moaned and wiggled against him. He grunted and caught my hip, urging me to follow his lead as he pushed his thigh between mine. Soon, I was riding the hard, solid muscle while he licked and bit at my nipple. Need gathered in my core, tightening my muscles and sending echoing pangs through my body. Clutching at his shoulders, I rocked harder and faster.

Luka muttered something against my skin that I couldn't make out, but I didn't care. I was too caught up in the sensations bombarding me, from between my thighs where I was already so wet, to my right nipple where he sucked and licked and bit, to my left, where he tugged and teased and stroked.

The orgasm hit hard, knocking me under unexpectedly as shocked, broken sounds escaped my throat.

When it ended, I was on my back with Luka bending over me.

My eyes cleared just enough to focus on him before he kissed me, tender and sweet and gentle.

"Sweet girl," he murmured.

I blushed, self-consciousness settling in. I was two seconds from apologizing—had I messed things up?

But then he moved down, and I gasped as he caught my left nipple between his teeth, like he had every intention of starting all over again.

And clearly, he did, paying my left nipple the same attention he'd given my right, but this time, the ache between my thighs went unrelieved, even as I wiggled and arched up against him. Each pull of his mouth, each scrape of his teeth added to that ache, like an invisible cord had been stretched between my nipple and my clitoris, and each successive touch had that cord drawing tighter and tighter.

The wetness, the ache between my thighs had me clenching my knees together. Shyness and nervousness kept me from blurting out, *Can we do it now?*

That was exactly what I wanted, though. That orgasm, shattering as it had been, hadn't been enough, and I wanted more, more, more...

Groaning, I gripped his shoulders, nails biting into the fabric of his shirt.

How much more of this was I going to have to take? How much more of this *could* I take?

He lifted his head, and I found him smiling at me.

"What's that sound for?" he asked before blowing a puff of air over my right nipple.

I whimpered and pushed my fingers into his hair, tugging him closer without thinking.

He resisted. Cupping my breast in his hand, he tugged on my nipple and that damn cord that ran all the way through my belly down to my clit twanged again, sending a pulse shuddering through my body.

"What was that noise for, Stacia? Are you not enjoying this?"

I could tell by the look in his eyes he knew better.

"You're teasing me," I said. The words came out harsh, accusatory.

"No." He rubbed his lips over mine. "I'm seducing you."

"Is there a difference?"

He moved then, settling between my thighs and rocking. "You're already so fucking wet," he murmured, lids drooped low. A shudder raced through his body, and he pumped against me, the ridge of his cock dragging the silk of my panties back and forth over swollen, slick flesh. "I can feel it."

He moved again, and another one of those strange noises escaped me. I sounded wanton and crazed.

Abruptly, he stopped and shoved off the bed, standing at the side. Confused, I lurched up onto my elbows and stared at him. Had I done something wrong?

He wasn't smiling now. The predatory, dangerous intensity on his face had my breath hitching. "You want to know if there's a difference between seduction and teasing. Should I show you?"

I wasn't sure if I should answer that, but Luka didn't bother to wait for an answer as he stripped out of his shirt, then reached for his belt. He didn't take it off, merely left it hanging open before freeing the button of his trousers and moving to drag the zipper down.

My face felt hot, and I was breathing far faster than I should. By the time he had freed his cock and wrapped his hand around the base, I thought I might hyperventilate.

Amber eyes bored into mine. He began to stroke, fist going up and then down, a slow, lazy pattern. Even though he wasn't touching me, every inch of my skin felt super-sensitive, too tight for my body. The blood in my veins grew warm, then hot, then what must surely be close to boiling.

Without realizing I'd done so, I sat up, staring as he pumped his cock. I clenched the silk comforter in my fists, kneading at it as I shifted, trying to ease the ache between my thighs.

"Do you see the difference, Stacia?" he asked, voice raspy now.

Maybe I could, although I wasn't sure I could explain it.

I gave him a slow nod, although I wasn't entirely sure I should—what if he stopped?

He didn't. He smiled once more, but this was an arrogant smile, and everything in me quivered, readied, even as I watched and licked my lips, staring at the head of his cock as his fist slowly swallowed it again and again.

Luka noticed. His eyes dropped lower and settled on the apex of my thighs. "Tease me, Stacia. Lay back and spread your thighs and slip your fingers inside your panties. Tell me how wet your cunt is."

"What?" I stared at him, shocked.

"Lay back down," he ordered. He edged closer to the bed, his thighs bumping into it. "Spread your thighs and touch yourself. You've done that before, haven't you? I already know you have. There's no way a woman as sensual as you are hasn't brought herself to pleasure before."

I started to argue that I couldn't do something like that. Yet, even as I fought to form the words, I found myself staring into his eyes...then sinking back onto the bed, lying flat.

I could do something like that.

And I did, trailing my fingers over my belly, then down, dipping them inside the waistband of my poppy red panties.

"Spread your thighs," Luka said, voice raw.

Shaking, I did so. The bed shifted under me, and I looked down as he settled himself on the bed, straddling my left leg as he continued to work his cock, his fist moving faster now, eyes locked on the wet, red silk of my panties.

I wasn't so sure this was a teasing game anymore, because it somehow felt even more intimate than what we'd already done.

Holding his eyes, I slowly circled my fingers over my clit before sliding them lower.

"You're so fucking wet," he muttered. "I can't wait to see for myself. To touch you, taste you."

I sucked in a breath, startled.

He laughed softly. "Do you honestly think I can look at you like this and not want to shove my face between your thighs and lick you until you're moaning and whimpering and begging me to fuck you?"

I couldn't speak now. I just couldn't. Staring at him, breaths ragged, I tried to picture what he'd just said, his head between my thighs and his mouth...I whimpered and clamped my thighs tight. The movement shoved my fingers more intimately into my pussy, and I cried out.

Luka shoved off the bed abruptly. I couldn't see him, but lust had me all but frozen, locked in place. Panting, trying to breathe around it, I lay where I was.

Seconds later, he was back.

His hands caught my knees, then slid up. I moaned as he caught my panties and dragged them off. He pushed my thighs apart and my face heated, apprehension trying to prick through, but instead of covering me, he stretched out between my thighs.

I froze as he lowered his head.

I was still frozen as he pressed his mouth to me.

But when he dragged his tongue through my wet folds, the spell shattered, and I lurched up, shoving my hips to meet him.

Then I jerked back, the sensation too intense as he flicked my clitoris. His hands held firm, and I couldn't retreat, and after a few seconds, I really didn't want to, anyway. I worked myself against him, any lingering hint of modesty or discomfort lost under the overwhelming onslaught of pleasure and sensation.

He took me straight to the edge, and I pushed my fingers into his hair, already anticipating the fall.

But...he stopped.

"Luka!"

He rubbed his stubbled chin against my inner thigh and pulled away.

If I'd had the energy, I would have grabbed him and hauled him back to me. I even tried to will my body to do just that, but he'd moved away from the bed, out of sight.

He was back before I could slide to the edge of the bed.

"That's a sight I won't forget any time soon."

Flushed, I looked at him, standing framed in the doorway. *He* was a sight I didn't think I'd ever forget.

He came to me, almost naked and gorgeous and confident.

And in his left hand, he held my little cross-body purse.

He tossed it onto the bed and cupped my face, bending to press his mouth to mine.

His kiss was different, and it startled me as I figured out why.

It was *me*. He tasted like me.

His fingers were like a brand on my face, his chest hot, the wall of muscle solid and heavy where it pressed into mine. And lower, I felt the ridge of his cock. I grabbed onto his hips, clinging desperately. Even with the sturdy presence of the bed under me, I felt off-balance and floundering, like I was going to drift off and spin away into nothingness if I didn't hold onto something—him.

He moved in closer, urging me to lie back. As I did so, he came down over me, settling between my thighs. The material of his trousers rubbed against my inner thighs, and I felt his cock, naked and hard, press against my folds.

He started to rock, slipping back and forth over me, and I was so wet, he began to glide, the pleasure already enough to wrack my mind. I didn't know if I could handle this...

Breathless, I tore my mouth from his, a sob rising in my throat.

He pressed a bruising line of kisses along my jawline, to my ear. "No last-minute second thoughts?" he asked.

"What...? No." I shook my head, wiggling, desperate for *more* because this was nowhere near enough.

As sweet as it felt to have his cock rubbing back and forth over me, as good as it was to have that pressure right there, it wasn't enough.

Luka pushed back, no longer touching me and frustration had me all but snarling. Shoving upright, I glared at him.

Amusement quirked his lips as he tore a foil packet open. "Easy there, love. I've got to take care of this."

This was the rubber.

Too needy to feel silly, I sank back onto the bed and gripped the silk under me, my entire being one hot, vibrating ball of want.

He covered me, hands pushing into my hair. "Kiss me, Stacia," he murmured as he pressed his lips to the corner of my mouth. "Let me have that pretty mouth again."

He didn't even have to ask.

Turning my face to his, I lost myself to his kiss as he settled between my thighs.

I whimpered as he rocked against me, but it was different this time. He'd pushed his trousers off, and these weren't teasing, taunting strokes anymore. He reached between us, and I tensed as he tucked the head of his cock against me.

"That's it," he murmured. "That's it..."

Fingers sinking into his muscles, I watched his face helplessly as he started to sink inside.

My heart skipped and trepidation rose inside, unexpected, but I shoved it down.

Not fast enough, or far enough, apparently.

Luka dipped his head and rubbed his mouth against mine

before sucking on my lip. He slid his hand down and caught my hip, lifting me up. I felt the pressure even though the pleasure still gripped me.

He thrust inside, hard, fast.

At the same time, he bit my lower lip.

As he started to withdraw, he let my lip go and soothed the hurt with his tongue. Then he penetrated again, his tongue taking my mouth as his cock filled my pussy.

His long-fingered hand gripped my butt and lifted me more fully against him just as he seated himself fully inside. His body pressed against my clitoris, and he lingered, swiveling his hips lazily in the cradle of mine, increasing the light pressure against my clit.

I moaned and reached down, clutching at his torso.

He withdrew.

This time, as he started to sink inside, I lifted to meet him.

The faint edge of pain was still there, but there were so many other sensations—his chest dragging over my nipples, his tongue teasing mine, his fingers molding to my butt as he lifted me just enough that I felt that sweet, sweet friction as he rubbed against my clit...and the way his cock stretched me, filled me.

My breath locked in my throat, and the need for air had me shoving at his chest until he lifted. Luka stared down at me, a question forming, but before he could say anything, I moaned, sucking in a desperate gulp of air. "Please..."

A broken whimper followed, and I clamped down around him as he started to withdraw.

"Please what?" He nuzzled my neck just below my ear. "Please stop...please don't?"

"Don't you dare stop," I said. Terrified he might, I wrapped my legs around him. It changed his angle, changed the sensations, and I whimpered, shuddering and writhing and wiggling, demanding more and more from him.

Luka groaned. He lurched up onto his hands, planting them by my head. Now his weight was balanced between where we joined and the bracing support of his arms. His cock pulsed and jerked inside me and the answering pang down in my core had the muscles of my pussy tightening around him, milking him.

He slid his hand down my thigh, palming my ass again. "Damn, Stacia..."

Through heavy-lidded eyes, he stared at me.

His cock pulsed again, then swelled inside me, and a savage look crossed his face.

I had no time to brace myself.

Luka unhooked my ankles from behind his back and caught my hips, using his hands to shove my thighs wide. That raw edge of pain flared as he thrust deep, hard, but it was gone in the next moment, lost under the onslaught as he began to ride me, hard and fast.

I went flying over, no time to prepare, propelled straight into a brutal orgasm that knocked the breath out of me.

Luka caught my mouth in a rough kiss, swallowing down my moan. I clung to him. He was the only thing real left in the world, and if I let go, I might go flying off into space and just keep spinning, spinning, spinning away.

I wasn't even sure if I'd mind.

OUR BREATHING HAD SLOWED.

I lay on my back with Luka next to me, his hand on my belly.

"Hopefully, your first time was worth waiting for."

My cheeks flushed, but I looked over at him. I'd invited a guy to my room, had sex with said guy. Surely, I could look him in the eye.

He had a faintly bemused smile on his lips.

It matched how I felt, and for some reason, it was reassuring.

"More than."

"Good." He leaned in and brushed his lips over my forehead. As he slid from the bed, I rolled onto my side and watched him. He disappeared into the bathroom and reappeared a moment later, dressing with easy grace. He caught me watching and flashed me a smile.

I smiled back.

What would he say if I asked him to stay the night?

Before I could summon the nerve to ask, he came over and bent down, kissing me softly. But it was a chaste kiss. Sweet, even.

Without saying anything else, he straightened and left.

Sighing, I rolled onto my back and stared up at the ceiling.

Well, I couldn't complain, I decided.

He *had* been worth waiting for.

EIGHT

LUKA

Exhaustion had my limbs heavy, but I couldn't stay in bed much longer. The alarm had already gone off twice, and I could only ignore it so many times. My personal assistant had cleared my morning since I'd planned to be out of the country for the race, but I still had lunch with Geraint and several meetings that afternoon.

A dull headache pulsed at the base of my skull, brought on, no doubt, by the fact that I hadn't crashed into bed until a little after five. It was now a quarter after eleven. Normally, six hours would be enough sleep, but I'd been on the move since six a.m. Sunday, and after nearly twenty-four hours awake, I needed more rest.

I forced myself upright, and everything protested.

Still, I smiled.

I would have gotten more rest if I hadn't spent most of the night with Stacia out in the garden...then a good hour in her room, one that stretched out well past two in the morning.

By the time I got back to the party, I'd been ready to call

it a night and head home, but a drunken Emmett had seen me and dragged me into a conversation with...somebody. A cousin of Princes Harry and William, maybe. Yes, that seemed right. The short, solid man had beamed at me and shaken my hand with a happy enthusiasm before telling me that he'd gone to college with my father.

That had made it even *more* problematic to separate from him, but the real kicker had come when Emmett slung an arm around my neck and told me that the man, a beloved cousin of the famous princes, was a fan of Formula One and looking to sponsor a team of his own. Emmett had been fucking with him, something I'd recognized easy enough, but the poor guy hadn't realized it, and I had to be diplomatic.

I had every intention of giving Emmett hell for it too.

Later.

Much, much later.

For now, I was too busy reliving those moments with Stacia.

"HOW MUCH DID you drink last night?"

"I'm fine, thanks." It wasn't until the answer left me that I realized it was a little off. "What I meant was, not all that much. I'm fine, Geraint."

My younger brother sat in front of me, amusement gleaming in his eyes. "Yes, I'm sure that's exactly what you meant, brother."

"Did your fiancée enjoy the party?" Deciding it was

better to change the subject, I reached for my water and took a sip.

"She did, very much. She told me to tell you she'd see you soon." Geraint snagged a roll from the basket near his plate and took a bite, eyes leveled on me. "Now...why are you so distracted? I don't think it's a hangover. You're not glassy-eyed. Did you meet somebody?"

"I thought we were going to discuss your wedding." I was tempted to lob my basket of bread at his head. I didn't need the reminders of Stacia. I'd never see her again. That was how she wanted it too. She'd made that clear. I had a night of sweet memories, and that was it. Frankly, that should be enough. More than enough.

"That wasn't an answer."

Geraint took another bite of his roll, then leaned back and gave me a measuring stare. "Distracted. You don't look like you slept well. I heard Leonor talking to Noah. You didn't get in until five."

"Are you keeping track of me, Geraint?" Taking a sip of water, I studied him over the glass. "Should I have called to let you know I'd be late? Were you worried I'd fallen in with a bad crowd and was out carousing?"

He grinned at me. "You most definitely hooked up with somebody. Not only are you completely distracted, you're touchy. You're *never* touchy...well, except at certain times. Like after a hook-up. Most guys are more relaxed after they get laid. But not you. I suppose you're worried somebody will be sniffing around, looking for a ring or something."

"For fuck's sake." Annoyed, I dropped my roll on the plate before I could throw it at him. "Yes, I...*hooked up* with somebody, and no, I'm not worried she'll be *sniffing around.* Grow up, Geraint. You're getting married soon. Women don't go *sniffing around.*"

Geraint scowled at me. "Some do."

"Would our mother be impressed to hear you referring to the opposite sex in such a manner?" Before he could respond, I added, "Would *Katrina?*"

"You've got a point. I guess you're serious about this woman. Who is she?"

"I'm not serious and it's none of your concern." The words came out quicker than I liked, harsher. Hoping to cover, I shrugged. "It was just a thing. But that doesn't mean you talk about women that way."

He gave me a skeptical look.

"I only got her first name, Geraint. I don't know anything more about her than the fact that she's American and visiting Monaco on vacation." Part of me felt bad for lying to him, but I'd made a big enough mistake sleeping with somebody who had even a tangential connection to the royal family of Monaco.

I didn't need Geraint to point my mistake out as well.

I picked up my fork to focus on my plate. "She has no idea who I am, either. We'll never see each other again."

Geraint's brows shot up.

Before he could form a question, our father strode in.

I started to rise, but he waved me back into my seat.

One of the servants rushed to the table, pulling out a seat while another set a place for him. "Would you care for a plate, Your Highness?"

"Just coffee, thank you." He smiled and nodded, and once

we were alone, he looked me over. "I hear your car did well in the race."

"Yes." I allowed a pleased smile.

"Your mother watched." He had a bemused look on his face. "She's developing a small obsession with the sport."

"I'll have to ask her to join me some weekend."

Now the bemusement melted away into a faint smile, and Gottfried Hahn, the Grand Duke of Luxembourg nodded. "She'd enjoy that. Did you spend much time talking with Prince Aeric?"

My mind immediately went to Stacia. Taking a sip of water, I said, "I talked to him a bit, but you know how those parties are, Papa. He was very much in demand."

"Of course." He grimaced. "I can't say I'm sorry your mother and I no longer attend the more...rambunctious social functions."

"Does that mean I have to have a staid and low-key wedding reception?"

The Grand Duke flicked a look at his youngest son. To my surprise, he chuckled. "I've come to know your young fiancée well enough to understand that she won't tolerate *staid* anything, Geraint."

I had to agree. It wouldn't necessarily even be by design. Katrina Von Brandt simply brought the world around her to life.

Geraint smiled at our father, looking pleased.

A cup of coffee was placed at the duke's elbow, and he took a sip before shifting his attention back to me. "You know we've been seeking to strengthen trade with other countries, particularly Liechtenstein and Monaco. With the upcoming marriage..." He lifted his cup toward Geraint before looking back to me. "And your friendship with Prince Aeric, it seems like the best time to move forward with the plans. I'm hosting a dinner on Friday that you'll both need to attend. Prince Aeric and others from Monaco will be there, as well as the royal family from Liechtenstein."

"Understood, Papa." I waited, wondering if he had anything in mind he wanted me to do to prepare.

But he pushed back from the table and rose, taking his coffee with him.

Once he was well out of ear range, I looked at Geraint. "I can't be *that* distracted. Our father didn't even notice."

"Like that means anything." He gave me a sardonic smile. "He loves us, of course, but we'd have to be bleeding, have severely disfiguring injuries, or be on fire for him to notice something was off. Distracted because of a woman? Never going to happen."

There was no point in arguing that. He was right.

NINE

STACIA

No matter how often I traveled, I could never manage to pack in such a way that left plenty of room for all the stuff I bought. I'd even brought along an *empty* suitcase— a packed carry-on tucked in the larger, matching full-sized piece of luggage. But was that piece enough?

Of course not.

A knock at my door interrupted my mental calculations, and I glanced over to see Aeric standing there.

He cocked a brow and looked around. "Are you having trouble?"

"This is *your* fault," I told him, pointing a red silk high-heeled shoe at him. It had a delicate row of crystals running across the diagonal strap that twinkled and flashed, catching the light and splintering into thousands of fractals. "I told you I didn't need to spend a day shopping in Milan."

"I didn't see you arguing too hard when you dragged me into the store where you found those shoes." He studied the heel pointedly before looking at the chaos around my room.

"Would you like me to send Gustave up? He's a genius at packing."

I scowled at him. "I don't need help packing, unlike *you*, Your Highness." With a sniff, I turned back to assess the madness. I wasn't about to tell him that the household's majordomo intimidated me more than a little. He was like a mix of Batman's Alfred, the Addam's Family's Lurch, and a nightmare amalgam of some of TV's *organizational experts*— the kind who went into a family's homes under the guise of *streamlining and organizing* and tossed out anything that interfered with the *minimalist lifestyle*. Okay, maybe that was exaggerating, but he still unnerved me.

"You're not exactly making a lot of progress standing there, my dear."

I flipped him off, and he laughed.

"You've been in a *mood* this week, Stacia," Aeric said, coming over to hug me. He dropped a kiss onto my temple before circling around to the side of my bed and picking up a dress I'd bought on our trip to Milan. "Are you just ready to get back home? Missing Mummy and Daddy?"

I stuck my tongue out at him. "Don't be an asshole."

He gave an unrepentant grin, still holding the pretty cocktail dress.

It was a simple sheath with cap sleeves and a modest neckline, but the black, scalloped lace overlay and the sheer design of the back gave it a modern edge.

"This would be perfect for the dinner I'm attending tonight," he said, displaying the dress in much the same manner used by the woman who'd sold it to me at the boutique. "Why don't you leave it out?"

I frowned at him. "What dinner?"

"In Luxembourg." He rolled his eyes. "My parents mentioned it a few days ago, and I forgot about it until they reminded me this morning. Why don't you come with me? I can't get out of it because we're discussing trade partnerships and such, but I hate for you to spend your final night here alone."

"So you'd rather me go with you so I can sit and listen to you talk trade partnerships." I gave him a dry look. "That's so sweet of you."

"I know." He winked. "Prince Geraint's fiancée, Katrina, will be there. You never had a chance to meet her. I think you'd like her. And trade partnerships will probably bore her to tears. She does a lot of charity work, and...oh, and her brother is married to an American actress. She's doing charity work that involves the theatre. You love the theatre, and you're always trying to find ways to get Uncle Wade and Aunt Willa more involved in more philanthropic causes."

I scrunched up my brow as I folded a scarf, a memory working free. "An actress...wait, you mean the Broadway Princess...Regan Elson?"

"You're just now making that connection?" he teased.

I grabbed the red silk shoe and threw it at him.

He caught it easily. "Hey...careful. You'd hate to have Blanche work you over for assaulting the prince."

"She'd probably slip me fifty and high-five me behind your back." Rolling my eyes at him, I held out my hand for the shoe and looked it over.

"If you were worried about damaging it, you shouldn't have thrown it," he said.

"Hush." Satisfied, I tucked it back in the box and closed it, removing it from temptation. The other pair of shoes I'd picked up that day sat next to it, and I tugged the lid off, looking at the Manolo Blahnik satin pumps with the jeweled asymmetrical strap. I really did like things that sparkled.

"You even have the perfect pair of shoes."

Flipping the lid back over the pumps, I met his eyes. "No purse. No jewelry."

"Oh, I'm sure my mother wouldn't mind helping you there."

I gulped at that idea. I had no doubt Princess Valentina would be happy to help, but the idea of wearing jewels from Monaco's royal collection made me a little sick to my stomach. "Ah...I don't know..."

"Relax." Aeric came around the bed and pushed the dress into my arms. "I'll let her know. Come on. You know you don't want to spend the night alone, and besides, for all we know, it could be several years before our schedules work out for us to visit again."

"Okay." I leaned against him with a sigh. "You have a point."

PRINCESS VALENTINA NICOLAI, my mother's older sister, swept into my room an hour later. A solid woman with a tight cap of gray curls followed behind her, carrying a silver tray with several wooden boxes on top.

I recognized Ana, one of her personal assistants.

Immediately, I clambered up from the floor where I'd been wrestling my suitcase closed.

Valentina gave me an amused look. "Aeric said you were having fun packing. It appears he wasn't exaggerating."

I'd always had a good relationship with my aunt. I got along better with her than I did with my own mother, but still, I was mildly embarrassed to be caught on the floor by the Princess of Monaco.

"I'm sorry, Aunt Valentina."

She waved a hand at me, unconcerned. "Ana, you may put those down on the dresser. Thank you."

Ana nodded and put the tray down, giving me a conspiratorial wink before leaving us alone.

Valentina walked over to the valet hook where the lace sheath dress hung waiting, the Manolo Blahniks waiting on the floor. "Is this the dress?" she asked.

"Yes." Apprehensively, I tugged my shirt down. "I have a couple of other options. One was the rose cocktail dress I wore for the dinner with you and Uncle when I first arrived."

"That was lovely. But so is this. Your mother doesn't give you enough credit when it comes to style, darling." She gave me a knowing look. "But I suspect perhaps you aren't as confident with your choices at home. Regardless, this dress is lovely. Aeric described it well, and I have the perfect pieces to accessorize with."

"Oh?"

She gestured for me to join her, and once we stood together by the dresser, she opened the smallest of the two wooden boxes. I gasped at the ring that lay inside, nestled on a protective bed of velvet.

"It's from the art deco period. It belonged to my grandmother. Your great-grandmother. They were passed onto me." She lifted her eyes to study me. "Do you like it?"

"Who wouldn't?" I asked, slightly breathless.

She chuckled and pulled it out. "Let's see if it fits."

I was almost too nervous to even try, but at the same time, the lustrous pearl framed by a hexagon formed of diamonds, then bracketed by gleaming onyx was prettier than anything I'd ever owned, whether I'd bought it for myself or had it given to me by my parents.

"It fits perfectly," Valentina said, sounding satisfied once she'd pushed it onto my right middle finger. "A wonderful statement ring, as they call them now."

"It's gorgeous, Aunt Valentina."

"Yes. And it suits you." She gave me a quick smile and waggled her fingers, her hand smaller than mine, daintier. "It never suited me, not with my stubby fingers."

"Your fingers are *not* stubby."

She laughed. "They are. Rings such as this don't flatter me. Here. The earrings work well with the piece." She flipped open the other box, revealing drop earrings, not quite two inches long, each with a shimmering pearl displayed elegantly from the tip of diamond studded pendants, accented with glossy black onyx.

"Again, wow." Knowing she'd want to see them on, I took one and turned to the mirror, slipping it into place before doing the same with the second. Looking back at her, I waited for her appraisal.

"Yes." She nodded. "You should wear your hair up. Would you like me to send someone to help you?"

"No. I can do it but thank you."

She leaned in and kissed me, once on each cheek. "It's been lovely having you visit. You'll keep those pieces, Stacia."

She was almost to the door before I processed that last part.

"Aunt Valentina?" I squawked.

She turned, one brow arched. "Yes, my dear?"

"I...I can't keep these."

"You can." She smiled. "They're a gift from an aunt to her niece, and you shouldn't argue over a gift, Stacia."

She left then, and I turned to look at what was probably close to a hundred thousand dollars in diamonds and pearls now adorning my body.

PUTTING on makeup was one of my banes in life. I rarely bothered with more than mascara and lip gloss unless it was one of my mother's more formal events, and for that, I usually went with the smoky eye I'd finally perfected after spending an *entire* afternoon practicing and watching YouTube tutorials.

But that was a bit much for a dinner with members of royalty. All those articles about the makeup that Meghan Markle and Kate Middleton wore to their weddings might have been a surprise to a lot of Americans, but not to me. There weren't as many strict rules on the various royals throughout Europe as there seemed to be in England, but there was always an emphasis on *natural*.

I didn't *mind* that, really, but it was a hell of a lot easier for me to achieve *natural* if I just didn't *wear* any makeup, but I knew better than that.

After twenty minutes I'd never get back, I swiped a neutral pinkish lipstick over my lips and stood back to check my reflection out.

"Good enough," I pronounced, then double-checked to make sure there weren't any stray specks of powder, bronzer, or eyeshadow on my chest.

Ten minutes after that, I had my dress on and gave my hair one more check, then put the earrings on and slid the ring onto my right middle finger. I was about to head out the door when I stopped and turned around, hurrying back into the bathroom to grab the lipstick and dump it in the little black clutch Ana had brought to my room earlier.

I opened the door in time to see Gustave approaching. He gave an approving smile. "The helicopter will be here in a few moments, Miss Stacia."

"Thank you, Gustave."

"Is your luggage packed for your flight home?"

I might have imagined it, but I thought I caught a glimpse of a hopeful gleam in his eye. Like he hoped I'd say *no*, so he could go in and organize my luggage and the contents down to the very last USB cord. "I have it all ready." I gave him a brilliant smile. "All that's left is my overnight bag."

"Wonderful." His polite smile never dimmed. "I'll have it all transferred down. I checked with Ann. She said we'll be laundering your dress from tonight and sending it to you once you're back in the states."

I opened my mouth to tell him I'd told Ann it wasn't necessary—I'd left room in the carry-on bag's concealed garment bag—but at the gleam in his eye, decided not to bother. What was the point? They'd clean the dress, the shoes if needed, and everything would be shipped back, ready to wear the next time. And I wouldn't have to argue with Gustave.

Not that I'd win anyway.

"Of course."

He gestured for me to precede him down the hall, and as we walked, he gave me an update on my trip the next day, letting me know he'd already arranged my ride to the airport, taken care of checking me in, then giving details about the weather throughout the entire journey.

"Should I let your parents know when you'll be arriving in New York?" he offered as we reached the hall leading toward the grand staircase.

"No." I managed not to blurt the word out. "I let them know before I left, so they're aware, but they have plans tomorrow night. I don't want them to feel obligated to change things because of my trip."

They wouldn't, but if I was lucky, they'd forgotten, and I'd have a few more days of peace before my guilt drove me to let them know I was home.

THE CASTLE CAME into view slowly, first hidden behind the terrain itself and a protective barrier of trees, particularly the large conifers that speared up into the sky. I caught glimpses of its pale exterior through the window and edged closer in hopes of a better view.

"You haven't been to Luxembourg before, have you?"

My uncle's voice pricked my awareness, and I gave him an embarrassed smile and slid back onto the seat. "No, Uncle. I haven't."

"It's a lovely country." He nodded to the window. "Kasteel Berg is beautiful. We'll make sure you get a tour while we're here."

I'd done some mad Googling on the flight, so I knew he was referring to Castle Berg, the home of the Grand Duchy. I hadn't bothered clicking on any of the links about the family, though. I knew all too well how easy it was for the *wrong* sort of information to get out there, and I'd rather form my own opinions on the people I'd meet tonight. "Thank you, Uncle. That would be wonderful."

He nodded and turned his attention back to Aeric.

They'd been discussing trade—textiles and technology, mostly—almost since takeoff, while Aunt Valentina had dropped bits and pieces about the Prince and Princess of Luxembourg and the upcoming wedding. That discussion had segued into the topic of Princess Katrina of Liechtenstein, and then Princess Regan and Prince Sebastian, the Hereditary Prince.

Her eyes gleamed with fascination as she talked about Regan, the woman who'd been dubbed the Broadway Princess by American media.

"I've only met with her a few times, but hopefully, we can talk more tonight. I'm fascinated by the theatre project she's building in Liechtenstein."

I nodded at her but kept my eyes on the window as we traversed a bend and came to a drive.

"We're here." My aunt patted my knee and settled back into her seat. "You won't be able to see much until we get through the gate."

She was right. After a few more moments of neck-craning, I gave up.

Aeric winked at me. "You're so impatient, darling."

"It's an American thing," I said loftily.

"It's a *you* thing."

"Behave, children," his mother said.

A faint smile tugged at his lips, but Aeric lapsed into silence.

Due to the angle the car took as it rounded the final bend and my position in the limousine, I couldn't see much more than I'd seen from the road but quashed the impatience as the vehicle came to a stop. I hadn't attended an event with my aunt and uncle before in another country, but I had no doubt there'd be some manner of pomp and circumstance, and I refused to embarrass them by fidgeting and bouncing up and down on my toes to better see the sights.

I even managed to keep from looking around with a wide-eyed stare once I was out of the car, standing next to Aeric. The large structure with its pale outer walls, along with the sloped, gabled roofs and numerous turrets gave it an air that seemed to be a mix between German and Swiss—or maybe they were the same. I wasn't an architectural expert. Windows sparkled in the sun, and every inch seemed to shine.

"Lovely," I murmured.

"Yes. But the Prince's Palace is lovelier," Aeric added

under his breath. "Come on. Introductions and announcements await."

He offered his arm, and I let him lead me from the car, taking the chance to surreptitiously take in another look at the castle.

But I had to snap my attention away from the big construction far too soon as Aeric came to a stop less than a minute later.

"That's the Grand Duke," Aeric said in a low voice as we took our place to the left of his parents. He didn't nod or gesture, but it wasn't hard to see who he meant.

The elegant couple descending the steps of the castle looked to be about the same age as my aunt and uncle, polite smiles set on their faces.

"You have the Grand Duke of Luxembourg, Gottfried Hahn, and his wife, Octavia Hahn, the Grand Duchess. They're a decent sort," he said. "They've got two sons...good men. Friends of mine. You know about Geraint. He's the one engaged to Princess Katrina. Here we go, they're coming out now too. You met Luka, by the way."

Luka...

I tensed, my eyes darting to the men following along behind the older couple.

"Are you all right?" Aeric asked, pausing his litany to look down at me.

"I...yes, fine." I swallowed, then nodded toward the castle. "Luka. He was at the party. I talked with him a bit." *Talked. And then some.* "I didn't realize he was Geraint's brother."

"Yes, well...he didn't appear to want it advertised. Luka is the Hereditary Grand Duke of Luxembourg. There's his brother, Geraint. His title is Prince Geraint. And there's his fiancée, Princess Katrina of Liechtenstein."

I was still stuck on what he'd told me about Luka. *Hereditary Grand Duke.*

"Hereditary Grand Duke?" I repeated, the words coming out a bit louder than necessary.

"Yes." Aeric covered the hand I had tucked into the crook of his elbow with his own. "Are you all right, Stacia?"

"I'm fine. Just trying to keep up. Go on, please." Swallowing, I jerked my attention away from Luka and studied the pretty, petite blonde standing next to the other young man who'd just descended the steps.

"Well, it can be a bit to keep up with, I know." He patted my hand, humor underlining the words. "We still have the Liechtensteiners to introduce."

"Lovely."

He continued. But I didn't process a word he said.

I was too busy staring at Luka.

I HADN'T INTENTIONALLY SOUGHT him out.

I wasn't even sure what to *say* to him. I knew how to *address* him, but it seemed very...weird to call a guy I'd slept with *Your Highness.*

But as I reached for the glass of wine I'd requested, he was just suddenly there. And the uniformed man who'd put the wine in front of me wasn't.

It was just Luka and me.

Feeling out of place, I looked at him. "Hello."

He inclined his head.

I hadn't done the proper greeting, I realized. Oh, well. Blame it on me being a crass American.

"I...ah...you're the last person I expected to see here. I thought Prince Geraint was the heir to the Grand Duchy. I... ah, well, I saw him briefly at the engagement party. I was there with Aeric. I guess I just assumed..." Feeling stupid, I let the words trail off and shrugged. "Well, I never heard you mentioned when they introduced guests."

Luka lifted a brow and gave me a look that was all too familiar—cool, condescending—judging.

He'd judged me and found me wanting.

Tightening my hand on the glass of wine, I fought the rush of blood creeping up my neck and decided I was thankful I'd taken the time with my makeup. It would mask *some* of my embarrassed flush.

"The engagement party you attended with Prince Aeric *was* in my brother's honor," Luka said, his tone dour. "It would be in bad taste for me to take away from him on a night that was for him and his fiancée. Naturally, I stayed in the background."

His amber eyes, the color of good whiskey, stared into mine.

It left me feeling naked and more vulnerable than I'd had when he'd covered me, then slowly pushed inside.

"Naturally," I said. "Excuse me."

A rush of emotions flooded me as I walked away, the feel of his eyes boring into my back.

Anger, hurt, embarrassment, resignation, they all vied for dominance, and I couldn't give in to any of them, not here.

That knowledge left me with an odd brittle sensation, one I knew too well.

I felt like I might shatter with the wrong look, the wrong word.

And that was something else I couldn't allow to happen here.

I should have stayed in Monaco. No, I should have just caught an earlier flight *home*.

TEN

LUKA

THE HALF-SMILE ON HER FACE WAS THE FIRST THING I saw when I stepped out of the castle.

I'd seen her every time I closed my eyes for the past week, and for half a minute, I wondered if I'd hallucinated her right into being. I hadn't been sleeping all that well, and lack of sleep *did* contribute to hallucinations, didn't it?

But then she turned her head and looked up at Aeric, and I knew I wasn't imagining anything.

Stacia was here, with her cousin. She was also with the Prince and Princess of Monaco.

I'd assumed she was a *distant* cousin, but I could toss that idea out the window because Prince Fortinbras of Monaco was too much a stickler for protocol. I couldn't see him inviting some distant cousin to dinner, even if the invitation *had* been extended to the Nicolai family.

Moments later, I was proven right.

Stacia was introduced as Princess Valentina's niece, visiting from America. My mother, naturally, had to ask, and Stacia, with that sweet smile she'd revealed to me several times throughout the night, explained that her mother was Valentina's younger sister. Willa had moved to America years earlier, and Stacia had always had a close relationship with her uncle, aunt, and cousins in Monaco.

Fucking perfect.

This is what you get for letting your dick overrule your common sense.

I spent the next hour lambasting myself, and yet, I couldn't even find any regret over what had taken place between us.

It had been...perfect.

What wasn't perfect was her being here and me not knowing what to say to her.

The ideal thing to do would be to stay away.

Yet when I saw her requesting a glass of wine while my parents mingled with the Prince and Princess of Monaco, instead of taking the route of wisdom and avoiding her, I found myself closing the distance until I was close enough to reach out and touch her.

I glanced at the sommelier who'd served her wine and jerked my head just as he set her wine down. He quickly withdrew, leaving us alone.

Stacia saw me, her eyes widening slightly. "Hello."

I had no idea what to say. I'd been worried she'd blurt something out about what had happened, or worse, call me *Your Highness*, which might erase the memory of her ragged whisper in my ear. "*Luka...*"

Her short, perfunctory *hello* worked well enough,

although I wasn't sure how to respond. Kissing her was definitely out.

"I...ah, well, I saw him briefly at the engagement party. I was there with Aeric. I guess I just assumed..." She swallowed and cleared her throat, eyes darting away before she looked back at me, clearly nervous. "Well, I never heard you mentioned when they introduced guests."

I cocked a brow. This was a first. I'd never had anybody mistake Geraint for me. As I watched, a faint blush crept up her cheeks, and I found myself remembering the blushes I'd seen Sunday night...where they started low on her breasts and rose up her neck, blooming like a rose.

"The engagement party you attended with Prince Aeric *was* in my brother's honor," I finally said, realizing I was staring. "It would be in bad taste for me to take away from him on a night that was for him and his fiancée. Naturally, I stayed in the background."

The flush on her cheeks deepened.

"Naturally. Excuse me."

She turned, wine in hand, and walked away, her strides clipped, the sound of her heels echoing angrily on the elegant marble floor before she reached the rich, woven rug where several couches were displayed.

Fuck. I'd bungled that one.

It shouldn't matter, I told myself, turning back to the drink service. The sommelier hovered in the background, and I nodded at him. I didn't want wine, though.

"Scotch," I said before he could speak.

If he was surprised, he didn't show it.

"Make it a double."

It couldn't matter. Bungling it was probably a *good* thing, really.

She was just an American, even if she was related to the Princess of Monaco. She'd leave and go back home, and that would be it.

ELEVEN

STACIA

When my aunt invited me to join her and the Grand Duchess for a tour of the gardens with Prince Geraint and his fiancée, Princess Katrina, I could have cried in gratitude.

I was still stinging over the slight from Luka earlier and doing my best to ignore him, although it seemed he was watching me at the oddest times.

Aeric, thankfully, was the only one who knew me well enough to realize my mood was off, and when he asked me if I was all right, I'd just told him I was tired.

He didn't entirely believe me, but he was decent enough not to press me—reason one million and two why I adored him so much.

Now, as we made our way back to the beginning of the maze, I fought back a level of anxiety I wasn't familiar with.

I didn't *want* to go back inside yet.

Aeric had texted me earlier, no words—just an emoji of a smiley face with a zzz above it. He was bored senseless, and I had a feeling they weren't even close to bringing their trade talks to any sort of resolution.

"I think I'm going to take another walk through the maze," I said abruptly, catching sight of the entrance ahead. "If you don't mind, Your Highness."

Octavia, the Grand Duchess of Luxembourg, gave me an understanding smile. "I don't mind, Stacia."

"If you don't make it out within an hour, I'll come find you," Geraint offered with a friendly smile.

We'd had an easy discussion over the past half hour, and I smiled at his jest. "You might need to do that, Prince Geraint."

"Would you like me to stay with you?" Katrina, the Princess of Liechtenstein, offered. "I'm not particularly fond of trade talk myself."

It was a surprisingly blunt statement from a royal, but over the course of the evening, I'd come to realize that Katrina was just...well...surprisingly blunt. I grinned at her. "Thank you, but I'm fine on my own."

A few minutes later, I was already lost.

Ten minutes after that, I was convinced I'd be stuck in the hedge maze until they indeed had to send a search party after me.

"That's fine," I mumbled, sitting on a bench so I could slip my heels off. Manolo Blahniks or not, they were *still* heels and uncomfortable as hell for somebody who preferred tennis shoes, loafers, or boots. After taking a few seconds to stretch my toes and flex my ankles, I rose, carrying my shoes.

I came upon one dead end after another. It was amusing, at first.

But after the fourth, I found myself staring at the wall of shrubbery like it had grown there on purpose, specifically to insult me.

"Lost?"

I jolted at the sound of his voice, and for a few seconds, blood rushed up my neck at the remembered embarrassment from our encounter earlier. I breathed deeply and reminded myself that having a *title* didn't *entitle* him or anybody else to be a dick.

Bracing myself mentally, I turned and gave him a cool look. "I believe that's the point of a hedge maze, Your Highness. I'll find my way through eventually."

"I could be of assistance."

Hah, no. But instead of going with my instinctive response, I said, "No need for you to waste your time, Your Highness."

His mouth spasmed.

Oh, was he feeling guilty for being a douche?

Good.

He took a step toward me.

Crossing my arms over my chest, my shoes still dangling from my fingers, I lifted a brow and stared him down.

"I was rude earlier."

"Of course not, Your Highness. You displayed immense courtesy, actually. I had no right questioning you, but you were kind enough to address my uneducated silliness." I infused each word with saccharine sweetness, pasting the most insincere smile I could manage on my face. "I appreciate the courtesy, Your Highness, and my apologies if I did anything to make you feel as if you were rude."

His eyes flashed and a muscle pulsed in his jaw. "Stacia—"

"Yes, *Your Highness*?"

"Luka!" He closed the distance between us, glaring down at me. "Luka. You fucking called me Luka just days ago. You all but screamed it a couple of times."

"I apologize. That was *wholly* inappropriate." Widening my eyes, I did my best to feign embarrassment. "If I'd known—"

A second later, I was in his arms, pressed against him. His hand curved over the back of my neck, arching my head up. Surprised...*thrilled*...I sucked in a breath just as our mouths collided.

Even though it was stupid and wrong, I dropped my shoes and reached for him, and the two of us were locked around each other, hands grabbing and tongues twined.

I moaned and pressed against him, jerking at his shirt where he'd tucked it into his trousers. Soon, hot muscled skin met my questing fingers as I shoved the material upward. He grabbed the hem of my skirt, and I shivered as his palms spread over my thighs before gliding up, moving higher and higher, until his big hands cupped my ass.

He pulled me against him.

My belly contracted as the ridge of his cock pulsed against me, all the muscles clenching while other parts of me went wet and hot and loose.

He nudged me backward, then stopped abruptly. Before I could figure out why, he broke the kiss and lifted his head, staring at me.

His hand, hot and hard, curved over my neck, and I could

feel the way my pulse lunged at his touch, as if to beg for more.

He pressed his lips to my ear. "Should I stop?"

I sucked in a breath, eyes locked wide on his face while indecision flickered to life inside. After a few taut moments, I said, "I should say yes. I should tell you to fuck right the fuck off...Your Highness."

"Are you going to? I deserve it." That same muscle pulsed in his jaw, and his lids twitched.

I felt his body tighten almost imperceptibly, too, as if preparing for the rejection. If I was smart, I'd tell him to stop. I'd walk back into the house, plant my ass at Aeric's side, and zone out until it was time to go home.

Somehow, with just a few words, Luka had managed to hurt me in a way I couldn't have predicted.

But, really, I was going home tomorrow.

He couldn't *do* that again. I'd never see him once I left Monaco, most likely. I'd make *sure* of that. No more parties with Aeric when I visited. No more Formula One races. I'd stay out of his orbit.

So...why not give in?

That was what my body wanted, no doubt.

I summoned up the smile I'd learned at my mother's knee. "I go back home tomorrow, and I'll never have to see you again, so...no. I'll wait until after."

"Good enough."

I had no time to brace myself before he hauled me into his arms.

It seemed to take a lifetime, but it likely was only a minute or two before he stopped and put me down. Apprehension—and an excitement I couldn't contain—flared to life as he turned me around then nudged me forward until I was bent over a pretty ornamental bench.

He shoved the skirt of my dress up over my hips, baring my ass, covered now only by black silk panties. The sensation of his fingers trailing over the silk covering the wet heat between my thighs made me gasp. He grabbed my hips next, and I whimpered, shivering as he thrust his cock against me.

He stopped after only seconds, and I moaned, pushing back.

He braced a hand on the small of my spine. "Patience... I'm just getting a rubber."

The words barely made sense, but I *did* process the fact that he wasn't leaving, and I locked onto that, curling my fingers around the wooden slats of the bench.

"One condom...fuck, Stacia. Had it for a while, but at least I've got one."

Again, the words barely connected, my spine undulating, need ripping into me.

Behind me, Luka swore, and abruptly, he caught my panties and yanked them to my knees before taking my hips in his hands.

"This tattoo, Stacia..."

I shivered as he traced his fingers over the seahorse that cavorted over my right hip, a few water bubbles trailing along behind, curling onto the top edge of my right butt cheek.

"So cute and sweet...so sexy and unexpected." He bent down and kissed it, and I shivered. "Just like you, darling. Sweet...sexy...unexpected." His voice roughened, the hands on my hips tightening.

I braced myself just in time, but not for the hard, deep thrusts I'd been hoping for. No, it wasn't his cock I felt.

It was his mouth.

He'd knelt behind me, and I cried out before I could stop it. Biting my lip to stifle the sound, I practically collapsed. If it wasn't for his hands, I would have. I locked my knees, shuddering as his tongue lashed, swirling over my folds, delving inside me.

It was like he wanted to *devour* me.

I swallowed another cry, then jolted when he brought his hand down hard on the right cheek of my butt.

A startled noise escaped, and I barely managed to muffle it.

He spanked me again, then thrust two fingers into my cunt, twisting and curling them.

It shoved me straight into orgasm, and before I even had a chance to calm, he rose and thrust inside. I arched my back, sucking in a breath and swallowing a scream that almost choked me.

He grabbed my shoulders and hauled me upright, my spine arching even more as the position drove me down on his cock. I was *impaled* on him, balanced on the tips of my toes, nothing to grab onto now, to brace myself on as his thick, heavy cock pulsed inside me.

He held me like that, like a butterfly pinned to a board, for long, interminable seconds, and each pulse of his dick made me shudder and clench around him.

"You've got the sweetest pussy," he murmured, sliding his free hand over my hip and seeking out my clitoris. "And you're wrapped so tight around my dick, Stacia. Still as tight as a fist, like you were last time. Tight as a virgin. So fucking hot."

His words, in his sexy as fuck accent, rolled over me, an aural caress that only added to the sensations evoked by his cock and the fingers strumming over my clit.

Another pulse of his cock had me jerking, the nerves in my pussy so sensitive it was almost *painful.* I moaned, desperate, and tried to move. I couldn't manage much more than a wiggle.

"What do you want, *ma belle?*" he murmured against my ear. "Tell me."

"Luka...please."

His fingers ghosted over my clitoris again. "Please...*what?*" An edge underscored his words. "Tell me what you want."

Confused, I shook my head.

"Do you want to come, *ma belle?*" he asked, his words teasing, sensuous...darkly delicious.

"Yes...*please!*"

"Do you want me to *fuck* you, *ma belle?*" He underscored those words with a light swat of his hand against my clit.

Shocked, stunned, I flailed, needing something to grab onto. I only found his hand, and with a whimper, I realized I was lifting my hips, begging for more.

He obliged, spanking my clit and the flesh of my pussy where I stretched so tight around him. "So sweet and hot," he whispered. "You like having your pussy spanked, don't you?"

"Yes...*please.*" My skin was so hot, everything in me too sensitive. I was going to come apart if he kept this up.

"Good...Tell me what else you like. What else you want,

ma belle. If you want me to fuck you, *say it.* Tell me. Say *Fuck me, Luka* and I'll do it. I'll ride you good and hard, and you'll come again and again before I'm done."

The words spilled out of me with no conscious thought.

"Fuck me, Luka...*please.*" I rolled back against him and said it again, *"Please,* Luka...*fuck me."*

He bit my neck gently, then urged me forward, bending me back over the bench.

His cock, so hard and swollen it almost hurt, pulsed inside me as he started to withdraw. I shuddered, trying to follow. He gripped my left hip but let the right one go. A breath later, I sucked in a stunned breath as he spanked me again. "It's time to get fucked, Stacia...be still and take it."

And that was all I could do. *Take* it. *Revel* in it.

Shuddering with each deep, bruising thrust, I bounced up onto my toes, lips rolled inward and pressed together to muffle the desperate, needy whimpers that tried to escape.

He muttered behind me, but he moved between French and German and another language I didn't know, and my mind was too overcome with pleasure to possibly keep up.

Sensation wracked me, and his cock filled me, and then the orgasm exploded through me.

I felt him swell even more, then he groaned. Finally, he said something I *did* understand.

My name.

TWELVE

LUKA

I woke early.

If I'd had my way, I would have slept in, with Stacia at my side after I spent the entire night between her thighs and getting my fill of her, but she'd left with her family less than two hours after we'd both gone inside—through separate doors at her insistence.

She'd barely spoken to me during that time, but her cheeks colored every time I looked at her, and I consoled myself that at least it was the memory of our minutes in the garden affecting her, not how I'd been an ass.

I'd apologized. She'd inclined her head, offering nothing else.

Two hours later, she was gone.

As I settled in for my third mile on the treadmill, I told myself it was over, just as I'd known it would be. She was returning to New York City, and we'd never see each other again.

But the memories were something I'd hold for a long time.

Hopefully, she would too.

I pushed myself through another two miles, then returned to my room to shower and dress.

On my way down to breakfast, I ran into Geraint. He was decidedly less clear-eyed and awake and greeted me with a grunt, rubbing at his right eye with a fist as if to knuckle away the dregs of sleep.

"Late night with Katrina?" I teased.

He flipped me off just as we entered the small, informal dining room we preferred to use when there were no guests in-house.

I sat down as one of the staff brought me coffee.

"What would you like for breakfast, Your Highness?"

I shrugged, nothing in mind. "Have them surprise me." I smiled at the young woman as my administrative assistant, Stuart, came in, carrying several newspapers that I followed, as well as the tablet he used to keep track of my daily schedule. "Good morning, Stuart."

"Your Highness." He nodded and placed the papers down.

Gesturing to the seat across from mine, I said, "Sit down, Stuart."

He hesitated, as he always did.

"Sit." I slid him a look. "I don't want to crane my head to look at you while we talk. You do realize that's a *literal* pain in the neck."

My brother smothered a chuckle, and even Stuart's lips twitched, although I knew he wasn't entirely comfortable with it. I suspected if my parents were to enter the small dining room, he'd jumped to his feet so fast, the chair would topple over. He glanced toward the door before finally taking the seat.

We did this every time we met over breakfast—and that was three times a week.

One would think he'd be used to the drill by now.

But he came from a long line of people who'd served as assistants to the Duchy. His father was still *my* father's assistant. Protocol was something bred into the bone, for him, for me. But I didn't see the point in making him stand and stare at the top of my head, or me get a crick in the neck as we went about our regular routine.

A few minutes later, Stuart started to go over the schedule for the week. I pulled out my phone to make sure the various appointments had synced to my calendar, then while he went into detail about the attendees at an upcoming banquet in Germany, I pulled up another app and started skimming the headlines for various countries.

I went from amused to annoyed to resigned, all in the span of two minutes, and was about to close the app when I scrolled past a picture, my eyes lingering but the connection not forming immediately.

I stopped and went back, staring.

Blood drained out of my head, and I closed my eyes.

Stuart said something. I held up a hand, needing a minute.

"Luka?" Geraint said gently. He touched my shoulder.

I hadn't realized he'd risen from his chair, but he was there.

Clutching the phone in a tight fist, I tapped on the article and waited for it to load. Although the internet connection was lightning fast, it *still* wasn't fast enough, and when it loaded within a second or two, it still felt like a lifetime had passed.

"Damn," Geraint murmured from just over my shoulder.

I swallowed as I read the article. It was only a few lines and ended abruptly.

"They don't even say how he is," I said bleakly, looking up at my brother.

"Go," he said softly. He nodded at Stuart. "I'll work with Stuart and take care of what I can, reschedule what I can't."

"YOUR HIGHNESS."

I looked at Stuart. He stood in the doorway, his ever-present tablet missing for once. "Have you learned anything?"

"Not much, I'm afraid." He shifted at the threshold of my suite before asking, "May I come in?"

I almost bit his head off but stopped before I could. It wasn't his fault I was more scared than I had ever been. "Of course, please."

I'd waved off offers of having my luggage packed, desperately needing complete privacy for a few brief moments.

Stuart looked at the minor chaos in my room, then wisely decided to ignore it, settling in a wing chair in the sitting area. "I've got some information about where he is."

Suddenly, exhausted by the stress, I dropped down on

the edge of my bed and waved at him. Nightmare thoughts had tripped through my mind ever since reading that Emmett had been in a crash during practice the other day. I didn't know why I hadn't been contacted—I *should* have been—and that was one thing Stuart would find out for me.

I listened as he updated me on what he'd learned, which wasn't much, then nodded. "Make sure you find out why nobody called me about this."

"I'm already working on it," he said softly. "I've got your trip arranged. Since your parents have the family plane, it proved to be more expedient for you to travel on public transport. Etienne will go—"

"No." I shook my head, even though I knew it would infuriate my parents. They didn't like it when I traveled outside Europe without security, but I wasn't dealing with the added hassle. "I'm going alone."

Stuart looked like he wanted to argue but shook his head slightly, as if to tell himself no. "Understood. The trip is taken care of, and I've synced all the information to your phone. I'm coordinating with Noah about shifting your meetings to Geraint for the next week. If you need more time, let me know."

"Thank you." I shoved myself upright and pushed my hair back. "When does the flight leave?"

Stuart checked the time. "You need to leave within the hour. You've got a layover in Barcelona before making your connection to New York, then onto Montreal." He gave me an apologetic smile. "Working on a time crunch, it's the best I can do. I had to pull strings to even get this flight. I wish it worked out better."

"It's fine." I checked the arrival time. It wasn't as fast as I'd like, but even if I was already *there*, I wouldn't be satisfied. "Thank you, Stuart."

He left me alone, and I rubbed the back of my neck, worry for Emmett a heavy weight on my brain. We'd been friends for so long.

"You better be all right, you stubborn bastard."

THIRTEEN

STACIA

Sitting in the window seat, I looked out at the clear skies spreading out over what little I could see of Paris. I should have arranged for a layover. I loved Paris. Not the parts my mother had tried to convince me to love, of course. It wasn't that I minded the art galleries or going to the theatre, but she didn't *go* because she enjoyed art or theatre or the opera. She went because it was the *thing to do.*

It was hard to enjoy all the culture and the history when you kept being nudged back into the present with reminders of, *Oh, look... it's the so and so family...I hear they're distantly related to Marie Antoinette...*

That was why I'd started traveling on my own as soon as I could, while avoiding family trips as often as possible. I'd taken my first solo trip abroad when I was seventeen—this very trip I was finishing now, in fact.

To see Aeric.

It had been the first taste of freedom I'd ever experienced. Even graduating early and attending Oxford at sixteen hadn't really been the same as being *free*, not with my parents.

"When is that VIP supposed to be here?"

The words, spoken in low, hushed French, caught my attention only because I was sitting in the last row of first class, and the airline attendants were standing behind me, preparing to do another walk-through, this time to offer gourmet snacks and fresh fruit, no doubt.

I'd noticed their hustling around earlier, letting people board earlier than what seemed normal. I hadn't thought much of it at the time, but now I glanced around, wondering if the frenetic energy I sensed in the air was related to this VIP.

"Soon," the other attendant said, this voice male.

Both were native French speakers. I'd traveled enough to be able to discern the difference, and I also knew that the French, in general, didn't *do* frenetic. It was beneath them.

But they were definitely excited about something. As I sat there and watched, their heads craned back and forth, going from the front of the plane back to the task at hand.

"Any idea what's going on?"

It was the first speaker again—the woman.

"No. I just know there were some diplomatic strings pulled. I overheard some talk in the background when I got the call and was told to let the pilot know we were to wait for his arrival. Period." He paused, then with jaded amusement, added, "It must be nice to have *that* kind of pull behind the family name."

His companion laughed. "We best get on the service so we're done before he gets here."

I studiously kept my attention directed outward, even as I pushed down annoyance. *Wait for his arrival.*

The implied arrogance that must come with such a decree set my teeth on edge. Shooting a look around the cabin, I then shifted my attention to the one empty seat available.

Right next to mine.

I was going to be sitting with somebody who had the arrogance to make an *entire plane* wait for him. And I'd be sitting with him for the next...I mentally counted the hours and winced. "That long?"

"Ms. Harden?"

I jerked my head up and met the gaze of the airline attendant, the man I'd overheard speaking. He gave me a polite smile and nodded at the proffered basket of goodies.

"No, thank you." I thought maybe the best thing to do would be curl up and sleep. The roar of the engines almost always lulled me into it on a plane, and it would be a great way to ignore whoever had *pulled strings* to hold up the flight. It was the kind of shit my parents—especially my mother—would do, and I had no desire to interact with the kind of people who did that sort of thing.

With that thought in mind, I pulled my purse into my lap. As I was pushing through it, digging for my earbuds, I heard the sudden commotion, followed by an abrupt silence.

Curiosity got the better of me, and I looked up just in time to see a man in a crisp polo, jeans and a blazer move down the aisle. He had a sharp gaze, and as he passed by, he shifted in a way that had his blazer falling open. I caught sight of the badge at his waist—and his weapon.

My eyes locked on that weapon even as my brain processed the badge.

He caught sight of me even as he reached down and tugged his blazer over the badge and weapon, striding past me on into the next cabin. My breath squeaked out, relief coming seconds later as I finally made sense of the badge. *Federal air marshal.* He was allowed to carry that weapon.

Maybe he was the VIP. Matters of law enforcement sometimes did warrant special consideration.

Of course, even as I considered that, my heart skipped a few beats, and I squirmed, nervousness blooming inside.

Was there somebody dangerous on the plane?

Was there—

Another commotion from up front caught my attention, and I looked toward the front of the cabin, watching as the airline attendants went rigid.

I rolled my eyes and went to look out the window, but before I could, the man in the front seat went rigid, too, and bemused, I watched as he fumbled with his seatbelt, red-faced. "Your Highness," he stuttered out in German.

I didn't even have time to puzzle through that before Luka appeared in the cabin doorway. He nodded at the man and waved at him, urging him to stay in his seat. "I've held you up as it is." He offered a nod, and while the man was still stuttering out a comment, Luka started down the aisle.

He saw me only seconds before he reached the seat.

He tensed, but it was so minute, I doubted anybody save me noticed.

I coolly shifted my attention outside.

He slid into the seat, and the airline attendants bustled

around him, hovering like honeybees over a flower. After he'd finally convinced them he was fine, and it was just the two of us, I could feel his eyes boring into me, but I didn't look at him.

"This must seem a little strange," he said, voice stiff.

"Does it?" I asked musingly.

"I...well. I'm not stalking you or anything. My administrative assistant just purchased the ticket a few hours ago. This is a last-minute trip. I'm..."

Swinging my head around to look at him, I cocked a brow.

"You're..." I prodded.

He just looked at me.

Annoyed, I huffed out a breath and went back to staring outside. He'd seemed so...down to earth. At least in Monaco. But the moment I'd arrived in Luxembourg, everything about him had changed, and he'd made no attempts to hide that indefinable air of superiority.

I was familiar with it. My parents had it. My uncle even had it, but he still treated people with kindness and respect. My aunt had it, although it was tempered. Aeric had some degree of it, but it came off more as an air of remoteness, which I could understand, and he did let himself engage with others outside the family and his circle of friends.

He wasn't a complete stick in the mud.

He was...Aeric. And once he got to know people, he let his guard down.

Luka had seemed open and easy in Monaco, but it had clearly been a façade. Now he looked at me with unreadable eyes, and finally, he shook his head.

Disappointed for reasons I couldn't explain, I focused on the simple task of digging my earbuds out and putting them in.

Once I had my music going, I looked outside.

It was going to be a *long* flight.

FOURTEEN

LUKA

THE COLD SHOULDER SHE'D GIVEN ME IRRITATED ME more than anything in recent memory, but it wasn't like I could press for details and ask what the fuck the problem was right here on the plane. Considering how our last encounter had gone, there was any *number* of explanations she could offer on just what the problem was, and an airplane where we were surrounded by others definitely wasn't the right venue for such a personal conversation.

Still, her silence rubbed me raw, and as I considered how easily we'd talked the night we'd first met, I only became more frustrated. Determined to distract myself, I pulled my phone out and powered up the screen.

It flashed on.

Then a warning came up. Groaning, I pinched the bridge of my nose.

I'd let the airline check the one bag I'd brought out of habit. The few times I'd ever flown commercial, the bag was always checked all the way through and transferred to my hotel, and I never had to bother with it, but now I wished I'd kept it with me.

I didn't so much as have a charging cable.

I eyed the TV in front of me, but I wouldn't be able to turn it on and get any news until we reached the predetermined height. Frustrated, I closed my eyes.

Immediately, my head filled with Stacia's scent.

I breathed her in, and my cock stiffened. Most commercial airline seats weren't made with the maximum of comfort in mind anyway, and although this was a nice craft, the seat still didn't allow for me to stretch out or do a damn thing to relieve my condition.

I shifted.

My arm brushed hers.

That didn't help.

I shifted again, this time pulling away from the armrest separating us, although I couldn't help but notice as she adjusted in her seat too. Was she as aware of me as I was of her? *Could* she be? I could hear her breathing, even above the noise in the cabin, and I wouldn't have thought *that* to be possible.

My peripheral vision had always been stellar, and I could see the rise and fall of her breasts under the teal material of her skinny-strapped tunic. Her skin glowed with a delicate tan, and I wanted to stroke my fingers along her arm, feel the silkiness there.

She shivered.

I almost asked if she was cold, then reminded myself she didn't want to talk to me.

Courtesy, though, demanded it.

Setting my jaw, I swung my gaze over to her. She was staring determinedly out the window.

Lost for words, I stared at her profile and watched as she brought her arms up, crossing them over her chest. My control was shot completely, eroded by the stress of worrying about Emmett half the day, and I found myself looking down, watched as she hugged herself. I had a flash of a second where I caught of view of her nipples, shielded by her bra and her shirt, but hard and erect, pressing against the teal fabric.

My mouth went dry. She hugged herself more determinedly, hiding her breasts more completely with her arms, and I jerked my gaze away, my cock now pulsing so hard and twisted into a position so painfully uncomfortable, I wasn't sure if it would ever straighten again.

I slumped low in desperation, and that brought some ease. Some. Not a lot, but I'd take what I could get. Easing back upright, I grunted uncomfortably and looked toward the front of the cabin, wondering if I had time to get up and hit the bathroom, just so I could adjust my fucking dick.

But the airline attendant took his position at just that moment, and I swore under my breath.

"If you're this impatient to get to New York, why didn't you just get a private jet?"

The sound of Stacia's voice was a welcome distraction, even if it did make my heart bump and jerk against my ribs. Swinging my head around to look at her, I said, "What?"

"You're clearly in a hurry. Why take a menial commercial

airline? Don't you have a private jet at your command, Your Highness?"

There was a look of disdain in her eyes I hadn't seen before, and it got under my skin, grating like sandpaper against my spine, but I pushed it aside, just glad she was talking to me.

"I couldn't wait. My parents took the jet on a trip to Papua New Guinea, and I have to get to Montreal as soon as I can."

"Why?" She cocked her head, a frown line appearing between her eyes.

I told her.

The story came pouring out unchecked.

Bit by bit, the cool set of her features faded until it was gone completely. Bit by bit, her eyes warmed, then softened with compassion.

And when she reached out and closed her hand over mine, I found myself clinging to her the way a child might cling to his mother.

"He's one of my best friends," I said, slumping in the seat. We'd finally reached cruising altitude, and the attendant had started serving us. I had a double serving of Glenlivet 12 in front of me. I had every intention of ordering more too. I'd offered to buy Stacia a drink, but she'd only wanted ginger ale. After one sip, she put it down, and it looked like she'd forgotten about it. "I can't stop imagining the worst."

"There hasn't been any more news?"

I grimaced and pulled my dead phone from the pocket of the seat in front of me. "No way to check. I left my fucking charging cord in my luggage."

"Well, I can help with that, at least." She reached down and picked up her purse, pulling a cord out within seconds. "Here."

Relief crashed into me. I took it, looking into her eyes. "Thank you."

"No problem." Her cheeks colored, and she cleared her throat. "Ah...so, how did you meet Emmett? Seems a bit of an odd match there, the heir to a dukedom...sorry, duchy." She smiled faintly in apology.

I wanted to catch that smile, kiss it until it faded to a moan.

"Anyway, it's an odd friendship. Or it seems that way. He's a racecar driver from Kentucky. You're in line to be the next Duke of Luxembourg. How did you even meet?"

I wouldn't have thought anything could make me laugh today.

But the memory of how Emmett and I had met did it.

"We got trapped in an elevator," I said, giving her a rueful grin.

"I..." She blinked and shook her head. "You what?"

"We got trapped in an elevator." I couldn't help but laugh again at the look of mild panic on her face, even though just thinking about the time was enough to make *me* feel a bit of panic creep back in. "I was on a trip to New York with my father. It was one of the first times I'd gone with him on one of his diplomatic trips, and although I had to attend several meetings with him, by early afternoon, I was bored out of my mind, and he let me go back to the hotel suite."

Stacia wrinkled her nose. "Uh oh."

I laughed. "Uh oh is right. As you can imagine, I didn't

stay long. I wanted to see the city that never sleeps, so that was what I did. I ended up in one of the big old department stores. Emmett got on the elevator with me. He was in town for a debate event and had gone out to do some shopping with his family that afternoon. The elevator didn't stop on every floor because several of the original entrances had been sealed off entirely. We were halfway between the first and fourth floor, and it just stopped. It took me a minute or two to realize it was stuck."

She gave an exaggerated shudder. "I would have freaked the hell out."

"The gene that allows for *freaking the hell out* was bred out of the family line generations back," I said solemnly. "It's frowned upon for a royal to engage in something so...common."

She narrowed her eyes at me, but slowly, a smile bloomed over her face. "You were scared, weren't you?"

"Yes." I shifted in the seat and took a sip of the whisky in front of me, swirling it absently as I remembered those first thirty or forty minutes. "I was scared out of my mind, but I couldn't show it. After all, this kid who was in there with me wasn't scared, and if *he* wasn't scared, I couldn't make out to be, either."

"So Emmett wasn't freaked out?" She gave me a skeptical look.

I laughed. "He drives racecars that go over 350 kilometers an hour, or over two-twenty for those of you who use *miles*," I teased. "He's been racing most of his life, started out with go-karts, then moved to stock cars as soon as he was old enough. It takes more than an elevator being stuck a while to scare him. He lives and breathes for his next adrenaline rush."

"I think I'd rather race a car at 330 *kilometers an hour* than be stuck in an elevator," she said, wrinkling her nose at me. "So...you bonded during tragedy?"

I laughed. "It...wasn't tragic. I was...well, I can't use the word *freaking out*, you understand."

"The gene thing."

"Absolutely. But I was...*mildly* concerned. He kept trying to talk me down. He'd already used the phone to call for help, and they'd located his parents. They were in town on a family vacation, and his family was in the store. Then I had to talk to the operator on the other end of the line about my father..." I hesitated, uncertain how to continue.

I didn't have to explain, though. After only moments, understanding lit her eyes. "You didn't know how he'd handle it, or how the operator would handle it, did you?"

"No. And I was scared of how my *father* would handle it. I knew he wouldn't be happy that I'd left the hotel." I grimaced, remembering *that* particular worry. It had all been for nothing. My father had already been on his way to the store because he'd had two of the security team watching me. Apparently, *he* had been young once, too, he'd told me later that day, giving me a stern look as he drank his second glass of whisky.

The team had known there was a problem almost immediately, and I'd been panicking about telling him something he already knew.

As I relayed that to her, she gave me a smile that was a mix of sympathy and laughter. "Were you really so afraid of how he'd act? He seems so kind."

"He is. Don't misunderstand. But both he and *Maman* can be very strict." I shrugged, taking another sip of whisky. "Neither my brother nor I were born into a life that would allow for undisciplined children. Monarchies don't tolerate it."

"You wanted to explore a city. It's not like you went out and got drunk, hit up your first drug dealer, and picked up a hooker."

"Well, there is that." I winked at her. "I waited to do all of that until my first trip to Paris."

"Ha, ha." She jabbed me in the arm with her index finger.

I caught her hand, not wanting to let it go.

She tugged free, clearing her throat. "So, how long were you in the elevator?"

"Hours. Some sort of electrical malfunction. They offered to bring us out another way, but..." I grimaced at the memory, "it was decided that, for privacy's sake, if the two of us were able to tolerate it and be patient, it would be better for the servicemen on site to handle the repair rather than risk bringing in more people who might talk about who all was involved. Papa hates publicity like that, and Emmett told us he was just hanging out...literally."

She wrinkled her nose. "Bad pun."

"Yes, he's lousy with them."

Blowing out a sigh, I checked my phone's battery status. At thirty percent. I told myself to check on my friend, see how he was. But fear made me wary. What if I learned something awful? Carefully, I turned the phone face down.

"We talked about everything," I went on, needing the added distraction of just talking to Stacia. "He told me about racing and Kentucky and badgered me until I finally told him who I was and why people were so worried about privacy and reporters finding out about two kids being trapped in an elevator. I told him and he...he just shrugged." I laughed, still thrown by his reaction even now. "He looked at me and squinted a little, like he wasn't sure if I was joking. Then he said, 'A duke? Like the guys in those historical romances my mom reads?'"

Stacia laughed, a full-on joyful sound that made me laugh too.

I elbowed her in her ribs before going on. "I've never read one, but a duke is a duke, I suppose. I said, 'More or less.' And he just shrugged, then asked if I'd ever been to a Formula One race since I was so close."

"Sounds like he already had his mind set on where he wanted to be, even then."

"He did." I tightened my grip on the phone.

I needed to look.

But I couldn't.

A soft hand covered mine, and when she gently tugged the phone away, I let her.

She couldn't unlock it, but when she held it up for me to handle it, instead of ignoring her, I obeyed her silent request.

And I sat there as she opened the browser.

"I see the article you were reading. You never closed it

out. There's an update," she said softly. Without asking, she started to read aloud.

Fifteen seconds later, I dropped my face into my hands.

She rubbed my back. "You said he was stubborn. Sounds to me like he's hanging on just fine."

I didn't let myself grab her and kiss her.

But I didn't stop myself from fantasizing about it.

FIFTEEN

STACIA

The relief on his face was so potent, it made my throat ache.

As he dropped his face into his hands, I put the phone back on his tray table and tried to fight the wave of guilt as it rose back up inside me. It was hard, though.

It wasn't like I knew his friend was in the hospital, I told myself.

It was the truth, too. But it only helped a little. Normally, I preferred to have people regard me as somewhat reserved. It had never mattered to people that I was shy and slow to open up. The Ice Princess rep I'd developed because of it had eventually helped, even if it had kept me more isolated after a while because who wanted to get to know an Ice Princess?

It had kept people at bay, but it had also protected me from their snubs and rejections.

And I'd just snubbed Luka.

Stop it, I told myself again.

He straightened in the seat, and I pulled my hand from

his back, tucking it in my lap. My palm tingled from the contact, but I managed to ignore it—mostly.

"Is there anything I can do to help?" I asked after he took another sip of whisky.

"No. You've done more than enough." A smile ghosted around his lips. "You listened. I feel like I can breathe again. Thank you."

My cheeks heated as he watched me, and self-consciousness washed through me. I tried to pretend that was all it was, but I knew better. Just sitting so close to him made me uncomfortable, and I couldn't pretend otherwise.

"Listening isn't so hard." I grabbed my ginger ale, half watered down by now, and took a sip to wet my parched throat. "Not really."

"You wouldn't think so," he said, voice light, almost playful.

Maybe that was why it took me off guard when he took my hand a moment later and lifted it to his lips. "But not that many people really know how to listen these days, Stacia. At least, that's been *my* experience in life."

Heat fluttered in my belly at the feel of his mouth on my skin again.

I'd told myself that, after last night, it wouldn't happen again. Even though this touch was chaste in comparison, I couldn't quell the rush of heat between my thighs. Or the abrupt uptick in the beat of my heart.

WE WERE a few hours from New York City when we hit bad weather.

I'd finally drifted off to sleep, but a rough bit of turbulence jolted me awake, and without thinking, I clamped my hand on the hard, muscled forearm so close to mine.

Luka covered my hand with his. "It's just a storm," he said, his voice low and soothing. "Nothing to worry about."

"I bet those words have been said before almost every major airline disaster," I said, trying to inject humor into the words and failing miserably.

He worked my fingers free of their death grip, then slid my hand down until he could press his palm to mine. "You probably have a point. I've got a brilliant idea. Let's go to the toilet and join the mile-high club before we die."

I gaped at him before breaking out into laughter. The airline attendant strode by just as I smacked his arm, and he went rigid, staring at me in horror. Luka sensed the reaction and looked over, waving the man on before shifting his attention back to me. "Be careful," he said soberly. "You'll have that man alerting the marshal on this flight, and you'll be handcuffed for the duration of the flight for assaulting my delicate personage."

"Ha." Cheeks flushing, I went to cross my arms over my chest, but he caught my hand, bringing it once more to his lips.

"You're laughing now. That's better than being afraid, Stacia."

"We're in a giant tin can flying hundreds of feet over the ocean while thunder rattles the plane." I rolled my eyes, trying to seem as unaffected. "It's perfectly *natural* to be afraid. Just like it was *natural* to be afraid while trapped in an elevator."

"Oh." He pressed a hand to his chest. "You wound me."

I rolled my eyes. "I don't think your ego *can* be wounded."

"Not true." He squeezed my fingers and lowered our joined hands to the armrest. "Let's talk. I'll distract you as you distracted me. It's the least I can do. Is family meeting you at the airport in New York City?"

I grimaced, his words reminding me I hadn't checked my mother's messages in...days. "I doubt it. They have standing plans and coming to meet me would be an *inconvenience*," I said, the words slipping out without me really thinking about just how much they gave away.

"Oh?" The polite inquiry hid a great deal.

I darted a look at him even as I grabbed my phone. Face heating, I said, "Ignore me. The storm's making me irritable. I told them not to worry about it, we could set up a lunch date soon." My face was hot as I clicked on the message bubble, the bright red notifications showing me what an ungrateful child I'd been, ignoring her texts.

Seven messages—three in the past twenty-four hours.

What time will you be in...dinner...blah, blah, blah...

Please respond, Stacia...plans...blah, blah, blah...

The last one had me straightening in the seat.

Let me know if you made your connection to New York. Tilly just reminded me that you're arriving today and informed me that there's a strike going on at JFK...

I shot her back a quick message to let her know I'd made

my connection and that I'd call her once I'd had time to rest. Dread churning inside, I looked over at Luka.

I didn't know if I should tell him now or not.

If it was me, I'd rather know.

I FELT his frustration as the small electric cart buzzed through the terminal at JFK. I'd ridden along with him to the customer service desk for the airline as they tried to get him on a flight—of course, the Hereditary Grand Duke of Luxembourg wasn't going to stand in line like other people. He was escorted to a quiet, elegant suite where several people hovered around him, offering cocktails, snacks, or a quick meal from the nearby restaurant. He'd declined all offers and just sat and waited, with me at his side in an elegant scoop chair that was easier to look at than to sit in.

As soon as we realized there wasn't any chance of him booking flights, I'd started trying to book him a rental car. I didn't have his information, but I knew how things worked. Money talked.

If I could *find* a car available...

I snagged what looked like an availability and called the desk, ending up on hold.

Tapping the driver's arm, I told him which rental agency, and he nodded when I spoke to the airport concierge sitting in the seat next to him. He whipped out his phone and dialed.

I wasn't surprised to hear him speaking to somebody at the agency, even while I continued to wait on hold.

The man's shoulders slumped, and I closed my eyes for a brief moment as I disconnected the call. There was no reason to keep holding anyway. As I put my phone into my lap, the trim, slim man in front of me straightened.

His name was Frank, I remembered.

He cleared his throat and turned to look at us, first at Luka, then at me. "I'm terribly sorry..."

Next to me, Luka slumped. I braced myself and picked up my phone once more, tapping out a message to my driver, Ricky. I wasn't going to commit his time without making sure he wasn't okay with it.

My parents did that.

I didn't.

It didn't even take him two minutes to respond.

If you need my help, Miss Stace, I'm there for you.

I knew him so well that even though I was reading a text, I could *hear* his deep, laconic southern drawl permeating the words, and I couldn't help but smile.

Next to me, Luka muttered under his breath, the words so despondent, I wanted to wrap my arms around him.

Instead, I took his hand and squeezed lightly. "I think I can help."

He looked tired and despondent but offered a faint smile. "How?"

I told him, and he listened, brows furrowed. Several times, he started to object, but I held up a hand.

His brows shot straight up.

I realized the concierge was still watching us—not only did *his* brows go up as well, his mouth dropped open.

Granted, he snapped it shut immediately after, but still, his shock was obvious.

"I'm sorry," I said, clearing my throat. Nerves crowded up, and I shoved them back. "I just...look." I nodded at the gathering crowds heading toward the rental car agencies. "It makes more sense to do it my way than for you to keep fighting to get a rental in a city the size of New York. It will be a nightmare. This way is simple."

Luka took my hand. "You've already helped so much, Stacia."

I hadn't, not really. "Luka, let me do this. You're worried sick about your friend, and you're clearly exhausted. We can get a few hours of sleep at my place, and my driver will pick us up in the morning, then we can get you to Montreal."

He wanted to argue. I could see it in his eyes.

"Think about Emmett. Even if you got there tonight, you shouldn't disturb him. He needs to rest."

"That's playing dirty," he said with a dark scowl.

"It's the truth. And you know it." I could see the acknowledgment in his eyes, and the exhaustion. I forged on before he could argue. "My driver is already here, waiting to pick me up. He needs to get some sleep before taking such a long drive, and he doesn't have his passport, but if you're willing to wait until morning, we can take you to Montreal. It's a six-hour drive, but if we leave around seven—"

"Enough." Luka took my hand and lifted it to his lips, pressing a kiss to the back of it. "You've convinced me. Where is your driver waiting? We need to get your luggage, yes?"

MY BROWNSTONE WAS quiet around us as I unlocked the door. Ricky brought up the tail end of the group, carrying Luka's single suitcase in one hand while pulling the handle of my stacked set of luggage behind him. I'd argued my way into carrying the second suitcase so he wouldn't have to make another trip. He needed to get home and rest, and I needed the same.

At least that was what I told myself.

But a few minutes later, after Ricky had deposited my suitcases in my room, then carried Luka's suitcase to the largest guestroom, I found myself loitering in the kitchen. The french doors opened up to the backyard and a garden that was abloom with a rainbow of colors.

Luka stood there staring into the night, hands in his pockets, shoulders rigid.

"I love it out there," I told him softly. "I mean, it's not the royal gardens at the Luxembourg palace or anything, but it's a nice place to find some peace in the middle of New York City madness."

"It's quite lovely," he said, but there was an air of distraction in his voice.

"Have you learned anything new about Emmett?"

He turned, his whiskey eyes meeting mine. "Very little. I did put in a call to his parents. They're at the hospital with him, but his father was so distracted, he couldn't do more than tell me he'd come through another surgery. But I know where he is, so that's more than I knew earlier."

"That's an improvement then." Uncertain, my heart

racing with things I just wasn't equipped to handle, I told myself to go to bed, but the thought of going to my big, lonely bed by myself just held no appeal at all.

"Ricky put your suitcase in one of the guestrooms. But..." A fist of panic locked around my chest, squeezing the words so that they stopped in my throat.

Luka cocked a brow and took a step toward me. "But?"

In his eyes, I saw a slow-burning smolder flicker to awareness. My belly heated, and the sudden rush of adrenaline bolstered my confidence.

"But..." I angled my head toward the stairs. "My room is bigger. You're welcome to join me."

He closed the distance between us.

My breath caught as he reached up to tug on my braid.

"Are you looking for somebody to keep you company tonight, Stacia? I can't claim to be in a patient, seductive mood if that's the case." He leaned, using his hold on my hair to draw my head upward until I met his gaze. He bent down and kissed me, hard, rough and impatient. "I won't be a tender lover today if I join you. Have you changed your mind?"

"No."

He dipped his head and murmured against my ear, "Say my name."

"Luka."

He kissed me again, swallowing down my moan. But when I went to press against him, he stopped me, his hands lightly gripping my upper arms and holding me back as he lifted his head.

Wordlessly, we stared at each other, unspoken things passing between us.

My heart sped up as he let go, then took the end of my braid, pulling the band off before slowly combing it free.

"I love your hair," he said, voice low and husky. "For a few minutes, that first night, you lay next to me, your head on my chest and your hair spread around us like a veil, soft and smooth as silk. I keep thinking about that moment."

He finished working my hair free, smoothing it down so that it spilled around my breasts.

"I want to see you wearing nothing but your hair, Stacia." He reached for the top of my blouse, giving me time to pull away.

I didn't.

I could hardly speak as he worked each button free, taking his time. Once he was done, he didn't push the shirt free, though. Instead, he swept me up into his arms.

Gasping, I wrapped my arms around him.

Taut seconds passed as he looked at me with a burning intensity that brought color to my cheeks. Finally, he looked away and started to walk. Unsettled by the way he watched me, I pressed my face to his chest and clung tighter.

In my room, he put me down by the bed, but he didn't finish the job he'd started. Instead, he sat on the edge of the mattress and leaned back, watching me from under heavy-lidded eyes. "Will you undress for me?"

"Will I...oh." I licked my lips, mouth suddenly gone dry.

"You don't have to."

"But you want me to." Although my face burned, I met his eyes, half expecting that charming smile to curl his lips.

It didn't.

A dark flush settled on his cheekbones, and his eyes deepened. When he answered, his voice was a low, hungry rasp. "Yes."

The sheer want in his voice gave me the confidence to take the first step, reaching up to push my blouse off my shoulders.

A hard breath escaped him, and his hands tightened in the fat, fluffy silver duvet beneath him, the bones under his skin showing white he gripped so hard. I started to reach for the waistband of my skirt but paused. "Will you take your shirt off?"

"Tit for tat?"

Instinctively, I glanced down, and he chuckled. I looked at him, almost grateful for the sudden lightening of the mood. "Maybe. Or maybe I just like looking at you too."

Luka sat straighter and pulled his polo off, draping it over the foot of the bed. "Good?"

I smiled and pushed my skirt down, focusing on the play of muscle and skin instead of the fact that I was stripping for this guy I barely knew. Straightening, I stepped out of the puddle of fabric and met Luka's eyes, but he was looking at my chest.

"Fuck...your hair. Take off your bra but keep your hair like that. I want to see your nipples peeking at me through those curls, darling."

A rush of heat gathered between my thighs, and my knees trembled, leaving me momentarily frozen, wracked by need. But finally, I pushed my body into motion and reached back to do as he'd asked.

His chest rose and fell on a rough breath, and the sight of his muscles bunching as he stared at me had the opposite effect on me—my thighs quivered, and my knees threatened to buckle. I peeled the lacy cups away, holding them in place a few seconds longer than necessary.

"Drop it," Luka said gutturally.

In the span of seconds, my nervousness was gone, and I found myself giving him the kind of smile I'd seen *other* women use—flirtatious and teasing. The kind of smile I never would have thought I'd have the courage to use, but there I was, easing the bra down bit by bit as I smiled.

How badly do you want me to drop it, Luka?

He made a low noise in his throat and sagged farther back on the mattress, using one hand to brace his weight. As I watched, he slid a hand over the ridge straining the front of his trousers.

I whimpered.

"Two can play the teasing game, Stacia," he said, dragging his eyes up to meet mine. "Drop the bra."

I did, still watching him.

The second the fabric hit the floor, I nodded at him. "Unzip your pants. I want to see..."

The confidence dried up.

"See what?" He tugged his belt open but went back to palming himself through his khakis, eyes bold.

"You. I want to watch..." Licking my lips, I started to cross my arms over my chest.

"Don't cover yourself, love. I want to see those beautiful tits. Look at yourself, Stacia."

Instinctively, I glanced down.

"No. Turn around. Look in the mirror. See what I see."

Face hot, I turned and found my reflection. His zipper rasped as he dragged it down, but I didn't turn around. Not yet. I couldn't. I was too caught up in the sight he'd instructed me to look at—my own reflection. My skin, tinted with just the faintest tan after my time in Monaco. My nipples barely visible through the tangle of my curls. And my face, flushed with passion.

"I see your tattoo...most of it. Push your panties down now, Stacia. Let me see that beautiful ass."

I was shaking by the time I'd complied, too raw to keep watching my own face and taking in the reactions he brought up inside me. Turning, I stared at him. He'd pushed his khakis down just enough to free his cock, and as I watched, he palmed himself, wrapped his fist around the heavy column of flesh and started to pump.

I quivered, and an ache deep in my cunt had me clenching my knees together.

He noticed.

Eyes running over me, he focused on the curls at the apex of my thighs.

"Does your pussy hurt for me, Stacia?"

"Yes," I whispered.

He stroked himself a little faster, his breath slightly rougher, but his voice remained calm. "Come here, then. I'll make it all better."

I started toward him but stopped just shy of where he could reach me, watching as he continued to fist his cock, the fat head disappearing inside his fist rhythmically. "I want something else first," I whispered, meeting his eyes.

His mouth parted. "Tell me."

"I..." My breathing hitched, and I shook my head, instead, going to my knees. My confidence had its limits, after all. Curling my hand around his wrist, I stilled his movements and leaned in, pressing my mouth to the head.

He mumbled something, but I couldn't translate the mash-up of hoarse German and French that spilled out of him as I opened my mouth to take him inside.

He tugged free of my grip and curved his hand over the back of my head, his grip light even as he tangled his fingers in my hair. I moved down a fraction then back up, down...up...

I fell into something of a rhythm, urged by the subtle movements of his hips and the way his hand tightened in my hair. Learning the taste and feel of him, I stroked my tongue over the thick, heavy vein on the underside of his cock, then sucked on the blunt, rounded head. He groaned when I scraped my nails over the heavy sac between his legs, cursed again as I went back and sucked on the head, releasing him with a slight pop so I could gulp in air.

But when I went to bend back over him, he caught my arms in his hands and hauled me up, eyes hungry and avid on my face. "Where the fuck did you learn to suck cock?"

"Um..." I blushed hot and red as I stumbled over the answer. "I...um...I read a lot."

His brows shot up. "About sucking cock?"

I shoved at his shoulders, although it was a useless gesture. He wrapped one arm around my waist, holding me firm against him, his eyes on my mouth while his cock pulsed against my belly.

"No." Huffing out a breath, I pointed out, "Romances have all sorts of information in them. And...maybe I watched a couple of dirty movies before."

"Ohhhh...how fascinating." A wicked smile curled his lips as he stroked my butt. "What did I say about unexpected, Stacia...you've got a bad girl streak in there, don't you?"

It was ridiculous that even the *suggestion* gave me a thrill. But it did. He saw something on my face too and nuzzled my neck. "You like that, don't you? Being a bit of a bad girl? I should have realized that the other night...you loved having me spank that perfect ass. Maybe I should spank you now. Bad girls need their punishment from time to time."

I couldn't have silenced my moan if I wanted to, and I didn't care enough to try.

Shaking, I let him nudge me around until I was bent over my bed, much as I'd been bent over the garden bench. He pressed his mouth to my tattoo again. Then he brought his hand down on my right cheek. Without pause, he shifted to the left, then back to the right, quick slaps that had me shuddering and quivering with arousal.

My knees buckled after the fourth, and he nudged me closer to the bed, letting it take my weight. I thought he might spank me again, but this time, after smoothing his fingers over the tattoo, he trailed one along the crevice between my cheeks, straight down until he could thrust it inside.

I stiffened, then clamped down around him, the utter surprise at the sudden invasion locking me down tight. He withdrew, and I followed, keening in disappointment.

"That's it, love...ride me. Show me how much you want me to fuck you. Show me how dirty and hungry you can be."

With words and strokes of his hand, he drew me right to the edge, and as I hovered there, so close to coming, he pulled away and bent over me.

Dismayed, I curled my hands into the duvet.

He bit my right shoulder. "Where are your condoms?"

The request didn't make sense at first. Finally, processing them through a haze of thought, I waved at my purse, which I'd dumped on the floor next to my suitcases.

He left me, and I felt his absence far too keenly.

He came back quickly, but the ache inside didn't think so, hunger already a ravenous monster. He tugged me up, urging me with his hands on my hips, then turning me. He boosted me back onto the bed and pushed gently until I was lying flat.

With slow, deliberate movements, he pushed my knees apart until I lay spread open before him.

I'd never felt so exposed, so vulnerable.

He could tell, too. I knew it in the way he stared me in the eye for long moments before letting his gaze caress me and slide down along my torso, straight down to the wet folds between my thighs.

"Look at how wet you are for me," he muttered, the words so low and quiet, I barely heard him.

He picked up something from the bed. He tore a condom open, and my heart stuttered as I realized his fingers were shaking.

Yes, I wanted him to the point that it *hurt*, but maybe this got to him too. He was shaking, after all.

Then I had no time left to think about it because he covered me.

SIXTEEN

LUKA

HER EYES, THE SOFT BLUE HAZY AND UNFOCUSED, locked on my face as I filled her. She saw too deeply, and there were things inside me that I couldn't risk her knowing. Desperate to be away from that insightful gaze, I cupped her chin, arched her head back and took her mouth.

She moaned into it, arching closer, her tight nipples rasping against my chest.

I went to withdraw, and her pussy tightened around me as if she'd hold me inside forever. The idea was all too appealing.

I gripped her hip, holding her steady as I withdrew before thrusting deeper.

She sobbed into the kiss, her nails biting into my shoulders.

Through the slick, thin material of the condom, I felt the heat of her cunt, and the honey from her pussy slicked all over me now as well. I wanted more of that, more of her, and the orgasm was already pushing closer.

Swearing, I rolled onto my back and urged her up into a sitting position until she rode me.

She gave me a startled look that slowly melted into one of rapture as she had time to absorb the different angles. Her mouth parted on an *oh,* although no sound came out.

I caught her hips and urged her to move. "Ride me," I told her. Then, desperate to keep the hot frenzy inside me from growing any more complex, I managed a smug grin. "You've read books after all."

She didn't smile back, lids fluttering low as she shifted, then leaned forward, her hands on my shoulders as she started to move, slowly at first, hesitant. Soon, though, her movements became fluid and easy as she found her rhythm, and the feel of her milking my cock, the sight as she rose above me, pleasuring us both as she rode me was an erotic sight I'd carry with me a lifetime.

Gripping her waist, I slid my hands up her sides, then plumped her tits together, watching as dark pink nipples pushed through her hair. I caught them between thumb and forefinger and felt her reaction, from the way her body tensed to the way her cunt tightened around me, giving me another full-length caress.

I tugged, and she cried out, shoving herself against me.

Fuck, the things I wanted to do to her.

Flipping us back over, I caught her right breast in my hand and shoved her nipple up for my feasting, taking it between my teeth and drawing it slowly away from her body.

Stacia set her nails into my shoulders, wrapped her thighs around my hips, clearly not wanting to let me withdraw. I reached out, unhooked her ankles, then caught one knee over my right elbow, moving higher on her body so that her ass now tilted up, deepening the angle. Impaled on my cock, she whimpered, spine arching. I hunkered over her, directing my attention to her left nipple this time.

She sobbed my name, and I withdrew slowly, bit by bit, until only the head was lodged inside. I sank back in partway, then withdrew again. Almost completely.

She shuddered, her pussy spasming now, so tight it was a chore to fill her, but what bliss it was to finally have her completely wrapped around me. I stayed within her this time, rocking back and forth, using my body to massage her clit and taking the cues from her reactions to see when I'd hit that spot buried inside her cunt.

She went taut as a bowstring when I hit it, the head of my cock bumping over it. "That's it there, isn't it, love?" Sweat stung my eyes, but I ignored it, watching her as her mouth fell open, a soundless noise escaping her. I bit her lower lip and began to move, keeping the thrusts short and rough, angled so that I hit her G-spot each time.

She exploded, coming apart in my arms, hot, liquid silk flowing from her as she climaxed.

I barely held onto my own long enough to see it happen, but once the convulsions had her locking around my dick, I gave in, thrusting into her hard, fast, the need leveling me.

"YOU CAN SLEEP IN HERE." Stacia murmured the words to me in the dark sometime later.

I'd gotten up to dispose of the condom and a rare moment

of awkwardness had settled over me. She lay on the bed, already under the covers, and when I looked at her, she'd smiled, then tugged back the duvet and sheets in invitation. "Turn off the light and come to bed."

Now, sleep drifting closer, I found myself considering her words and wondering if I should.

"I can," I said softly, staring up at the night-darkened ceiling. It was done in a simple, soft ecru, a ceiling fan the only decoration.

I found it incredibly appealing.

I found *her* incredibly appealing...and I shouldn't.

I knew that.

"But should I?"

She was quiet a long moment, and when she answered, it was obvious she'd chosen her words with great care.

"It's just an offer, Luka. Tomorrow, we'll get you to Montreal, and you'll see your friend. I'll head back here to my life and you'll...continue on with yours, being the heir to the Grand Duchy of Luxembourg, one of the richest countries in the world. That's for tomorrow...if you want. Tonight, we can just be Luka and Stacia. But it's up to you. Stay...or go."

Her words were carefully neutral.

I couldn't tell if there was hurt in them or not. I couldn't even pick up a trace of any emotion.

Part of me found myself wanting...*something.*

Well, something more than the idea of a night where we were just Luka and Stacia. She clearly knew who I was now and yet had no expectations of me.

I wanted a night with her, an entire one. But I wanted something more too.

The bed shifted next to me, and when I looked over, she'd turned onto her opposite side, settled into what looked like a comfortable half-sprawl. I turned toward her, moving into the curve of her body, aligning myself with the shallows and dips and lines.

"One night. Just Luka and Stacia." Kissing her shoulder, I murmured, "Thank you."

She didn't answer.

But when I slid an arm around her waist, she covered my hand with her own.

SEVENTEEN

STACIA

I gave Ricky a dirty look when he arrived at the doorstep with a sleek black full-sized SUV, the black Lincoln Navigator my father favored for longer road trips. He gave me an innocent expression before taking Luka's luggage down and putting it in the back.

"It just seemed more fitting for a long trip, Miss Stace," he said, his deep southern drawl friendly and easy.

"I better not get a call from my *mother*," I muttered to him.

"They don't even know it's missing," he assured me. "I talked to Robert. Your mother and father left for Philadelphia last night on the private jet. A last-minute dinner party with a client, Robert said."

I huffed out a breath, then nodded. I had a good idea why he'd chosen the Navigator. It was outfitted with a number of security features, including bulletproof paneling and windows. My father was a bit paranoid, but those safety measures were probably wise if one was traveling with a member of royalty and all.

And if Robert said my parents were out of town, then they were out of town. Robert had been my father's driver for years, and he was friends with Ricky.

Although I'd insisted taking over handling Ricky's salary after I received my inheritance at twenty-one, my car, the one he used as he ferried me around town, had been a gift from my parents, and I stored it at their estate in Tarrytown for the most part. Ricky stayed on salary, but I only needed him a couple of times a week, and there was no point keeping the car in the city for that.

If they were out of town, they wouldn't even know I'd made use of the Navigator, so no point in making a fuss.

Neither of them had checked in to see how I was, even after I'd sent a text letting them know I'd landed. I'd expected them to be attending an opera, or a ballet, or maybe some speaking engagement by a visiting professor—although nothing too provocative or politically skewed. That just wasn't acceptable.

Such events made up their Saturday night social plans and had been for as long as I could remember.

Feeling Ricky's gaze, I pasted a disinterested look on my face. "What is it?"

He said nothing but patted me on the shoulder.

Both annoyed and touched, I turned away, taking care not to let the emotions show on my face as I looked for Luka. He'd gotten a call from his father just as Ricky had arrived, and I'd slipped out to give them some privacy. I knew they'd had a few texts exchanges the evening before but with his parents being three-fourths the way around the globe, the time difference must make for some interesting juggling for them both to be awake.

As if summoned by my thoughts, Luka appeared in the doorway, cellphone in hand, but no longer at his ear.

"Everything okay between you and your parents?"

"Of course." He gave a polite smile, the distant one I'd seen from him too often, but I decided it was because of Ricky. Aeric was often the same way, friendly in public, yes, but with far more reserve than was his true nature.

After an awkward silence, Ricky stepped to the curb and offered his hand to me. "Miss Stacia." After I'd joined him, he looked at Aeric. "Your Highness." He gave Luka that polite, deep nod of the head I'd seen others overseas offer him and Aeric, which made me aware I'd been woefully lacking in...*proper* etiquette, but...well. It was hard to think of him as the next Grand Duke of Luxembourg when I'd been on my knees in front of him, learning the feel and taste of his cock with my mouth.

My cheeks heated and I turned away. "I need to lock up. You can get settled, Luka."

But when I turned back, Luka was still standing there, hands clasped in front of him, a brow arched.

I sighed because I knew why he hadn't climbed in. I had no idea if this was a protocol thing or just a gentlemanly thing, but if he was anything like Aeric, he wouldn't get in that vehicle until I did. He'd done the same thing last night.

I strode quickly to the SUV and Ricky opened the door, giving me a bemused look. Trying to cover, I said, "I never did get coffee this morning. Is it okay if we grab some on the way?"

LUKA SAID nothing as Ricky climbed out to get coffee for us from my favorite local shop.

I kept to myself, watching Luka from the corner of my eye as he worked on his phone, fingers flying. If the tension in the air was anything to go by, whatever he was reading didn't leave him happy.

Ricky returned with three cups. He always surprised me, an old tradition, and I took a sip, making a stab at the concoction as he settled in his seat.

"White chocolate and caramel?"

He winked at me from the front seat. "I'm going to have to start trying harder, Miss Stace. I'll put the screen up but buzz me if you need anything." He shifted his attention to Luka. "Your Highness, I have the hospital already programmed into the GPS. Since it's so early, and on a Sunday, the drive itself should only take about six hours. Just let me know when you'd like to stop for a break or food."

"Thank you," Luka said.

The screen went up, and next to me, Luka let out a pent-up sigh, tension evaporating.

"Are you afraid my driver is going to interrogate you?" I asked without thinking about it. The idea amused me, and when Luka whipped his head around to look at me, I laughed. "You've been so stiff, it's like somebody glued a steel rod to your backbone. As soon as the screen went up, you relaxed. You don't need to worry. Ricky's harmless."

Luka lifted a brow. "He's military-trained and carries a weapon. I assume he also acts as your bodyguard. That's not what I'd call harmless."

"Um." Blood rushed to my face, and I squirmed.

"Your family has money, I take it."

Now, I *really* wanted to squirm. Squirm, or maybe just crawl into the very back of the vehicle and hide. "My dad's in finance," I said vaguely. "You can't be in finance in New York City without doing well."

What I didn't say was that he'd gone *into* finance already ridiculously rich and had only gone on to make more for the family, for his clients, often on the backs of people who had little to begin with. I loved my parents, but at the same time, I hated who they were and what they stood for.

"Not a happy relationship there?"

Hearing the compassion in his voice, I looked over at him, forcing myself to relax. He wasn't really prying, after all, and I doubted he was going to run to the nearest gossip reporter and chat about how the Ice Princess was an ungrateful bitch who didn't appreciate her parents.

"It's not that it's...*unhappy*," I finally said. Stalling, I took a sip of the hot, frothy confection Ricky had gotten and glanced at him. "My parents just have...certain expectations of me. And I never fail to disappoint."

His eyes roamed over my face, and after a moment, he said, "I can't see how anybody could be disappointed in you."

I blushed and focused on the coffee again. "They have views of the world that I don't share. I'm expected to be finding an ideal husband. After all, isn't that why *most* women in my position go to college in the first place?"

"I'd always assumed the point of college was for an education?"

I shot him a look and caught the smile quirking at his lips. "Heaven forbid."

"It sounds like your parents don't understand you."

"Do parents ever understand their kids?"

He took his time before answering. "I think many of them try."

"Do yours understand you?" I shifted in the seat to look at him more fully.

"I'm in a complicated position there," he said wryly. "My life was predetermined the moment I developed a Y chromosome. I've had a path set before me my whole life, and while my parents love me and have indulged me to an extent, almost every choice is made with the knowledge that I'll one day step into my father's shoes."

"Including hanging around a Formula One racing track?"

A laugh burst out of him. "Well, perhaps not that. I'll admit, I've been luckier there than some. Both Geraint and I have. They encouraged us to have hobbies that truly interested us, not just something that was...considered acceptable by those of our station."

"So, you didn't grow up playing cricket and polo?"

"I kick ass at polo," he said, gesturing to me with his coffee cup. "At least, I used to. I don't play much anymore, but that's because time doesn't allow for it as much."

"But you can spend weekends in Monaco at the track with Emmett."

His eyes gleamed. "And you'd know that how, Stacia?"

"I might have looked," I said defensively. I took another sip of coffee.

"Looking for information on me," he murmured. "Darling, I'm an open book. Just ask."

I slanted a gaze at him. "Yes, you're so very easy to figure out, Luka."

"Well," he said with a faint smile. "Perhaps not for many, but I'll make exceptions...for some."

THE HOURS FLEW BY.

When Ricky stopped for gas, we both climbed out to stretch and headed into the store. Since I knew he was eager to get to Montreal, I suggested grabbing something to snack on after we'd used the restrooms, and he looked around the big, open convenience store with a look on his face that left me thinking he'd never been on a road trip in America before —maybe never.

"Come on," I said, tugging him along with me to the bagged chips. "Fresh fruit is almost always safe, but you decide how adventurous you're feeling about the hot food like pizza and hotdogs."

"I like pizza." His eyes slid to the front.

"I'm from New York." I managed not to shudder as I considered the small, already-packaged slices sitting under heat lamps. "That's not pizza."

He laughed. "I'll defer to the expert." He grabbed a bag of chips and a snack pack of mixed nuts. I did the same, doubling up for Ricky. "Should have grabbed a basket."

Luka simply scooped everything out of my hands, and I gave him a once-over. "I bet the gossip rags in Europe would have a field day if they had a picture of you right now."

"Hush." To my surprise, his cheeks flushed.

Charmed, I did as requested and led him over to the refrigerated units. "Water or soda?"

"Soda?"

"Ah...Coke. Pepsi. That sort of thing. It's this English to English language barrier."

"We could just speak German or French," he said, sliding easily into the latter. "I noticed you're quite fluent. Except under certain circumstances."

Knowing exactly what he meant, I resisted the urge to make a face at him. "Does that mean you want soda?"

"Water is fine," he said, going back to English.

"You're incorrigible."

"You bring it out," he said with a wink. "What can I say?"

A few minutes later, we carried the bags out to the SUV, and I passed a water and the snacks for Ricky onto him. He dropped a kiss on my forehead then nodded to the vehicle. "If you're ready?"

"You want to run inside first?"

"I'm good."

I rolled my eyes but didn't offer to go in with him so he wouldn't worry about me being grabbed. It had happened to the daughter of one of my father's business associates a few years earlier, and Ricky had been more watchful than ever since.

Once we were back on the road, I peered at the GPS. "It won't be more than a couple of hours as long as traffic is decent."

We sat back to munch on snacks, and although the silence was comfortable, it wasn't long before he filled it, asking about college and what I'd studied before moving on to what I wanted to do with the degree I'd earned.

The rest of the trip flew by, passing through the America/Canada border with little hassle, although the agent on guard at the station did a doubletake after running our passports—I assumed because of Luka.

He asked us to wait a moment and called his supervisor over, and the supervisor spoke to Luka in French, likely because he assumed neither Ricky nor I would speak the language.

I smiled to myself but had to admire the thoroughness Luka's staff had undertaken after learning of his change of plans. They'd already contacted the supervisors at the various borders who were to be watching for the passage of the Hereditary Grand Duke.

Luka assured him everything was well, and we were wished an excellent journey and ushered on our way.

We quickly fell back into our conversation, and the rest of the drive passed so quickly, I was surprised to see the Montreal skyline fill the horizon ahead of us.

An odd pang tugged at my heart—not sadness, exactly, because I knew how anxious he was to see Emmett. Bittersweet. Maybe that was what I was feeling. I'd accepted the fact that I wouldn't see him after leaving Monaco, then again in Luxembourg, then he was dropped back into my life, but fate wasn't going to keep playing this dance.

He'd lapsed into silence, and as the city grew larger in front of us, I did the same. I wanted to take his hand, but I didn't let myself.

As he'd already said, his life had been predetermined before he'd even been born.

He was *basically* a prince.

I was just...me.

The Ice Princess of Manhattan, surely, but still not a match for a duke.

THERE WERE several suited men waiting at the curb as Ricky pulled the Navigator in front of the hospital. He'd lowered the screen a few minutes earlier to let us know that we'd be met at the door.

Luca had frowned.

Ricky explained that Luka's assistant had been in contact with him and they'd arranged for several members from the Protective Policing arm of the Royal Canadian Mounted Police to provide protection while the Hereditary Grand Duke was in Canada.

Luka looked like he wanted to scowl, and the expression deepened as Ricky added, "From the conversation, I'm thinking that the protection detail is being...*strongly urged* by the Canadian government, Your Highness."

Now Luka stared out the window at the four men, all clad in black suits with earpieces curling up over the left ear with a resigned expression. "It's probably for the best," I told him softly, touching his arm. "I don't know much about Montreal overall, but it would seriously suck if something were to happen. I mean, I'd feel bad."

"You'd feel bad," he said, chuckling. "Then, for your peace of mind, I'll be gracious."

I gave him a sunny smile as Ricky climbed out, moving to greet the men waiting. He hadn't unlocked our doors, so unless I wanted to crawl into the front seat, we were stuck there. I watched, unsurprised, as Ricky checked IDs, comparing each picture to the man who passed it over before returning the credentials.

"Your driver takes his duties seriously."

"He does." Soberly, I added, "He'd feel bad if something happened too."

"I'm touched."

Ricky unlocked the doors, turning toward us, but Luka had already shoved the door open, climbing out. The protective detail moved forward to greet him, but he shook his head. "I wish to see my friend first. If you want to discuss other matters, we can do so after I've seen Mr. Finch."

I wouldn't have been surprised to see them snap out a salute in response to his firm, commanding tone.

Trailing in his wake, bracketed on both sides by stern-faced men in suits, I wrapped my arms around my mid-section. I hadn't thought to ask what was going to happen after we got here. I probably should have. I didn't want to intrude but leaving him here before knowing what his plans were, whether his assistant had made arrangements, felt wrong.

We all crowded into the elevator, and I tried to catch Luka's eye, but he was focused on the digital display of floor numbers, and the doors slid open.

Fifteen feet down the hall, I saw a uniformed officer standing outside a door, and I knew without asking where Emmett was.

I started to say Luka's name, but he quickened his pace until I had to trot just to keep up. The guard at the door went to stop him, but the suited cop on Luka's right waved him off.

"Luka—"

He looked back at me, an expression on his face like he'd forgotten me.

It stung.

"Thank you for getting me here, Stacia," he said, voice formal and polite, exactly as it had been when he'd spoken to the protective detail and when he'd greeted Aeric and his family. Polite. Formal. Distant.

That really stung.

"I need to see my friend," he said, inclining his head.

"Ah..." Blood rushed to my cheeks, a sharp retort rising to my lips, but I bit it back. I wasn't going to embarrass myself just because he'd been cool to me. Taking a page from my mother's book, I cocked a brow and gave him a polite nod. "Of course, Your Highness. I'll leave you to it. I'm going to visit a friend while I'm in the city. Ricky will make sure your luggage is dealt with. I'm sure your assistant will make satis-factory transportation arrangements for you from here on out."

He went to speak, but I turned, not wanting to hear anything else.

I'd *stupidly* let myself start to feel something, even after telling him last night that everything would go back to normal today.

The time for *just Luka and Stacia* had already ended. I just hadn't realized it.

Stupid, stupid, stupid.

EIGHTEEN
LUKA

THE FLICKER IN HER EYES ALMOST MADE ME APOLOGIZE, even with these four strangers standing around us, but I bit the words back. Still, if she hadn't turned and walked away when she had, I doubted I would have been able to hold back a second time.

Before I could give into the temptation to say her name, I turned and strode into the hospital room.

It was better that she left. I knew that.

I needed distance between us. I never should have slept with her again, shouldn't have spent hours laughing and talking with her.

I hadn't realized just how stupid those actions had been until we'd reached Montreal and I'd found myself thinking something so incredibly tempting, so incredibly impossible that I discovered how foolish I'd been.

I'd found myself thinking about inviting her back to Luxembourg.

What kind of madness had fallen over me to think that?

But I'd been so close to asking.

Even though it scraped raw that she'd turned and walked away, I couldn't risk there *not* being distance between us because the more I was around her, the less distance I wanted.

But now that I had it, I hated it.

Shoving the emotional turmoil aside, I eased into the room, my gaze on the man in the hospital bed before me. His vivid red hair was the only real color. Everything else was muted, from the sheets to the casted arm lying across his abdomen, to the dull, faded bluish gray gown that only covered part of his chest, the snaps that were supposed to hold it closed undone on his right.

He also had a leg elevated, a cast starting just below the knee. His eyes were closed, and I moved quietly, not wanting to wake him.

"Mom, Dad...I told ya...get some food, get some air."

"I've been called a lot of things in my life, but this is the first time anybody's ever called me Mom or Dad."

Emmett lifted his lids and turned his head, giving me a good look at his bruised, scraped face. His dark blue eyes seemed even darker, thanks to the double set of black eyes, and his lower lip was swollen. He grinned at me, then winced, lifting his good hand to press to his mouth. "Fuck you for making me smile, Luka. What are you doing here? Mom told you I was okay."

"What am I doing here?" Annoyed, I took the seat next to the bed and glared at him. "I understand why you're perplexed, Emmett. My best friend was in a wreck that could have killed him, and I learned about it in the fucking newspaper since nobody on the team thought to call me, but it was silly of me to want to see you, talk to you personally to reassure myself."

He winced. "Okay, I sounded kinda like an asshole there, didn't I? I just...hell, man. You got enough going on in your life. You don't need to be worrying about me."

"And if the situation was reversed?"

He took his time answering, reaching up to scrape his nails through the gingery brown growth of stubble that darkened his face. "Well, I guess I'd be busting my ass to come check on you too," he finally admitted.

"Well, then. That's why I'm here." I studied the bruises, then looked at the other obvious injuries. "How badly are you hurt?"

"I'll heal." He went to shrug, then stopped, pressing his good hand to his side. "Bruised ribs. You should see what I look like under this gown, it ain't pretty. I'm bruised so bad, you'd think somebody beat me with a lead pipe. They...ah, well, they did have to do surgery. I ruptured my spleen, and they had to take it out. It was laparoscopic, so I don't even have a sexy scar or anything from it."

"A sexy..." I rubbed my hand over my face. "You son of a bitch. Priorities."

"Hey, I'm the one who got thrown around like a ragdoll in that fuckin' car. I can make all the morbid jokes I want." He shot a tired sneer at me, careful not to move his mouth too much. "Ribs aren't broken, though, so that's good. If it wasn't for these two fucking casts...I'm out for the season, man."

"It could be worse," I told him.

"That's what *we've* been telling him."

At the familiar feminine voice, I looked up and rose to greet the woman. Emmett's mother, Ellen stood in the doorway. Her red hair, a shade or two brighter than her son's, framed her round face in a tangle of ringlets instead of her normally smooth coif, and there wasn't even a hint of makeup on her face. I couldn't imagine how she had to feel for that to happen.

In all the time I'd known her, she'd never looked less than perfectly put together. Emmett told me she wouldn't even get gas without "putting on her face."

She looked younger than she was and despite the obvious exhaustion, she smiled at me, walking toward me with her hands outstretched.

I pulled her in for a quick hug and nodded at her husband, Dale.

"You didn't need to come, but I'm not surprised to see you, sir," he said.

"Of course, I came."

"I'm *so* sorry nobody from the team contacted you," Ellen said, giving me one last squeeze. "I've been onto the manager about it, and he's just not telling me anything."

"I'll handle it," I assured her.

"Y'all quit standing by the door. I can't hardly hear anything you're saying."

"He's always been so nosy," Ellen said, smiling at me.

"I'm aware." Together, we returned to Emmett's side, and I had the pleasure of watching him stoically tolerate it as his mother fussed over the sheets, tugging at his gown until she could refasten the snaps before whipping out a brush to tend to his hair.

"Come on, Mom. I can do tha—"

She smacked him sharply on his right shoulder, one of the few parts that didn't look battered. "Hush, you. I can too, and it gives me something to focus on besides seeing that wreck play out in my mind over and over."

"I'm sorry, Mom," he said immediately, looking as contrite as he could possibly be.

I grinned, unable to stop it, and his father smothered a laugh.

We both received a dirty look from Emmett as Ellen finished and turned away, tucking the brush back into her purse.

The exchange wasn't enough to distract me from thoughts of Stacia, but I had a feeling I'd be thinking about her for a long, long time, so I'd take the distractions where I could.

NINETEEN

STACIA

I paused as the woman next to me held up a hand. Her gaze moved away to linger on somebody else standing behind me.

A deep male voice, touched with a faint German accent, had my heart skip a beat, even as I told said stupid heart to stop being silly. *It's not him.*

I turned and looked at the man there, a good-looking guy, but not Luka. He wore work coveralls and had a handcart in front of him.

"I was told to bring these up here," he said, looking from me to Belinda.

Belinda, my mother's favorite event planner, hustled around the table. "Daniel...it's been a while since I've seen you!"

He just smiled and passed the clipboard over for her signature. "Where do you want the boxes, Ms. Morris?"

She gestured to the far wall where a small city of boxes already sat. "Over there. Thank you so much, Daniel."

He nodded. "Yes, ma'am."

As he pushed off with the handcart, she looked back at me. "My team arrives in two hours. And..." she checked her watch, huffing out a breath, "I *still* haven't heard back from the catering group."

She shot me a speculative look.

"I hope that's not a *can you cook* look," I said, smiling. I liked Belinda. Mom described her as efficient and energetic. I found her friendly and easy to work with. It was the only reason helping with these events wasn't a chore—and the main reason I'd agreed. Mom's backhanded comments about how I wasn't *really* doing anything since I wasn't involved in any committees or such had rubbed me raw, but I'd decided not to point out that I was currently on the hunt for a job.

"It's not." She beamed. "It's an *are you busy* look. I know we were just running through the schedule and doing a walk-through so you could update your mother." She chuckled. It was a long-standing joke that Mom wouldn't *need* me updating her if she'd bothered to read the daily emails or let her assistant, Tilly, read them for her. "But I have to deal with the caterer problem and get in contact while they still have people in the office, and I'm supposed to be meeting one of the guests that was hired for the children. He was coming here straight from the airport so he could take a look around and get an idea what we were doing."

I cocked a brow. "I guess I can do that. Where were you supposed to meet him?"

"In the coffee shop downstairs. In five minutes." She went to pull something from one of the many files, but her phone rang. "The caterer! Finally."

She answered, and I hesitated. I didn't even know who I was looking for.

Belinda's mouth pursed, and she grabbed a pen, scrawled on the file, then held it up.

E. Finch. HURRY.

With a nod, I turned and did just that, glad I'd gone with a pair of comfortable flat-soled shoes since I knew I'd be on my feet most of the day. It took every bit of the five minutes just to navigate my way to the elevator bay, and once there, I elected to take the three flights rather than wait for the elevator.

Through the glass, I could see the large hospital and the pedway connecting the two buildings. Once Belinda's team got to work, that walkway and the ballroom I'd just left would be transformed into a kid-friendly circus extravaganza, complete with popcorn, cotton candy, hot dogs as well as healthier food options and plenty of vegan and vegetarian alternatives, assuming Belinda worked out whatever issues with the caterer.

I had no doubt she would.

My mom only worked with the best, after all.

It was one minute after three when I reached the coffee shop, and I peered through the crowd, wondering how I was supposed to locate an *E. Finch.*

"Well, fancy meeting you here."

I spun to my right and stared as Luka's friend Emmett rose from a table, grinning at me.

Finch, I remembered. Emmett Finch.

"Please tell me you're here to meet Belinda," I said.

"Okay. I'm here to meet Belinda."

"You're not just saying that, are you?"

He laughed. "You just told me *to* tell you that."

We hadn't spent more than a few minutes talking during my time in Monaco, so it was hard to tell if he was joking, and the affable smile on his face didn't make it any easier.

He scratched his jaw, and I caught sight of a fading bruise on his jawline. There were a few more yellowish shadows around his eyes, and I winced instinctively, noting the cast on his left arm and the boot on his left lower leg. "That must have been some wreck you were in."

"You aren't kidding." He sighed and took a sip of his coffee, then said, "By the way, yes, seriously, I am supposed to be meeting a Belinda," he squinted, clearly thinking hard, "Morris, I think."

"Excellent. She had to deal with a call from the catering company and asked if I'd escort you to the event hall."

"Lead the way." He gestured to the line in front of the counter. "Could I buy you a coffee first?"

"No." I pressed a hand to my stomach. "I've been here since eight. If I drink much more coffee, I won't ever sleep again."

He chuckled, and we made our way to the elevators. Thankfully, the crowd was thinner now, and we only had to wait a few minutes before a car opened up for us. Several others joined us, so following the unspoken elevator rule, we didn't discuss business until we'd stepped off.

Gesturing to the pedway that led over the busy street below, I said, "This will be decorated to look like part of the circus."

"Circus." He looked at me with a grimace. "I guess there's going to be clowns."

I grinned at him. "You're one of those."

"Don't make fun." He popped the plastic lid of the coffee cup and dropped it into a bin for recycling before tossing the cup into the one set aside for paper. That done, he pointed at me. "Coulrophobia, the fear of clowns." He snorted. "A misnomer, if you ask me, has a pretty solid base in science."

We'd stopped walking, and I turned to look at him, trying not to smile but not succeeding very well. "Okay. Elaborate. Why is coulrophobia a misnomer?"

He cleared his throat and spoke with a deeper, slower voice, sounding more like an old-school southern orator now. "Because, Ms. Harden, the word *means* an irrational fear of clowns and if you understand the science, it's a very, very rational fear."

"I'm all ears."

A smile tugged at his lips, but he continued, still in his role. "There's some debate about whether the true reason behind the fear lies in pattern recognition or because the clown hides his true feelings behind a mask or paint."

"It's a job."

He flapped a hand at me. "If I may continue, young lady?"

"Of course, professor."

He winked. "Now, first you have to understand the science behind *pattern recognition*. Your eyes recognize patterns, and sometimes, say with a *clown*, something is just off." He folded his arms over his chest, the casted one braced on his belly while he went to stab at the air with his other finger. "For example...have you ever heard that some people believe children react to dangers or threats without really understanding there *is* a threat? How can they perceive a danger before even adults do? It's because the *pattern* the child recognizes is off, and the child's instincts give a warning."

"Basically, the lizard brain."

He snapped his fingers, reminding me oddly of a professor from high school. "Exactly. The lizard brain reacts to something about the clown. Say, the too-big smile but mean eyes as being wrong."

"But what if the eyes aren't mean?"

"Nonsense. The eyes *have* to be mean, otherwise, why hide behind a mask? Now, the other theory has to do with emotions. Clowns represent unrealistic, exaggerated emotions. It's like dealing with somebody who *smiles* all the time." He shuddered dramatically.

I broke out into laughter. "I think you missed your calling. You should have been an actor."

"Maybe." He gave a bow. "But I prefer to spend my days racing around a track. That's *sane*. Who wants to live their life being scrutinized in front of a camera?"

EMMETT TURNED out to be as charming and funny as he'd first appeared, and after I'd escorted him around the venue and gone through the schedule of events, I asked him what plans he had for the rest of the evening.

"Room service." He rolled his eyes and added, "I'm

limited as to how much walking I can handle without paying for it later, and I've reached that point for the day."

"How about if the only walking you had to do was to and from a car?" I checked my watch. Ricky was in the city since I'd planned to go to my mother's house and update her on the event. I might just call her instead. I'd rather spend the evening talking to Emmett. "I'd love some company for dinner."

He considered the idea, then nodded. "As long as you let me buy. It's the least I can do after talking your ear off the past few hours."

"That's fine with me." There wasn't anything romantic about the offer, I told myself. He was a cute guy, and *so* easy to be around, but I didn't *want* anything romantic. Not when I still found myself doing a doubletake if a tall, leanly built man with hair just the right shade of brown passed by me on the street, or if I heard a voice with the faintest hint of an accent.

No, romance was *not* what I was looking for.

But a distraction?

A friend?

That was more than welcome.

IT WAS FAR EARLIER than I liked when I rolled out of bed the next morning.

I'd sent my mother a text, letting her know I'd call her later with an update, and she'd insisted I come to the house and give it. When I'd explained I was having dinner with a friend, she'd waved it off and told me to come anyway as I knew she was a night owl.

Fine, *she* was. I wasn't. But she didn't care.

I'd been tired enough, and unlike my mother, *not* selfish enough to demand Ricky wait for me, so I'd stayed the night in my old room and simply selected an outfit from among the clothes I still kept at the house. This was far from the first time my mother had insisted I drive out to speak with her late at night.

Now, as Ricky pulled up in front of the hotel, I smothered a yawn.

"You should try to get more sleep, Stacia," Willa Harden said, studying me from dark brown eyes that were just now starting to show the faintest signs of wrinkles. "You must care for your body now if you want to keep it in good shape your entire life."

"I had planned to get more rest last night, but it didn't work out," I said, resisting the urge to tell her I would have gotten plenty of sleep if I hadn't had to drive out to the estate to update her on the event in person.

Next to her, my father tapped away on his phone, oblivious.

"How long is this supposed to last, Willa?" he asked, tugging his glasses off as the car stopped.

"The event ends at three. We can leave around one, as Stacia has agreed to stay until everything is wrapped up." She gave me a tiny smile as Ricky opened the door. "I'll send Ricky back once he's dropped us at home."

"There's no need. I'll take a Lyft."

She looked like she wanted to argue, but I climbed out of the car before she could.

My father was behind me, and he'd wait for her. Knowing they'd move at a measured pace—mustn't be seen hurrying!—I strode quickly on ahead, tossing Ricky a wave over my shoulder. I'd text him later, just to make sure he didn't head back. I didn't need a driver for the twenty minutes it would take to get back to my brownstone.

I was grinning by the time I stepped into the fairytale circus that had been created overnight.

"I have to admit." Emmett's voice had me turning. He pushed off the wall and gestured to the silks overhead where a clown in an exaggerated tutu was pretending to climb. "These clowns aren't too bad."

"They were hired to entertain kids," I said loftily. "They better not look scary or have mean eyes."

He offered his arm. "How about I take you around the big top, pretty lady? Show you the sights?"

TWENTY

LUKA

"You didn't eat much."

I looked at Geraint where he sat across the table, his plate of food all but scraped clean. "You ate enough for us both."

He took a sip of coffee and gave me a pensive look, eyes slightly narrowed. "That's about the third time this week you've spent more time pushing your food around than actually eating. What's going on with you, Luka?"

"Not a thing." I sipped my coffee and directed my attention back to the tablet in front of me. I had it open to the *New York Times*, scanning it more out of habit than actual interest.

Lack of interest had plagued me for the past two weeks, and I could no longer blame it on worry for Emmett. He had been discharged days ago and was expected to make a complete recovery.

I needed to get my head in the game, but it was proving to be harder than it should be, yet one more sign of my distraction.

I had to get past it.

So, do it already, I told myself.

I blew out a rough breath and cleared my mind.

"You want me to believe *not a thing* is wrong." I flipped my brother off without looking at him. "Keep that up, and I'll tell *Maman* how poor your manners have gotten."

"Keep *that* up, and I'll tell *Maman* you were sneaking off to Katrina's suite while she was visiting." I wouldn't. Neither would he. But brothers had to fuck with each other. It was a rule.

"You're smiling, you dick."

I shot Geraint a look. "Am I?"

He laughed and shook his head. "I've got a meeting in a few hours. I need to get going."

As he left the room, I refilled my coffee cup and focused back on my tablet. The stock markets were going crazy. It had been like this for the past couple of years. Luxembourg wasn't in any danger. Our economy was stable, and even if things outside our borders devolved, it wouldn't affect much here.

Still, it was concerning. A true leader, my father had always told me, didn't just concern himself with those directly under his leadership, because the reality was that we were all connected.

I believed he was right.

Annoyed with the headlines from the front page from one of the world's largest papers, I went to exit, but a voice distracted me.

"Is there anything else you'd care for, Your Highness?" Marta, one of the kitchen staff, stood in the doorway, a smile on her round face.

"No." I smiled in return. "I'm fine, thank you. I'll just sit here and read."

She nodded and disappeared through the door.

Looking back at the tablet, I went to exit as planned and froze.

Two familiar faces stared out from the screen, a thumbnail image down on the side. "What the..."

I tapped on it and the link opened.

Emmett and Stacia.

I stared at their faces, the smiles, for a long, long moment before shifting my attention to the headline below.

Emmett Finch, Formula One Driver, and New York City Native Stacia Harden Enchant Children at Local Event.

I skimmed the article, a pulse throbbing in my temple, reading, hoping for an answer to...something.

I didn't even know the question.

But I was looking for it.

The article didn't tell me anything, though. Well, except for what I'd already figured out. The two of them had been photographed together at an event.

A charity gala. Emmett had been brought in for the children at the hospital benefiting from the event. I didn't know why Stacia was there, but judging by the list of people mentioned, it was obvious a number of people attended, from local celebrities down to politicians.

They could have just been there together.

It wasn't like there could be anything there anyway. Emmett had just gotten out of the hospital a week earlier. Stacia had left me in Montreal just two weeks ago.

This didn't mean anything.

Besides, it wasn't like it really mattered in the end. It couldn't. We were who we were, and it wasn't like I'd been particularly kind to her, especially after she'd helped out the way she had.

I shifted my gaze to Emmett, the wide, familiar smile on his face.

I couldn't be mad at him either. He didn't know.

Because I hadn't told him. I hadn't wanted to talk about her when I was there with him in Montreal. I'd told myself if I stopped thinking about her, it would be easier to just...stop thinking about her.

And here I was glaring at the screen because the woman I wanted was smiling at the man I considered my best friend.

TWENTY-ONE

STACIA

"Hello, Mom." I rubbed my temple with my free hand, holding the phone to my ear as I walked through the brownstone, searching for my black heels. Of course, I'd already found two pairs of black heels, but neither were the ones I was looking for—I wanted *that* particular pair.

Emmett and I were going to dinner and then hitting a club, and I wanted my comfortable, sexy heels.

"Darling. I'd like you to join us for dinner tonight. We'll be meeting a couple of friends and their son."

"I've already got plans, Mom, but thanks. Besides, I'm joining you for brunch tomorrow."

"Just because we're seeing you tomorrow doesn't mean we can't see you today. But if you already have plans..." She kept her voice light. Her pause was so slight, it was hard to pick up on, but I knew her too well. I wasn't surprised when she asked in a frost-edged voice, "Are you going out with that...racer again?"

"His name is *Emmett*, Mom. And the last time I checked,

racer wasn't a dirty word." Irritated for reasons I couldn't describe, I said something else I never thought I'd say. "It's not like I'm going out to dinner with a pimp or a drug dealer."

"So, you *are* going out with him." She huffed out a breath. "Really, Stacia. Do you have any idea what people think?"

"Do you have any idea how little I *care*?" Even as I said it, I was surprised.

She was too. Her sharp intake of breath made that clear.

"I'm sorry," I said stiffly. A part of me was, even as another part wasn't.

"I'd *hope* so. What has gotten *into* you?"

Irritation still prickled at me, needling like a fine row of teeth, and I clamped it under control before answering. "I'm just a little frustrated at how you're talking about a friend of mine, Mom. He's a nice man, and we have fun together. I don't see why you have problems with him."

"I'm sure he's perfectly *nice,* and if it's just friendship, of course, that's acceptable." She hesitated.

I knew why she waited. She wanted me to tell her that, of *course,* Emmett was only a friend.

I kept my mouth tightly closed.

"Well." She huffed out a breath. "Well, I guess I'll see you tomorrow. Good night."

She ended the call. I rolled my eyes and sat down on the couch. And there were my shoes, the heels barely visible under the coffee table. Just in time. I checked the time on my phone, then dropped it into my lap, glad I'd timed returning her call so that I'd just have a few minutes before Emmett showed up.

He'd spent most of the past five weeks traveling back and

forth between Kentucky and New York City, visiting his parents and coming back up here.

We'd had fun together, more fun than I'd had in...well, maybe ever. I showed him around the city the way only a local could, and he gave me insights that somebody, a New York native and a wealthy one at that, would never likely gain on their own.

The museums we visited weren't new to me. Most of them, I'd been to probably three or four times at least. But they were a new experience with him.

Lots of things were.

And I was enjoying it.

Sliding my feet into the shoes, I flexed my ankles and stood. As I smoothed my skirt down, the doorbell rang. Grabbing the phone, I tossed it into the small clutch purse.

After checking to make sure it was him, I opened the door and greeted Emmett with a smile.

Red hair spilling down into his dark blue eyes, he smiled back.

Moving closer, I wrapped my arms around his neck. He pulled me in closer for a hug. He turned his face toward me and kissed my temple, then pulled back and grinned down at me. "I've spent the past week down in small-town Kentucky, but as much as I love it there, I don't fit in quite the way I used to, and I never fit all that well anyway. I'm ready to go hit a club, dance with a gorgeous woman, and have some fun. So...are you ready?"

THE HEAT GOT TO ME.

At least I thought it was just the heat.

Like most clubs, the air was humid and thick, and the packed bodies made it seem even worse, but the heat wasn't any worse than normal. Still, it was the only reason I could think of to explain the sudden lightheadedness that came over me, the film of sweat that broke out across my brow and the back of my neck. I was incredibly glad I'd pinned my hair up, although, at the moment, the weight of it was giving me a massive headache too.

Emmett noticed right away, escorting me off the dance floor and toward one of the wide-open terrace doors that led out onto the roof-top garden. The air was marginally cooler, but far less thick, and there weren't as many people pressed in around me, so I sucked in a gulp of air.

"Are you okay?" Emmett asked, guiding me over to the chest-high balustrade that looked out over much of the city. A bit of a breeze kicked up, cooling the sweat on my face, and I started to feel better.

"Just a little too hot, that's all."

"How about I get you a soft drink?" He brushed a stray lock of hair back from my face. "I could use something myself. And I'm hungry."

"I'd love something cold. Just a soft drink, though." The thought of eating just then made my stomach churn.

"Okay. Hold on, let me..." He looked around, then held up a hand. I saw where he was looking.

"Emmett, don't. I'm fine."

He just winked at me.

Annoyed and appreciative at the same time, I watched as

he went over to a nearby collection of low seats and couches. The seating area could have held maybe ten people, but only seven sprawled there. Emmett stood there a few minutes, talking, then gestured toward me, beckoning for me to come closer.

They all scooted in a little closer.

I sat down as Emmett walked off. The woman closest looked me up and down before giving me a smile. "That's a nice man you got there, honey. And those eyes..."

Not feeling good enough to answer, I just gave her a wan smile.

She seemed to understand and patted my shoulder.

I breathed in, feeling a little better as the breeze picked up. Conversation wafted around me, a soothing lull that was oddly cathartic. I lost track of time, might have even nodded off, although I didn't know how.

"Hey."

Emmett sat down next to me, and I stirred, trying to smile at him.

He pushed a drink into my hand, and I curled my fingers around it, the cool, frosty condensation a welcome relief. My first sip was tentative, but my belly welcomed it, so I took another before lowering it, holding the chilled glass between my hands.

"Want one of these nachos?"

Emmett held the dish closer to me. The scent of peppers, spicy meat, and cheese rose to fill my nostrils.

I slammed the glass of lemon-lime soda down so hard it splashed out. Bolting upright, I took off from the group, although I had no idea which way. I didn't make it to a bathroom.

I made it to the hallway outside where the rooftop bathroom was, and the sight of the line there made it clear I wouldn't have any chance of making it inside.

But a server caught sight of me, and she must have recognized the look on my face. She caught my arm, swung me around, and nudged me into a hall I hadn't even seen.

"There, baby...right there..." She nudged me toward a garbage can, and I bent over, just in time, emptying my stomach. I wretched several times more before the spasms mercifully stopped.

I straightened slowly, head pounding, saliva pooling in my mouth.

The server, a tall, skinny woman, her dreads pulled into a regal looking crown, stood there. She had a glass of light gold, sparkling liquid in her hand. "Ginger ale. Try it. It might help."

I took the glass and sipped mechanically. "Thank you."

"Better?"

I looked at her, embarrassed, but thankful. "I don't know yet.

"You don't look so glassy-eyed." She pursed her lips as she studied me. "You're not drunk, that's obvious. Did you eat something that upset your belly?"

"No." I blanched at the thought and added, "My friend had some nachos and just the smell of it..." I gulped hard, the memory almost as fresh as the experience.

"Oh, honey." She laughed and patted my arm. "I

remember those days. Take another drink, give it a few minutes. Those first couple of months can be a pain."

Not thinking about what she said, I did take another sip.

Those first few months...

Just as Emmett came around the corner, I realized what she meant. And I realized something else, too. I'd missed my period.

"Son of a bitch," I breathed to the kind server. "I'm pregnant."

Emmett's eyes popped wide.

TWENTY-TWO

LUKA

Accepting a glass of wine, I tried to focus on the conversation drifting around us, tried to focus on the woman I'd been partnered with for the night.

Her name was Violet Bourne, the daughter of one of my father's oldest friends and a member of one of the oldest noble families in Europe with ties to the British monarchy.

I had no doubt that my mother had at least something to do with this particular seating arrangement. She'd dropped what I believe she'd assumed were subtle hints about the young woman. While my mother had many skills and *could* be subtle, match making and subtlety didn't go well when she tried to pair them together.

"How is your friend?" Violet paused, then added, "The Formula One racer, Emmett?"

The question was the only one Violet had asked that generated any interest from me all night, although I'd feigned it anyway.

"He's doing better, thank you." I gave her a brief nod. I

hadn't talked to him much, but we texted a few times a week. He'd called a few days ago, and although I felt like an ass, I kept the conversation brief, claiming I was supposed to be taking a conference call with a diplomat who didn't even exist.

Talking to him was hard right now. As much as I wanted to, I hadn't let myself ask about Stacia, or what was going on between them. Just trying to keep things feeling...*normal* between us was proving to be harder than I'd thought.

"I heard he'll be out the rest of the season," Violet said, smiling shyly.

"Yes." I swirled my wine, staring into the rich red instead of her pale green eyes. I could feel her watching me, felt the nervous interest and her shyness, and I just wanted to be away from all of it.

Feeling Geraint's gaze on me, I looked up. He raised an eyebrow, the look telling. I bit back a sigh, then looked at Violet with a smile. "He's actually quite lucky. A broken fibula, radius, and bruised ribs. A few other complications, of course, but it could have been much worse."

"You must have been worried."

"Yes." I took another drink of wine, a bigger one, and wished it was something stronger. "It doesn't help that he was clear over in Canada when it happened, and it took far too long to get there."

"You're very close?"

"Yes. We've been friends since we were teenagers." The open look on her face made it clear she was interested in hearing more, but I really had no desire to *offer* more. I checked the time and smiled. "I think I'll walk around a bit. It's been lovely talking to you again."

Ignoring the look Geraint gave me, I pushed back from the table and escaped into the small crowd. There were only a few families at the dinner party Aeric's parents had organized. I knew everybody there, so finding a few minutes alone wouldn't be easy, but I needed those minutes.

I headed outside to the terrace, and it wasn't until I was out there that I thought about how damn stupid it had been to come *here*. The last time I'd been out on this terrace, I'd been with Stacia.

My blood thickened and heated. Dragging a hand down my face, I muttered, "Don't think about her. *Stop* thinking about her."

Standing on the terrace made that next to impossible, so after only a few minutes, I slipped back inside. Violet was still sitting at the table, talking to Geraint and Katrina, and I had no doubt my brother would give me an earful. I needed to go back over there. Blowing out a breath, I headed in that direction.

"Luka!"

I paused as somebody cut in front of me. I didn't recognize him at first, which was weird. I should, considering the gathering. Also, he'd used my given name, which was something very, very few would do.

Recognition and annoyance hit at roughly the same time.

The man was a distant cousin on my father's side, someone I saw only rarely, but whenever I did see him, Alain went out of his way in his attempts to ingratiate himself to me and Geraint. I'd been tempted more than once to tell him that he was wasting his time. His father had once worked alongside mine, but some unsavory business contacts had ended that.

Those unsavory business contacts were still in play, and Alain used the same network.

He flashed his blinding smile at me, arms spread out as if expecting a hug. Cutting that off, I stuck my hand out for a quick shake. "Alain, hello."

"It's been a long time." He accepted the handshake easily enough, but before he could cover my hand with his and drag the handshake on, I broke away and flagged down a server to scoop up another glass of wine. "Are you enjoying yourself?"

As predicted, he started to talk.

Tuning him out was easy. I simply nodded every fifteen seconds or so while my attention drifted. I was about to end the man's annoying ramble when a familiar voice caught my ear.

Aeric's.

I glanced over and saw him just a few feet away, standing at a slight diagonal as he spoke to his sister, Anne.

"...talked to her lately?"

Ignore them.

"No. I keep meaning to call her, but time slips away. How is she?"

Aeric's annoyance was obvious. "Fine, but...fuck. Her parents are giving her more trouble than ever."

"They can be horrid," Anne said, her voice short. "Our cousin is so sweet. How did she *come* from them?"

Cousin—

"How about you, cousin?" Alain clapped me on the shoulder.

I focused back in on him. "About the same as always, Alain. Listen, I better get back to my table," I told him, thoughts still focused on the conversation between Aeric and Anne. "I don't want to neglect my table companions."

I smiled at him and strode off.

Our cousin is so sweet.

"Stop it," I told myself.

Aeric had a large family, a number of cousins on his father's side. They could have been talking about any number of *sweet* cousins who had parents who treated their daughters less than stellar. And it wasn't like Stacia had outright *told* me her parents were, as Anne had put it, *horrible*.

TWENTY-THREE

STACIA

I checked the test again.

It was still sitting on the counter from last night. Emmett and I had stopped by a pharmacy to pick it up on the way home from the club, and I'd taken it while he sat in the living room waiting.

So far, he was the only one who knew.

Personally, I was just fine with that, but I had lunch with my parents ahead of me, and I'd spent the past few hours trying to figure out what to tell them, *if* I should tell them today, and if not *today*, then when...

It was all enough to give me a massive headache, and in the end, I made the decision based off one simple thing. I was tired of walking on eggshells around them. If I didn't tell them *today*, I'd be walking on those eggshells and worrying about their response until I *did* tell them.

Who needed that in their life?

Just *thinking* about the conversation with my mother the

night before irritated me all over again, that faint edge of disdain in her voice as she discussed Emmett.

A nice guy who made great money and did good things for people, but it wasn't good enough for her—or my father.

Nothing was good enough for them, and I could only imagine their reactions when I told them about the baby.

Looking at my reflection, I reached down and covered my belly with my hand. I wasn't showing yet. When would I? I had no idea. I hadn't looked up any of that, afraid I'd end up on one of those stupid sites that would convince me everything was wrong, then I'd curl up in the bed and not come up until the doctor's office opened on Monday.

No. I had enough worrying to do. My parents weren't going to be on that list too. I already had a lot of things to figure out over the next few months and dealing with my parents' reactions shouldn't even be a consideration.

I'd have Ricky stay handy to drive me back to my brownstone in case they didn't take it well—and I knew they wouldn't. I normally didn't ask him to work on weekends, but this wasn't a normal day.

He knew something was up when he knocked on the door. He took one look at me and frowned, but before he could ask, I held up a hand. "Later, okay? I've got to keep my cool so I can deal with Mom and Dad. I'll talk to you about... everything later."

He hesitated, then nodded, concern clear in his eyes. "Let's get on the road."

I WAS *STARVING* by the time we got to the estate, despite the nerves tangling my belly into knots. As we came around the final bend and the big estate, a sprawling construction of stone and sparkling windows, came into view, I made an executive decision.

I was going to eat first.

I didn't feel remotely close to how I'd felt last night when I'd gotten sick, not hot and sweaty, not nauseated.

I doubted lunch at my parents' would involve anything remotely close to nachos or spicy meat or peppers, whatever it was that had set my stomach off.

Of course, if I went in there and something didn't past the smell test, I'd have to reconsider the eating thing, but as long as nothing set me off, I was going to eat.

"The final meal of a condemned woman," I murmured.

"What's the sentencing, Miss Stacia?"

I looked up to find Ricky glancing at me in the rearview mirror. "You're stubborn."

He winked at me. "Only with the people who matter."

I smiled back. "I'll tell you later. I might need you to take me someplace where I can cry it off, actually." Concern flashed in his eyes, and I leaned forward, patting his shoulder. "It's okay, Ricky. Or it will be. I just have to tell my parents something that will surely upset them."

He looked like he wanted to push, but he didn't, and I was grateful. As he came to a stop in the circular drive in front of the big house, I took a deep breath and braced myself. I even sat inside the car and let him come around to open the door, something I rarely did. I needed every last second to gather my nerves.

He held out a hand to help me out, then squeezed it gently. "You call me when you're ready. I won't be more than ten minutes away."

"Thank you." I gave him a grateful smile.

"Of course." He lingered behind, watching as I made my way up the stairs.

Theo, my parents' butler, had the door open before I cleared the first step, and I nodded at him. He gave me a stiff smile in return.

The two of us had never gotten along well, not that he'd ever said anything antagonizing toward me. But he had about as much warmth and personality as a dead houseplant—a poisonous one—and trying to engage him in even polite conversation resulted in withering stares. It was as if he wanted to relegate you to the same dead, poisonous houseplant status.

"Your parents are in the small salon," he said, holding out a hand for my purse.

I turned it over, keeping my muted phone tucked in the pocket of my skirt. My parents had an unwritten rule about cellphones and other devices at the dinner table, but if I had to get out of there in a hurry, I wasn't hunting down Theo just to get my purse so I could text Ricky.

Without waiting for Theo to escort me, I started through the house. The small salon—only called that because it was *smaller* than the main one—was across from the small formal dining room. Neither the small salon nor small formal dining room was especially small. A party of ten could sit comfortably in either room and had, many times. As I neared, I caught scents of food drifting from the kitchen and breathed a little easier. No nausea. If anything, it only made me hungrier.

"Darling."

"Hello, Mom. Dad." I went to where my mother sat and bent to kiss her carefully powdered cheek.

My father rose from his chair and came to drop a kiss on my brow.

"Ma'am."

The voice behind me was a welcome one, only because I knew what it signified. Turning, I saw Mattie, the head chef, smiling at my mother. "Lunch is ready if you'd like to proceed to the dining room."

My father held out a hand to my mother, and I trailed along behind them on their way across the hall into the room where three place settings waited. Although only three of us were dining at the large, ten-foot-long dining table, my dad sat at the head and Mom sat at the far opposite end, while I had a place in the exact middle. All other seats had been removed.

It was cold...distant. Just like the relationship we shared. I'd thought about it before, but it had never struck me as hard as it did just then.

I'm not raising my child like this.

"Is something bothering you, darling?" Mom asked as I lingered in the broad, arched entry.

"No." I gave her a blank smile and circled the table to take my seat.

Our meals were brought out, already plated. Chicken with a lemon-herb butter sauce, sautéed vegetables, a rice pilaf, a salad. Nothing terribly exciting, which was standard for my parents, but I was grateful for that.

One of the staff went to put a glass of white wine at my elbow, and I held up a hand. "None for me, please. Do we have any ginger ale?"

After a brief pause, the young woman nodded. "I believe so, ma'am. I'll check."

I felt my mother's disapproval but didn't look at her, reaching for the glass of ice water instead.

My father broke the silence, asking her about an upcoming charity gala, which would keep her distracted for at least ten minutes. She barely noticed the drink placed by my plate, and I took a sip before cutting into my chicken.

I kept my attention on my food, not looking up until Mom said my name.

"Yes, ma'am?"

She studied me over the rim of her wine glass. "You're rather quiet today, even for you."

"Am I?" Putting my fork down, I reached for my glass of ginger ale, taking another sip. The food I'd managed to consume grew heavier in my belly. I'd eaten almost half, probably could have eaten all of it, but that look on her face made it clear she'd picked up on something, and I knew she wouldn't let this go until she'd figured out what it was.

"Yes." She took a drink of wine. "Are you still upset with me over your racing friend?"

I met her eyes levelly. "I wasn't the one who was upset. My relationship with Emmett bothers *you*, not me, and that's your issue. So...no. I'm not upset with you over it."

Her lids flickered slightly.

It was petty for me to feel smug, but I did. She was so set in her ways about *proper* friendships, *proper* relationships. I wondered how often she'd ranted to my father about Emmett. Suppressing a smile, I took another sip from my ginger ale then put the glass down.

"However, since you brought it up, I do have something on my mind, and I might as well tell you both now." I looked over at my father, then back at Mom. "I'm pregnant."

Mom had been holding her fork, and it fell from her suddenly limp fingers to hit the plate. Her eyes, wide and stunned, locked on my face. "What did you say?"

That had actually been much easier than I'd thought.

Saying it a second time? Easier still.

"Mom, Dad." I looked over at him this time. "I'm pregnant."

"Stacia..." My mother sucked in a breath, sounding appalled. "How can you...you're not even *married*."

"Mom." Sighing, I looked over at her. "It's the twenty-first century. Unmarried women don't get stoned in our society for having babies anymore."

My father still hadn't said anything, but at those words, he shoved back abruptly from the table and crossed over to the beverage service and uncapped the whiskey decanter, splashing himself a healthy serving.

"Who is the father?" he demanded after taking a swallow.

"It doesn't matter."

My father shot me a hard look. "I fail to see how *that* is possible."

Meeting that look without wilting wasn't easy, but I

managed. "He won't be part of the baby's life. And before either of you ask, *yes,* I'm keeping the baby."

"What do you mean, the father won't be part of the baby's life?" Mom half-shouted.

"I believe you heard me."

"I *heard* you, but that's not an explanation, young lady," she snapped.

I rose from the chair.

"Sit down." She pointed to the chair like I was eight and had refused to eat my vegetables.

"No, thank you. It's clear you're both upset about this. I'm sorry for that. But I refuse to sit here and be scolded like a child. I'm *not*. I'm an adult, and I can make my own decisions."

TWENTY-FOUR

LUKA

"You remember we have the party in Monaco this Saturday."

I looked at Geraint, frowning. "What party?"

He stared at me. "You've misplaced your brain this summer. You can't blame it on Emmett's accident, either. It was misplaced *before* that. *Aeric's* party. His birthday party. We've already RSVP'd."

I resisted the urge to swear. I didn't want to go back to Monaco, and I definitely didn't want to go back to the Prince's Palace and be assailed with memories of Stacia.

Speculatively, I eyed Geraint.

"No." He pointed at me. "Get that look off your face, brother. *Now.*"

"What look?"

"*That* look." With an annoyed glare, he flapped a hand at me. "You're giving me that look you always give me when you're about to try and pass something off on me."

"How often do I do that?" I demanded.

"Not often," he conceded. "But you've done it more in the past few months than you *ever* have, and it's almost always events that have to do with making public appearances. In case you've forgotten, you're the face of the Grand Duchy. You're the *heir*, not me. Whatever it is that has you shying away from parties and such, you need to get over it."

I wanted to tell him he was imagining things, but I couldn't.

He *wasn't*. I *had* avoided a few events over the past few weeks. There had been an engagement party in Paris for one of the Formula One drivers I was friendly with, and I hadn't gone, sending a gift instead. It wasn't unheard of, really, because I had a full schedule, but I *would* have gone if I hadn't worried about seeing Emmett...and possibly Stacia. Together.

Emmett had even texted me, asking why I hadn't been there.

I'd responded that business in Luxembourg had kept me tied up. He said he understood, but it had been a lie.

I could have gotten away for a few hours, easily.

I'd also avoided a charity event in Milan that many on the Formula One circuit supported. I send a large donation instead and somebody else in my place.

Geraint was right about this, though. Aeric and I were friends, and Monaco was one of Luxembourg's allies. It could be seen as a slight if I didn't go. Fuck it all.

Emmett may well be there.

Aeric was a big supporter of the entire Formula One sport, and while he and Emmett weren't close personally, I knew they got along well. Emmett had attended Aeric's bashes in the past.

And Stacia...

Would she be there? It was likely. Not only was she dating Emmett—their fucking pictures kept showing up online—but she was Aeric's cousin.

Would they be there *together?*

Clenching my teeth, I pushed the thought out of my mind and looked at Geraint. "You're right, of course."

"You sound like we're attending a funeral. You'll be a fun one to be around that night." He rolled his eyes.

"You'll be sneaking off with your pretty bride-to-be, so you won't have to concern yourself."

"I'm afraid not. Katrina has a fundraiser that's been in the works for a while. Both she and Regan have been working on it for months. It's the first play Regan's little group will be putting on, for the Prince and Princess of Liechtenstein, no less." He gave me a smug smile. "If you try to pass Aeric's birthday off on me, I have a handy escape already in mind. *Maman* would certainly understand if I felt I needed to show my support for my future wife's charitable endeavors."

"I already told you I was going." I flipped him off, resigned to the coming weekend.

"Good." He grinned, looking as smug as I'd ever seen him. "Just keep in mind my escape route if you start having second thoughts. If you try to get out of it and send me, I'll tell our mother I've changed my mind and won't be going."

"LUKA." My mother, Octavia, stood in the doorway of my office, a smile on her face. She nodded at me, then looked at my personal assistant. "Stuart. How are you this afternoon?"

"Quite well, Your Highness." He was already on his feet, offering a short bow.

"The same. I was wondering if I could have a few minutes of my son's time."

"I...of course." Stuart scrambled to collect his things, looking at me. "We were almost done for the day, weren't we, Your Highness?"

"Yes, I believe so." It wouldn't do any good to say otherwise, would it? I couldn't exactly tell my *mother* I had other things to do. That would just be rude.

Stuart left after giving another quick nod, shutting the door behind us. I still stood behind my desk, but now that he was gone, I came out from behind it and went to greet her, giving her a quick kiss on the cheek. "What can I do for you, *Maman*?"

"I just wanted to talk about the birthday party you're attending this weekend for the Hereditary Prince of Monaco. Have you found a gift for him?"

"I was thinking about giving him a peacock."

My mother blinked. "A peacock."

"Yes. I was actually inspired by a gift given to Prince Harry. He was gifted two macaws on a trip to the Caribbean in 2016."

My mother pursed her lips, still studying me. "I don't think a *peacock* is a proper gift, Luka."

"Have you *met* Aeric, *Maman*?"

A smile quirked at her lips. "I said *proper*, not *fitting*."

"You're taking away my fun."

She sighed and shook her head. "I'm almost tempted to allow it. You're not having a great deal of fun lately, it seems."

That struck me silent, and I realized I hadn't been hiding things as well as I'd thought. Geraint had realized something was bothering me, but he...well, he *looked*. My parents had always seemed a bit more distant. But perhaps they saw more than we realized.

"I see we won't be discussing it." She nodded. "Very well. Have you considered asking Violet to the party?"

The swift change in subject matter might have thrown me, and although I was grateful she hadn't decided to linger on the matter of what was plaguing me—*a beautiful, blue-eyed, American brunette I'll never have*—I really didn't want to talk about Violet, either. She was sweet, and I had a bad feeling somebody had planted ideas in her head that she and I could become some sort of match. The way she looked at me made me think she was already picking out wedding cake flavors.

"I mentioned it briefly, but she can't come to the party."

"Oh?" Giving me a quizzical look, my mother cocked her head.

"No. Besides, I...well. *Maman*, Violet is a nice girl, but she and I aren't compatible."

"I see." She gave a small nod. "I take it you have something else in mind besides a...peacock for Prince Aeric."

Glad she'd decided to let it go, I nodded. "Of course, *Maman*." I pulled my phone out from my pocket and pulled up the picture of what I'd finally decided to give to Aeric. "He goes there every year," I told her, passing over the phone.

"It seems to be something he cares for a great deal, so I decided we'd help out."

She studied the image for a long moment, then passed me the phone and kissed my cheek. "Perhaps he's a bit more than a peacock. And so are you."

Embarrassment heated my face, but she didn't say anything, just rose and left the room.

———

"YOU WENT and funded two wells in Africa," Geraint said, grumbling. "I gave him a bottle of Stoli Elite Himalayan Edition. Why didn't you tell me about the fucking wells? I could have gone in with you, and we'd have funded three or four."

I shot my brother an amused glance as I sipped at my serving of the Stoli. It was *very* good vodka. "If I'd done that, I wouldn't be standing here with you enjoying this fine vodka."

"You've got a bottle of it back in your suite at home," he pointed out. "I gave it to you for your birthday."

"You're getting predictable."

He grumbled again, this time too low for me to hear. Still, I smiled. I was in a relatively good mood.

The party had been underway for a couple of hours, and I still hadn't seen Stacia.

I was taking it as a sign that she wasn't here.

I hadn't seen Emmett either.

A part of me felt guilty for not wanting to see my best friend, but I needed to accept the relationship between them before I could deal with seeing him again. I didn't want to do or say something that would tarnish a friendship I valued.

Somebody called Geraint, and he nudged me on the shoulder. "I'll see you later. Enjoy yourself for once, will you? Even if you are enjoying *my* birthday present."

"You gave it to Aeric!" I called out behind him before retreating to the recessed sitting area where Aeric was currently enjoying his second serving of Stoli Elite and laughing as he recounted some story.

He caught sight of me and lifted his glass cheerfully. I tipped mine in return and started to sit but made the mistake of glancing around the big ballroom. I told myself I wasn't looking for Stacia, even though I knew I lied.

What's the harm, though? I thought. *She's not here.*

Except...she was.

Light flashed off a woman's beaded dress as she descended the steps, and my gaze lingered, first out of appreciation for the way the fabric draped over a hip, highlighting the elegant curve lovingly. But the skin on the back of my neck prickled, and my heart thumped, and I looked up and found myself staring at a familiar face, one that haunted my dreams.

Stacia.

TWENTY-FIVE

STACIA

I MIGHT HAVE JUST STAYED IN MY SUITE THE ENTIRE night, but I'd promised Aeric I'd make an appearance.

Just an appearance, I'd warned him. "I might only come down for five minutes, so don't grumble at me if I don't stay."

"Have I ever grumbled at you?"

I was sure he had, a time or two, but I hadn't responded, and he'd hugged me and told me just to come down if I wanted to.

In the end, it was guilt that had me descending those stairs. I was *here*, after all, and he *was* having a party. It wouldn't take me that much time to put on a dress and go mingle for a few minutes.

After all, I was hiding out in Monaco—again—to get away from my parents...*and* all the gossip that was sure to start in their circle as soon as people realized I was pregnant.

I had no doubt my parents would keep it quiet as long as they could, but I wasn't about to start hiding away in my brownstone. I'd finally figured out the whole *being social* thing with Emmett, and I'd come to enjoy having a social life. I'd even made some new friends, and I didn't want to creep back into my empty life as the *Ice Princess* because it made things easier on my parents.

It wasn't like they'd ever made anything easier on me.

"Miss Stacia."

"Hi, Blanche."

She waved me down into the sitting area where my cousin and his friends waited. "I'll have someone bring you a drink." She raised an eyebrow. "Ginger ale?"

Blanche was the only one who knew in Monaco. She'd found me getting sick in my suite the day I arrived, and I'd confided in her only after she'd promised to keep it to herself.

"Thank you."

She nodded and waved down a server as I descended into the pit.

Aeric saw me and made room on the wide, plush couch. As I sat, he lifted something from the floor and brandished it. A bottle of vodka. "Want some? It's from Geraint."

A warning echoed in my head even as I shook my head. "No. None for me. I'm holding off on alcohol as tired as I am."

"Aw...just a drink, cousin. It's quite wonderful."

But I nudged the glass he urged at me away. "Not tonight, Aeric."

"All right." He heaved out a sigh. "But remember, I offered. This is fine vodka, and I've only shared with a few select people. Isn't that right, Luka?"

My heart skittered, and blood roared in my head. I looked up in time to see the familiar, tall, lean form circle around the firepit in the middle and settle in a seat a few feet away from us. He glanced casually at me, then nodded at Aeric, lifting his glass. "Of course, Aeric."

"Miss Stacia."

Jolting at the sound of my name, I looked over to see one of the staff standing just to my side with a tall, slim glass filled to the top with a pale gold liquid. "Thank you." I smiled at her and took the glass, bringing it to my lips. I was parched, my throat gone tight with nerves, but I only allowed myself a sip before lowering it.

"How are you doing?"

Feeling his eyes on me, I looked over at Luka. He was pointedly staring at me. Aeric was talking to the woman next to him, and despite the crowd, the way Luka watched me was strikingly intimate, giving me the impression it was just us in the room.

Just Luka and Stacia.

My heart ached, and I pushed the stupid, weak thing aside, forcing myself to recall how Luka had acted in Montreal. And the way he'd acted when I'd gone with Aeric to visit Luka's family in Luxembourg. What *intimacy* Luka might want to convey was illusory. He'd made that clear.

"I'm fine, Your Highness."

His lips twitched, eyes burning into me.

I sat there a few more moments, nursing my drink, then leaned over and tapped Aeric's shoulder. "I think I've mingled enough."

His dark brows rose up. "You weren't kidding when you said you'd only stay a few minutes."

"Well, I warned you." I gave him a teasing smile, then

kissed his cheek. "Happy birthday. I'll see you in the morning, okay?"

Leaving my drink on the platform behind the couch, I rose and headed for the pit's exit, already thinking about getting out of the shoes, the dress and washing off my makeup, then slipping into some pajamas so I could watch Netflix and brood until I was tired enough to sleep.

Somebody bumped into me.

"Oh, please excuse...Stacia!"

I looked up and met a familiar pair of eyes.

"Ger...Your Highness." I dipped into a quick curtsey at Luka's brother. "Excuse me, I didn't see you."

"I bumped into you, Stacia." He gave a mock bow and offered a charming smile. "How are you doing?"

"Ah...I'm well, and you?"

Before he could answer, a taller form appeared in my line of sight. "Still tripping over your feet, brother?"

"Learned from the best, Luka." Geraint grinned at him. "Look who's here. You remember Aeric's cousin, Stacia, don't you?"

"Indeed. I was actually looking for you, Stacia." He held out a hand. "Care to join me for a dance?"

I wanted to punch him. What was the etiquette for refusing to dance with a member of royalty? I had no idea. I'd never researched that. I wouldn't have minded finding out, but I realized more than a few people were watching us and I wasn't about to draw any more attention.

"Of course." I nodded at Geraint, and just for the hell of it, dipped into a much lower curtsey for the elder prince. Luka narrowed his eyes before leading me onto the dance floor. The moment he pulled me against him, my body started to melt, which didn't help my irritated mind at all. Or my ego.

I kept my hand on his shoulder and stared at a point just over that, glad my heels were tall enough for that mercy. I didn't want to look up *at* him and just staring at his chest seemed cowardly.

He had one arm wrapped around the small of my back while his free hand grasped my right one.

The music was still relatively formal, but more and more couples were moving into decidedly *less* formal styles of dancing as it grew later. Luka held me close enough that the fronts of our bodies touched lightly, close enough to bring back all the aching memories I kept trying to bury and forget.

"You're angry with me," he murmured in my ear.

My skin broke out in goose bumps at his soft words.

I didn't know how to respond, so I stayed quiet.

He dipped his head closer.

The feel of his lips brushing my ear elicited a sharp gasp, and under the double-layered silk gown, my nipples tightened into hard points.

"Not even going to speak to me, Stacia?"

My lips were stiff as I answered. "What's there to say, Luka? You asked for a dance. We're dancing. Once this dance is over, I'm going to my room. In a few days, I'm going home, and I'm certain you'll do the same."

"You'll go to your room." He drew the words out slowly, almost teasingly. "Are you going alone?"

Irritated now, I lifted my head to glare at him.

"What, are you expecting another invitation? After the way you acted in Montreal?"

His lids flickered, and his mouth went tight. "I deserve that."

"Yes." I didn't look away. "You do."

He sighed. "I'm sorry. I was worried about Emmett, and there were other things on my mind. But I shouldn't have been so curt with you. I know that, and I'm sorry."

The song ended, and another one came on. But when he tugged me up tighter against him, I didn't pull away.

Why?

Because I seemed to be helpless when it came to him.

I couldn't explain it.

But I was helpless.

"I've missed you," he murmured, lowering his head to mine once more, murmuring the words into my hair.

I closed my eyes, telling myself not to let the words mean anything. They *couldn't* mean anything. I kept on telling myself that even when he whispered my name again, and when I noticed the music had grown fainter, and that the air was cooler.

He cupped my chin in his hand, and I looked up, realizing that at some point, he'd maneuvered us onto the terrace, where we'd been the first time he'd kissed me.

"Luka—"

He kissed me again.

And just like the first time, the feel of his lips on mine stole my breath away.

I shuddered in reaction as he caught my lower lip between his teeth and sucked as he tugged, then let go. I whimpered as he dipped his tongue inside my mouth in a slow simulation of lovemaking.

And when he finally lifted his head to stare at me, I was clinging to him.

He tugged the top of my dress.

I stiffened, and he murmured, "Shhh...nobody can see us."

I looked around, panicking, but he was right. He'd led us into one of the alcoves, and he stood with his body blocking me completely from view.

"Look at your tits, Stacia. Fuck, your nipples are already swollen...see how hard they get for me?" He dipped his head, using one hand to lift my breast completely from the dress, and I sagged as he took me into his mouth, sucking and swirling his tongue over the sharp point, then biting down lightly.

I saw stars.

Clenching my thighs together, I whimpered. My pussy ached already, for him, for this.

"Is there any reason you can't come to my hotel with me?" he asked, his mouth pressed to my ear.

TWENTY-SIX

LUKA

Moonlight gilded her flesh, turning her pale skin to alabaster. Her nipple was wet from my mouth, and her eyes were wide and hungry.

"Stacia." Swiping my thumb across the swollen curve of her lower lip, I asked again, "Is there any reason you can't come back to my hotel with me?"

It had to be my hotel.

I still hadn't seen Emmett, and at this point, I didn't *care* if they were together. I had to have her again, but if I saw any sign of them being a couple, whether he was here, any sign at all, I'd lose it.

But I had to have her.

Her lashes fluttered, like they were just too heavy for her lids to bear the weight. Then she swallowed and shook her head. "No."

That *no* could mean any number of things, and I wasn't going to risk common sense or decency getting in the way of having her again, so I didn't question her. With a few brisk tugs, I had her gown back in place, then taking her hand, I led her to a side door near the end of the terrace.

I'd been to the Prince's Palace in Monaco often enough that I knew my way around, and I led her through a side hallway that ran alongside the ballroom where the party continued.

It took only five minutes for us to emerge from the grand entrance, and one of the many valets hustled to me, but I ignored him, striding to one of the black cars lined up for random party-goers.

I didn't want my personal car brought around, because that could mean one of the staff taking notice of Stacia.

The driver leaning against the car closest to me saw me bearing down on him, and he straightened, offering me a bright smile. "Would you care for a ride, sir?"

I gave him the name of my hotel, and he nodded smartly, opening the door for us. We were inside before any of the valets reached us.

From inside the car, I texted my brother to let him know I'd taken a private car back to the hotel. I also texted a member of my traveling party who'd stayed behind at the hotel so they'd be out front to pay the driver. After that, I put my phone on silent.

Pulling Stacia into my lap, I laid my hand on her knee and toyed with the beading on her dress. "I saw you from across the ballroom, saw this dress, and even before I saw your face, I knew it was you. The slope of your shoulder, the dip of your waist...I think I could find you blindfolded in a crowd of a thousand people, Stacia."

"Luka..." She whispered my name.

But if she had anything else to say, it was lost against my mouth as I kissed her, pushing my tongue past her lips, while slipping my hand under her skirt and sliding it up along her thigh.

She sagged against me, her body lax and warm, pliable. She whimpered as I curved my hand over her hip, the material of her dress pushed all the way up to her butt now. Catching her lip between my teeth, I tugged. "It's a good thing my hotel is only a few minutes from the palace, Stacia. Otherwise, I might do something that would turn your pretty cheeks red."

Her lids flickered up as I lifted my head to stare down at her.

"Something...?"

"Something like push your thighs apart to see how wet you are. Or have you take my cock in your hand...or your mouth."

Her gaze darted to the man in the front seat just as he pulled into the circular drive of the big hotel that served many of the country's more prestigious guests.

He wasn't looking at either of us, but her cheeks still flushed hotly red.

Easing Stacia off my lap, I peered out the window, then directed the man where to park. "He'll handle paying you."

The man didn't question me, and as one of Stuart's men paid the driver, I took Stacia's hand and led her into the hotel, straight to the private elevator. In moments, we were in my room, and I grasped the back of her neck, tugging her close to kiss her again as I fumbled with the door's locks blindly.

We fumbled and moaned, and finally, I pulled my mouth

from hers and nudged her against the door, much as I'd done earlier in the garden, so I had her pinned in, my body pressing into hers, enjoying every soft, sweet curve. I tugged the dress down once more. "Where were we?"

Her breasts were completely exposed this time, and she moaned as I dipped my head.

I echoed the noise when she pushed her hands into my hair, clutching me closer. I felt her hips moving against me, and I caught the material of her gown, tugging it up. When I slid a hand between her thighs, I found hot, wet silk and even hotter, wetter pussy. She cried out as I slid my fingers over the wet material, dragging it over her folds.

"You're so hot," I said against her mouth. "Is this all for me, Stacia?"

"Yes..." She pushed insistently against my hand.

"Tell me. Say, 'I'm hot for you, Luka.'"

She lifted her heavy lids and licked her lips. "I'm hot for you. But you already know that."

The words, so simply spoken, should have been enough to reassure me, but they weren't. "Do you want me to fuck you?"

"Yes..." She moaned and rolled her hips against my hand, seeking relief.

I pulled the panties aside and plunged two fingers into her wet cunt.

She cried out.

The sound of it was the sweetest thing I'd heard in weeks. "Come for me, baby," I whispered against her ear, twisting my fingers, moving faster, desperate to remind her who'd taught her what it was like to feel like this.

She clung to me, half-wild, riding my hand and whimpering.

I stroked my thumb over her clitoris, and she broke. Slamming her head back against the door, she erupted into my hand and came.

Savage now with need, I tore open my trousers and exposed myself, then shoved her dress all the way up. I caught her hips and lifted her, staring into her flushed face. "Look at me, Stacia."

Shuddering still from her orgasm, she did just that. Eyes wide, lips parted, she watched me, and I tucked the head of my cock to the mouth of her pussy and thrust up and in, filling her completely.

She cried out and arched against me, taking every last inch.

Her hot, silky wet pussy clamped tight around me, milking me, and I swore.

"*Fuck.*"

She flinched at the tone of my voice.

I shuddered, telling myself I had to do it, that I had to pull out. "I...sorry, but...I need to stop. I forgot a condom, Stacia. I have to have a condom."

She stared at me with solemn eyes, then in a shuddering voice said, "I'm clean."

"I...fuck. So am I, but that's not the only issue. Pregnancy is."

Her lashes fluttered, a faint pink flush rising to her cheeks. "That's not something you need to worry about tonight."

Stop. You can't be this stupid.

I even started to pull out. But that required *moving* inside the tight fist of her slippery, sweet cunt, and instinctively, as she clenched around me, I stroked back inside her.

"I shouldn't do this," I muttered, shaking my head.

She smoothed her hands down my shoulders. "Then stop. But it won't matter if you do."

I withdrew...then sank back inside, because having her wrapped around my naked cock was pure, sheer bliss. I groaned and gripped her hips, tilting her closer so I could go even deeper.

She whimpered, and I looked at her, watching her eyes widen in shock and pleasure. "It feels just as good to you, doesn't it?"

"Yes...Luka...please!"

I couldn't have stopped then. Not for anything.

I thrust deeper, harder, and she clung to me, whimpering, crying and pleading for more.

She stiffened, her orgasm catching her, and as she started to clench rhythmically around me, I couldn't hold back any longer. Burying my face against her neck, I came, shuddering with the intensity of it and clinging to her, every bit as tightly as she clung to me.

TWENTY-SEVEN

STACIA

THERE WAS A ROBE HANGING ON THE BACK OF THE bathroom door, and I pulled it on, snuggling into the warmth and enjoying the lingering scent that I immediately identified as Luka's. Woodsmoke, the forest, and musk. I had no idea just what all contributed to that unique scent, but if they could bottle it and sell it, the mastermind behind it would be rich, and women across the world would be forever grateful.

Hearing movement out in the main room of the suite, I told myself to stop sniffing the soft, fluffy cotton and open the door. After checking to make sure my face wouldn't give anything away, I did.

Luka stood in the middle of the room, a phone pressed to his ear. He had his back to me, and I was treated to a full view of his excellent butt, the high, hard curve so unbelievably perfect, I had a sudden wish to draw, just to memorialize it. But I could barely manage stick figures, and that was no way to do justice to such a fine ass.

As if sensing me, Luka turned, a smile curling his lips as our gazes met.

I smiled back, leaning against the door as he finished his conversation.

"I hope I'm not interrupting anything," I said as he hung up, shoving my hands into the robe's pockets, nerves creeping back in.

We hadn't been alone together in almost two months and those last few minutes hadn't been...comfortable.

"No." He tossed the phone toward the large wingback chair without looking.

I wasn't surprised that it landed. If I'd tried that, it would have hit the table, or the floor, or the window behind the chair.

My throat went tight as he closed the distance between us, reaching up to curl his hands in the thick cotton lapels crossing over my chest. "You're wearing my robe."

"I...well, I needed to put something on, and my dress is out there."

"Who says you needed to put something on?" he countered. "Maybe I prefer you naked."

My cheeks heated. "I'm not walking around naked."

"What if I insist? I could give a royal decree." He slid a hand down and tugged gently at the tie knotted at my waist.

"We're not in Luxembourg." My voice, breathy all of a sudden, caught in my throat, and I had to clear it to even finish the sentence. "This is Monaco, and you can't *make* decrees on foreign land."

"Not even pretend ones?" Giving me a slumberous look, he tugged the belt again. "Not even if I say pretty please?"

The heat in his eyes threatened to burn me, and my heart raced. The need he'd just slaked flared back to life, and I curled my hands into fists to keep from reaching for him.

Staring at him, I tried to figure out how to respond.

He clearly expected *something*.

"What sort of decrees would you make?" I asked, surprising the hell out of myself.

"Take off the robe and find out," he said, a wicked grin flashing across his face.

"How about I *open* the robe?"

He gave me an arrogant look, then a slow, regal nod. "I'll allow that."

Utterly naked, he backed up several steps then walked over to the bed, settling on the edge. He lounged there, legs spread out, and I had a full frontal view of his semi-erect cock, the curls at the base and the heavy weight of his sac between his thighs. The solid muscles in his chest, arms and thighs drew my eye as well, but my attention kept going back to his penis, and it wasn't my imagination that he seemed to be lengthening with every passing moment.

My mouth watered and cheeks grew warm. Other parts of me went hot and wet too.

"The robe, Stacia."

With clumsy hands, I loosened the belt and let it fall open. The lapels caught on the curves of my breasts, but I didn't spread it open farther, smiling inside as hunger lit Luka's eyes, almost making them burn.

"That's fucking sexy," he murmured. "The soft white of the robe, clinging to your nipples and covering your breasts while letting me see this strip of flesh all the way down to your cunt, those pretty curls covering you. Touch yourself, Stacia. Are you wet?"

I didn't react right away, and his eyes slid to mine in challenge.

"Are you done obeying me already?"

"No," I said, voice shaking. Sliding my hand down, I covered myself.

"Not like that...don't make it to where I can't watch while you slide a finger inside your pussy."

A whimper burned its way up my throat, and I pressed my lips together to silence it, then did as he asked.

"Look at that," he whispered.

I did, even though I didn't think it was one of his... decrees. My heart stuttered at the sight, and I was overwhelmed by how erotic it was, simply watching as I stroked a finger across my clit, then down lower, through the wetness slicking my pussy. Was it because he watched? Or because he *wanted*?

"Come here."

I looked back at Luka and saw him watching me, flags of color riding high on his cheekbones. My muscles quivered as I walked to him. He caught my wrist and brought my hand up, closing his lips around my finger, the one I'd used to touch myself.

"Sweet..."

He curled his tongue around me and sucked, finally letting go with a little *pop*. After releasing my wrist, he leaned back on his hands and studied me, that faint, arrogant smirk still lingering on his lips.

"I want your mouth on my cock."

A rush of heat gathered between my eyes. I couldn't speak. I'd end up babbling or stuttering out anything I tried to say. So, I held his gaze as I went to my knees in front of him, still wearing the robe hanging open from my shoulders.

The muscles in his thighs tensed as I leaned forward, wrapping one hand around his erection to hold him steady.

His breath rasped out as I dipped my head and pressed a hot, open-mouthed kiss to the head.

"Damn..." The word came out in a low, reverent whisper that sounded equal parts praise and plea.

I felt his hand on the back of my head, tugging and pulling lightly for a few seconds before my hair went tumbling down my back, then he shoved both hands into my hair and held me still.

"I'm standing up, Stacia."

He did, and then he began to slowly, thoroughly fuck my mouth, talking to me the entire time. "I've wanted to do this to you from almost the first time I saw you...your mouth was made for this, Stacia...such a pretty...perfect..." He pressed down on a spot near my jaw and angled my head. "Breathe now...take me deeper...*fuck*, like that...pretty, perfect mouth. Just right for fucking. Suck on me now. Swallow me..."

The words could have sounded crude—maybe they should have.

But the litany of them raining down on me as he thrust his cock into my mouth, the head bumping against the back of my throat, it was all so intense, I found myself rocking hungrily, seeking release from the rising, burning ache between my thighs.

"I'm going to come," Luka said gruffly.

Abruptly, he pulled me off, using his grip on my hair.

He looked down at me, the skin over his cheeks pulled taut. "I'm just seconds away from losing it. Do you want to swallow it? Should I come on you, Stacia? Or do you want me to stand you up and bend you over?"

"I..." Lightheaded now, I stared at him. "I don't know. I don't care. What do you want to do?"

He cupped my chin, stroked his thumb over my lip. "Open your mouth, darling."

I shuddered and did as ordered.

He filled me once more, moving rougher this time, gripping my head in a way that didn't allow much movement, but I didn't care. I'd had no idea how erotic, how hot this could be. I reached up and clung to his wrists, my clit pulsing between my thighs and my nipples so tight, they hurt.

He pushed deeper, almost too deep, then his cock jerked inside my mouth, and he started to come. I jolted, but he held me in place, muttering to me in a raw voice, "Just take it... swallow for me...please...just like...*fuck*, you're sweet, Stacia..."

I gasped when he pulled away, slumping forward to rest my head on his knee as he sagged back onto the bed.

Sweat dampened my forehead and the back of my neck.

My heart pounded like I'd just finished running three miles on the treadmill.

And I *burned*...for him.

I went to stand, thinking only about easing that ache.

A knock sounded from somewhere.

Close.

Luka lifted his lids and gave me a lazy smile. "There's the treat I ordered for you."

I could barely think past the burn of lust riding me. "Treat?"

"Hmmm. After we refuel, I'm going to return the favor you just did me." His lids tracked down over my body, lingering on the curls between my thighs. "Maybe you can even talk dirty to me, beg me to eat your pussy."

I blushed so brightly red, it almost hurt.

Luka chuckled and stood. "Let me use my robe. Get in the bed and cover up."

On autopilot, I did as asked and watched as he slid into the robe and walked out of the room. "Coming!"

Struggling to regain control of my breathing, I closed my eyes and pressed my left cheek into the pillow, relishing the soft, cool material against my skin.

A sound had me opening my eyes, and I only barely managed to contain my squawk of surprise when an unfamiliar man pushed a cart into the room, one laden with a champagne bottle chilling in an ice bucket, several flutes, and a covered dish. He didn't even look at me as he swept the metal dome of the top off the dish and bowed to Luka.

"Perfect," Luka said in flawless French, giving the man a short nod. "Thank you."

As the man hustled out, Luka picked up the champagne, all ready uncorked, and poured. Trepidation tripped through me, and I sat up slowly, watching him.

He shot me a look, still grinning, although the smile started to fade when he saw me.

"Not fond of champagne? I thought I saw you enjoying a glass the night we met."

"Oh, well, I like champagne," I hedged, then immediately wished I'd lied and claimed I'd been drinking a champagne cocktail of some sort that first night. Too late now. "I just... well, it's a mood thing. I'm not much in the mood right now."

Luka chuckled. "You will be after you try one sip of this, trust me. It's nectar from the gods."

He brought two glasses around, along with the dish that had been on the cart, and I saw it was full of fat, ripe strawberries.

Strawberries and champagne.

My heart hiccupped even as the nerves twisting my gut drew into ever tighter knots.

"Here." Luka extended his hand, offering one of the glasses, and out of habit, I took it.

Saliva pooled in my mouth, and I wondered if maybe I'd luck out at this *very* moment and get hit with a case of morning—or in my case, evening sickness. Then I could just claim...something. Exhaustion. Food poisoning. Even the stomach flu, if I had to.

But none of the nausea I hoped for made an appearance, and worse, as I stared at the ripe, lush berries, my belly gurgled in demand.

"Take a sip, Stacia," Luka urged.

"I'm not in the mood for champagne."

He eyed me curiously, lifting the glass to his lips before leaning over and kissing me.

The kiss was tart and sweet at the same time, and the taste of champagne on his lips was divine, no doubt. As he pulled back, I licked my lips and tried to blank my face. "I think you like the taste of it just fine." He dipped a strawberry into his glass and lifted it to my lips, but I turned my head.

Frustrated, I put the flute down and rose from the bed, forgetting I was completely naked until I felt his eyes burning over me. There was more than just lust in his gaze, though.

I'll distract him, I told myself, desperation working its way in.

I moved over to him and plucked his flute away, putting it down by mine, but when I went to straddle him, he caught my hips and held me steady in front of him.

"Something's wrong," he said in a level voice.

"No." I shook my head a little too quickly.

"Don't lie." The tone was implacable and hard—the tone of a man not used to being ignored. *Or disobeyed.* "It doesn't suit you, and you're not very good at it."

Knowing my blush would be my undoing, I twisted away from him and stepped away from the bed. I felt completely exposed, and he wore the only robe. There was a soft throw that looked to be chenille draped over the wingchair, and I grabbed it, wrapping it around me like a sarong. "I just don't want the champagne, Luka. Why is that such an issue?"

"If that was the *issue*, fine. But it's not." He rose and closed the robe, loosely tying it at his waist. Crossing his arms over his chest, he skewered me with a look that seemed to go right through me. "There's something else. I can see it in your eyes. Something you don't want to tell me. What is it?"

A headache pounded at the base of my skull, and the wary, watchful look in his eyes only added to its intensity. I'd come here to get *away* from judgmental looks and doubt, and now I was getting it from the *one* man I absolutely couldn't handle it from.

Clenching my jaw, I stared at him for a long moment, then averted my eyes. "I think I'll go back to the palace now."

He caught my arm as I went to pass. "I want a fucking answer!"

"I'm pregnant!" I half-shouted at him as he swung me around.

His face went slack, mouth falling open.

"I can't drink the champagne because I'm pregnant! Okay?" The words spilled out of me, and I jerked out of his grip, his fingers suddenly lax.

Setting my jaw, I glared at him, not certain how he'd respond.

"You..." He straightened and looked down, his hair falling into his eyes and shielding his face. A shudder went through him, then he went incredibly still, deathly still.

A chill went down my spine, and I stopped breathing for a few seconds.

When he looked back at me, his entire expression had changed. He'd never looked at me like that. His eyes were nothing but chips of amber ice, set in a face harder than stone, his mouth flat and unsmiling.

"Get out," he said.

He turned away, and I gaped at him.

"What?"

"I'll take some of the blame here." He glanced back at me, raking me up and down with a disdainful look. "I knew you were dating Emmett, which was why I *asked* if there was any reason you couldn't come back to my hotel with me. If it was serious between you two, I would have *thought* you'd consider him a reason. A *baby* damn well should have been a reason. At least in *my* mind. And I know him well enough to say that Emmett would consider a baby a good fucking reason not to come to my room with me. But I was stupid and wanted you enough to think that maybe things weren't serious between you two, that you'd be honest with me. Clearly, I was wrong. But I'll rectify that mistake."

I felt like I'd been hollowed out, completely scraped empty, with nothing but ragged, bleeding gouges left as evidence to show there'd once been something more inside me. Throat locked down so tight, I shook my head and cleared my throat twice before I could even speak. "Luka, I don't know what it is you're thinking, but—"

"Don't you?" He cut me off and gave me a bored, derisive look. "Stacia, darling, you're good in bed, but *nobody* is that good, and you're far from the first to try and pull this sort of scheme."

My blood went cold at the expression in his eyes. Predatory and hostile.

"I'm trying to decide what your goal is here...money or marriage." His lids drooped, a look that had been so seductive and enticing earlier was now enough to make me sick inside. "I bet it's money. You're connected to a royal family yourself...barely. But you're smart enough to know there are rules when it comes to marriage among royals and marrying *well* is one of those rules."

That was it. I was going to vomit. I knew it. I pressed my lips together and tried to control the impulse, thankful the nausea was brought on by...*this*, instead of the baby inside me. Instinctively, I placed a hand over my belly, staring at Luka as I thought, *I'm glad you can't hear this right now, little one.*

Luka noticed, and his lip curled.

I flinched and curled in on myself as he stalked closer.

It took all of my courage not to look away when he bent down and glared at me, staring me right in the eye.

"Let me make one thing absolutely clear...*darling*. You fooled me once. It won't happen again." He jerked his chin toward the door and bared his teeth in a cold, mocking smile. "Now, get the *fuck* out of here before I have you thrown out. Aeric's a friend, so right now, I'm restraining myself out of respect for him and his family, but my patience is about to snap. Much longer, and you'll end up as gossip fodder because *somebody* will witness security dragging your lying, manipulative ass out of here."

That hurt enough, drove the knife in deep enough, that I reacted, sucking in a breath that sounded more like a sob.

Cutting around him, still clutching the chenille thrown to my breasts, I headed for the other room where my gown, shoes, and clutch purse waited. I gathered them all up, holding them to my chest and hoping desperately that nothing fell—especially the throw. But if it did, it couldn't humiliate me any worse than what Luka had done.

"Get dressed out here," he said in a surly tone. "I don't want to see—"

Ignoring him, I opened the door to the suite. "I'll stop by the front desk and pay for the cost of the throw," I said in a wooden voice, staring straight ahead and not once looking at the man glaring daggers into the back of my head. "You're wrong, though. The baby isn't Emmett's. You're the only man I've ever been with."

Holding my gown, shoes, and what remained of my pride, I hurried out and headed to the elevator.

One of my shoes fell, but I didn't bother to grab it.

Two men had been standing outside Luka's doors. Bodyguards, I assumed.

One of them called to me as I jabbed the elevator's down button, but I didn't look back.

The doors opened instantly, and I darted inside, hitting the button for the lobby before the bodyguard could reach me.

I was getting the hell away from there. I'd go by the restroom on the lobby level and change there. The front desk could either send the throw back up to Luka's room, or I'd pay for it. I had cards in my purse. I was tempted to just sail out while wearing the damn thing, but Luka just might try to claim I'd stolen it.

My eyes burned, tears threatening, but I shoved them down.

I couldn't cry.

Not yet.

TWENTY-EIGHT

LUKA

"I think I'll go back to the palace now."

Like hell, I thought. Catching her arm as she strode by, I whirled her around, glaring at her. "I want a fucking answer!"

"I'm pregnant!"

I felt like she'd struck me, straight in the gut.

"I can't drink the champagne because I'm pregnant! Okay?" She jerked away, twisting easily out of my grip. She squared her shoulders and firmed her jaw, glaring at me.

I couldn't figure out the look in her eyes, but at the moment, I was having a hard time even understanding my own thoughts.

I'm pregnant.

All the pictures I'd seen over the past few weeks, her with Emmett at another New York charity function. Them at a party. A baseball game. Laughing at a gala to raise funds for the Bronx Zoo.

I'm pregnant.

I heard my own voice asking her, "Is there any reason you can't come back to my hotel with me?"

Had it even been two hours since I'd asked?

She'd said *no,* and I'd been ecstatic and not just because I'd soon be buried balls-deep inside her again, but because of what *else* it could mean—it meant she couldn't be serious about Emmett. Not really. She might be dating him, but if they were serious, she wouldn't sleep with me.

That was what I'd thought.

How fucking wrong I'd been.

"You..." Unable to keep looking at her as I gathered my thoughts, I stared at my feet. My heart hammered in my ears, blood rushing, roaring like one of the Formula One engines I loved so much. All I wanted now was blessed quiet—and about a thousand miles between me and this woman I'd become so obsessed with.

Lifting my head, I stared at her. A part of me committed each feature to memory while another started mentally castigating myself for what happened this evening. I couldn't blame *only* her, either. I'd asked her to come to my hotel. I'd stabbed my own best friend in the back.

"Get out," I said, so disgusted with us both, I couldn't think straight. So *hurt,* I wanted to puke.

Behind me, Stacia spoke, and damn her, she actually had the nerve to sound *stunned.* "What?"

"I'll take some of the blame here." I looked back, and again, the beauty of her, of her soft blue eyes, the curve of her jaw, the elegance of her cheekbones, struck me like a fist. "I knew you were dating Emmett, which was why I *asked* if there was any reason you couldn't come back to my hotel with me—if it was serious between you two, I would have *thought* you'd consider him a reason. A *baby* damn well should have been a reason. At least in *my* mind. And I know him well enough to say that Emmett would consider a baby a good fucking reason not to come to my room with me. But I was stupid and wanted you enough to think that maybe things weren't serious between you two, that you'd be honest with me. Clearly, I was wrong. But I'll rectify that mistake."

"Luka, I don't know what it is you're thinking, but—" She shook her head, her face pale, save for the harsh red flags of color on her cheekbones.

I had no idea what she was going to say, but I knew one thing—I wouldn't listen to it.

She'd spent almost *two months* with Emmett, and yet she'd told me there was no reason why she couldn't come back here with me, and now she tells me she's *pregnant?*

And she had the nerve to look *hurt?*

I thought I'd be sick, but I clenched my jaw and stared at her, trying to think past the sense of betrayal. "Don't you? Stacia, darling, you're good in bed, but *nobody* is that good, and you're far from the first to try and pull this sort of scheme. I'm trying to decide what your goal is here...money or marriage."

Her throat worked, and her gaze fell away for a brief moment. Money, then. It had to be. Besides, she was Aeric's cousin. She had to know marriages in royal families were complicated. She was too intelligent not to be aware of it.

She'd fucking *used* me. Was she even *pregnant?*

"I bet it's money. You're connected to a royal family your-self...barely. But you're smart enough to know there are rules when it comes to marriage among royals and marrying *well* is one of those rules."

She backed away a step, and I had a feeling she didn't even know she'd moved.

A vague wave of disgust—directed at myself—washed over me, and I shoved it aside. I was entitled to be angry, wasn't I?

I was, naturally.

But that righteous decision turned to ashes on my tongue as her shoulders curled in protectively, her head slumping just a bit...and she placed her hand on her belly.

Fuck.

Viciously jagged claws of envy tore gouges from my heart as I recognized the action for what it was.

A mother instinctively acting to protect a baby. Even one still forming in her womb. She *was* pregnant. A baby...

Envy and rage twined to form a monster.

Fuck this.

Crossing the floor, I dipped my head and stared into her soft blue eyes, now as blank as a doll's. "Let me make one thing absolutely clear...*darling*. You fooled me once. It won't happen again."

I nodded toward the door and gave her a cold smile. "Now, get the *fuck* out of here before I have you thrown out. Aeric's a friend, so right now, I'm restraining myself out of respect for him and his family, but my patience is about to snap. Much longer and you'll end up as gossip fodder because *somebody* will witness security dragging your lying, manipulative ass out of here."

A noise escaped her, something like a low moan.

The pained, animalistic keening cut me deep, but I steeled myself against it.

She'd used me. Lied to me. Was she playing Emmett and me against each other? Was she trying to trick me into marriage? Was she jealous her cousin had a title but not her? I had no idea what this was or what her game was, but she'd used and manipulated me.

I refused to fall for her lies any longer.

She shoved around me, walking straight toward the main entrance of my suite, the ends of the throw dragging behind her like a cloak.

Abruptly, it hit me that her gown was in the main room. She had to change.

Fine.

I trailed after her, gripping the edge of the door that separated the living quarters from the bedroom. Staring at her narrow back, I watched as she gathered her belongings.

"Get dressed out here," I ordered. "I don't want to see—"

I broke off as she walked to the door of the suite, a slow, awkward shuffle, clutching the blanket *and* all her things.

"I'll stop by the front desk and pay for the cost of the throw," she said, her voice so faint, I could barely hear her.

Look at me. Suddenly, I wanted her to *look* at me.

But she didn't. She stared straight into the hall as she continued to speak. "You're wrong, though. The baby isn't Emmett's. You're the only man I've ever been with."

The door closed behind her, and I squeezed my eyes shut, gripping the wooden frame in my hand until the corners gouged into my palm.

When a fist hit my door, I sprang into action, something

that was both relief and fury rising to fill me. I stormed to the door, already talking before I even opened it. "I *told* you—"

The words died.

It wasn't Stacia standing there.

It was Thierry, one of the men from my security team. He had a sheepish look on his face...and a woman's heel in his hand. "Forgive me, Your Highness." He held out the shoe and offered a small bow.

Without any conscious decision on my part, I took the shoe, looking at the logo inside. *Tom Ford*. As Thierry started to talk, I shifted the shoe in my hand, now looking at the pale satin blue exterior and the crystals scattered along the side, like stars in the night sky. A pretty shoe. One a woman wouldn't carelessly leave behind.

"I tried to stop her so I could return it to her, Your Highness. But she didn't stop. Should I call the front desk?"

"No."

I closed the door in his face and put the shoe down on the table just inside the door.

You're wrong, though. The baby isn't Emmett's. You're the only man I've ever been with.

She was lying—*still* lying. She had to be.

I'd always worried someone would get too close to me and use me, try to get something out of me simply because of my station, and it had finally happened.

Turning away from the elegant, lonely shoe, I strode into my bedroom.

An inane thought hit me as I flung myself down on the bed.

If I'd done as my mother had wanted and brought Violet,

none of this would have happened. But I hadn't, because I didn't want to get involved with a nice, sweet young woman while I was obsessing over Stacia.

"Problem solved," I muttered. "Obsession *over*."

To prove it to myself, I picked up my phone and checked the time. It was almost eleven, but it was Saturday.

I sent her a text.

ARE YOU AWAKE?

VIOLET ANSWERED ALMOST IMMEDIATELY.

I AM.

I SHOT BACK A SIMPLE QUESTION.

CAN I CALL?

WHEN SHE RESPONDED WITH A YES, I hit the phone icon to dial her number.

Obsession over.

TWENTY-NINE

STACIA

I SUDDENLY UNDERSTOOD THE APPEAL OF COUNTRY music.

I hadn't slept more than a few hours, and after waking for the third time just after four, I'd given up trying and just plugged in my earbuds and turned on the music app on my phone.

None of my regular favorites appealed. Even the moody, melodic strains of artists like Adam Hurst didn't do it.

Stumbling on the twangy tunes of Dolly Parton as she sang *I'll Always Love You*, I felt the ache in my chest expand, and all the tears I'd been holding back broke free. It had been a quiet stream at first, as Dolly's sweet, gentle voice trailed away and another song by an artist I didn't recognize came on. *I Fall to Pieces.*

By the time *that* one ended, I pretty much did just that—fell to pieces.

The songs came on one right after the other, and the

stream of tears turned into a river that soon soaked the pillow-case beneath my head.

Crying's *exhausting*, though. The sunrise found me dry-eyed and tired, fighting a headache as I scrolled through search results on my phone trying to find a simple fricking answer to a simple fricking question.

What can you take for a headache when you're pregnant?

Acetaminophen looked to be safe, but then I made the *big* mistake of clicking on one of those stupid ads on the sidebar of a website.

Those damn ads were why I'd avoided looking at websites before going to see the doctor. I should have known better, but what did I do?

I clicked.

STOP! The big, bold red letters practically shouted at me, and by the time I got done reading what I *knew* had to be nothing more than scare tactics, I was so sick with nerves, I ended up puking up the water I'd drank, hoping to ease the headache into tolerable levels.

And *that* just made the nausea worse.

In desperation, I wet a washcloth with cool water and turned off all the lights, hiding in the bed.

After a little while, the headache receded, and I was able to fall into a fitful sleep.

THE KNOCK, soft as it was, jerked me out of that fitful sleep as surely as if somebody had rung a gong over my head.

I bolted upright, immediately regretting the action as I cradled my aching skull.

Swearing, I bent forward and tried to think beyond the pounding.

The knock came again.

I opened my mouth to snarl like a demented, rabid animal and just barely managed to control it. Clearing my throat, I gingerly called out, "Come in."

The bare sliver of light that penetrated the gloom of my bedroom was too much.

"Miss Stacia?"

I recognized Blanche's voice and muffled a groan. "Hey, Blanche."

"May I come in?" she asked.

"As long as you don't turn on the light."

"Of course not."

I heard her soft footfalls over the carpet, and even though I knew it was coming, I winced as she sat down next to me, making the big, soft bed shift oh so slightly under her weight. My belly dipped, and my head protested. Thankfully, nothing threatened to come up, even though a fine film of sweat broke out over the back of my neck.

"Morning sickness?" she asked softly.

I almost lied and said *yes*. But I was too tired and too... hurt. "I don't think you could call it that."

"What would you call it, then?"

But I didn't want to tell her. As kind as Blanche was, as much as I liked and trusted her, I just couldn't spill all of this, this whole, humiliating mess onto her. And it *wasn't* just the mortification I'd suffered as Luka lashed out at me.

271

It was the hurt, too, and it went even deeper than that in ways I still struggled to articulate. Swallowing the knot in my throat, I finally managed to say, "I don't know, Blanche. It's just...complicated, okay?"

She stroked a hand down the back of my hair, which I knew had to be tangled beyond all belief.

I didn't shrug her touch away, though. It was...soothing.

She kept it up for several moments, and I found myself moving in rhythm with her, lids growing heavy once more. It wasn't until I started to sway, and she had to steady me that I realized I'd almost crumpled forward, off the bed and onto the floor.

"There, there..." Blanche murmured, her voice as gentle as if she were speaking to a child.

Light pressure from her hand had me looking at her. I blinked owlishly as I stared into her concerned eyes.

"Miss Stacia—"

"Stop it," I said, cutting her off, irritated, tired and just... fed up. "I'm not some southern belle or rich old woman in a period novel. You're *ten years older* than me, Blanche. This *Miss Stacia* crap reeks of elitism and classism."

Her lips twitched, and her eyes twinkled, but she replied in a level voice, "I work for the Hereditary Prince of Monaco, and you are his first cousin. It wouldn't be proper—"

"I'm his *pregnant, American* first cousin, and I don't have a fucking title." I glared at her. "Indulge me."

"Very well." Amusement danced across her face, but only for a few moments before her expression softened. "Stacia. But only while we are alone, as long as you agree not to tell anyone...*and* if you let me help you now. Something is wrong. Will you talk to me?"

Flushing, I looked away.

She took my hand and squeezed gently.

"I'm not ready to talk about it," I said tightly. With my free hand, I gingerly touched my aching head. "At least not the emotional stuff. Physically, though? I feel like I've been beaten up and down with a tire iron."

"I'm not entirely sure what that is." I looked over at her, and she gave me a commiserating smile as she added, "But it sounds very unpleasant."

"I've never been beaten, with a tire iron or anything else, but you're right. It sounds *extremely* unpleasant." Drained, I dropped my head on her shoulder. I was both surprised and touched when she echoed the gesture, angling her head until it brushed mine. "I'm tired, Blanche. And I feel empty, like I've been scraped out raw, not just physically but emotionally. My head hurts, and my stomach's all twisted into knots, and I'm just..."

Tears rushed to my eyes, and I squeezed my lids shut against them.

"Fuck. I'm *tired*. That sounds whiny and small and bitchy, but I am. My parents are being so ugly about the baby, and I don't know what will happen when I get home, and I'm *tired*."

She wrapped her arm around me, hugging me close.

Turning my face into her shoulder, I let myself cry a little.

BLANCHE LEFT A LITTLE WHILE LATER, promising to bring me some ginger tea. I was reluctant to accept the offer until she showed me some information and promised to call the doctor who routinely provided care to the royal family. She must have seen my panic because she promised the woman would be discreet.

I had a plane to catch in a few hours, and although the last thing I wanted to do was spend hours flying, I most definitely didn't want to stay in Monaco another minute. I didn't even want to be in Europe right now.

Remembered humiliation made my bones ache as I made my way into the bathroom, dimming the lights so they didn't singe my already sensitive eyes.

I wet a rag with cool water, hoping it would ease my headache as it had earlier. On my way to the divan by the window, there was a knock at the door. It swung open before I could call out, but I didn't mind. It saved me the annoyance of my own voice.

"Stacia."

I stiffened instantly, then forced myself to relax. "Hey, Aeric."

"I ran into Blanche. She tells me you're not feeling well."

I sank down on the divan, turning to look at him. I froze at the sight of the cup in his hand. A hot, steaming cup.

"Ginger tea," he said, smiling crookedly. The smile faded as he looked at me. His mouth firmed out, and he approached silently, offering the tea.

Dread filled me as I accepted the cup. I wasn't surprised when he sat next to me. The tea had a spicy scent to it, and I breathed it in, surprised when it didn't immediately turn my stomach. I took a small sip, then lowered it, staring into the pale amber liquid.

Next to me, Aeric sat and waited.

I took another sip and squeezed my eyes shut, wondering if maybe I should go back to bed, beg off and tell him I was just feeling too bad. He'd have somebody on staff handle my travel arrangements, and I'd have some time to get myself together before dealing with this.

Dealing with it, I thought, disgusted.

How did I *deal* with the knowledge that the father of my child thought I was just a mercenary, money-grubbing bitch?

Money or marriage...I bet it's money.

I had to swallow back the noise that tried to escape me, had to fight back hot tears.

Aeric could tell, too. He covered my shoulder with a comforting arm. "You're not just feeling poorly, sweetheart. You've been crying."

"I'm fine," I told him. I even managed to keep my voice steady.

"I didn't ask if you were fine. I said you've been crying."

I didn't respond. Taking another sip of tea seemed wiser.

He sighed and shifted on the divan next to me, stretching out his long legs and leaning back on his hands. "All right, cousin. Don't tell me. I can wait."

I got up, moving too fast, causing the tea to slosh out of the cup. I took another sip, then put it on the table. "I need to be getting ready for my flight home."

"Tell me why you've been crying."

Spinning around, I glared at him. "Damn it, Aeric! You're the Prince of *Monaco*, but I'm an American!"

"Impressive." He cocked a brow and gave me an arrogant, smug grin. "But you know I'm not asking because I'm a prince of anything. I'm asking as your cousin."

"You haven't *asked* anything." With a sullen look, I crossed my arms over my chest and stared him down.

"Very well." He rose and came closer, his face sobering. "Stacia, will you please tell me why you've been crying? I hate it when one of the people most dear to me is hurting."

The concern in his voice landed on all the raw, ruined places inside, and I closed my eyes, covering my face with my hands. I didn't want to do this, didn't want to tell him. I knew how he'd react, and how it could affect things between him and Luka.

"Stacia."

I jumped and lowered my hands, not realizing he'd come so close that we were now only inches apart.

"Do you remember a conversation we had once? It was the summer after you turned nine. You'd come over to spend a month. Remember?" Aeric caught my arms gently in his hands and lowered his head, pressing his brow to mine. Without waiting for me to answer, he continued. "You were visiting for the summer, and we were out with my mother. We ended up at some boring society lunch, and a classmate of mine was there with his father."

I remembered. "Otto." I sighed and hugged him quickly before backing away. "Of course. How could I forget Otto? He was an asshole."

"He still is. He'd heard you talking and knew you were American but hadn't realized who you were...remember what happened?"

I huffed out a sigh and glared at him.

He tapped my nose. "Of course, you do. But I'm going to finish my story. We were at the window, talking and bored out of our minds, and he comes over, all but pushes you out of the way so he can talk to me about the polo team."

"And then I pushed back between you two," I said, taking over. I managed a faint smile because the look on that obnoxious teenager's face still managed to amuse me. I'd been skinny and several years younger, but he'd made me mad —*and* my mother hadn't been there to scold me for not being a *lady*. "Then I told him that if he wasn't intelligent enough to realize when two people were having a conversation, then he wasn't intelligent enough to play polo and maybe he should focus in improving his observation skills." I rolled my eyes. "And he got all angry about it and tried to push me again, and you grabbed him and shoved him back, and he ended up falling over a table, then tripping over his feet and landing on his ass, right as his father was bragging about how close the two of you were."

"He looked like he'd swallowed an egg whole," Aeric said, clearly thinking back to it with fondness. "And while the old idiot was sputtering about boys being boys, Otto gets up and starts yelling at you and how rude Americans were, not knowing who their betters were." He hugged me, then eased back. "You looked like you wanted to poke him with something sharp, but you just looked at him and said that I was your cousin, and it didn't matter to you if I was going to be a duke or not, that I wasn't allowed to be friends with people like that. Then you looked at *me* and said I'd *never* talk about people not knowing who their betters were. Oh, and we would always be friends before we were anything else. My mother was hard-pressed not to laugh. It could have been quite the scandal except most of her acquaintances had seen how Otto pushed you, and two of them had already been moving to intervene, but I just beat them to it."

The look he gave me brought tears to my eyes, and I blinked them back before glaring at him. "What are you getting at?"

"I won't stop being your friend, cousin. Don't stop being mine." He caught a lock of my hair and tugged. "Talk to me."

I closed my hand around his wrist, but he flipped it around just at the last second so that we ended up with our hands loosely linked. The concern on his face proved to be my undoing. Without any idea it was about to happen, I dropped my head forward to rest on his shoulder. "I've fucked things up, Aeric. I mean *bad*."

"It can't be that bad." He gave me a reassuring pat on the back, then urged me to look at him. "Come on, talk to me."

Talk to him. Where did I begin?

I hesitated, trying to find the right words.

Somebody knocked on the door. Aeric sighed and stepped away. "I had the kitchen get breakfast ready for you. You'll eat, and we'll talk."

Warily, I eyed the door as he opened it.

One of the kitchen staff pushed in a cart. That familiar cold sweat broke out over the back of my neck while my face began to heat. Shit.

"Just set it up over there," Aeric said, unaware of my imminent run for the toilet.

I started to shift toward the door to the bedroom—and

the bathroom. The man in his pristine white uniform placed the tray on the table and whisked off the silver dome.

The scent of food filled the air, and my belly revolted.

Spinning on my heel, I rushed for the bathroom, ignoring the startled voices from behind me. I barely made it to the toilet and bent over, emptying my belly.

Ginger tea and water rushed out.

I was vaguely aware of Aeric, and after the second spasm, I heard his footsteps as he came over. Saliva pooled in my mouth, and I groaned, another spasm twisting my stomach. This time, as I bent forward, Aeric held my hair.

My belly calmed after a few more seconds, and I eased away. He helped me to my feet, and I took great care not to look at him as I went over to the sink. I rinsed my mouth out with water, the weight of his eyes on me unbelievably heavy. Brushing my teeth bought me a few more minutes, but that was it.

Finally, I blew out a sigh and turned to meet his gaze.

Aeric was leaning against the door frame, arms crossed with a troubled look in his eyes.

"You're pregnant, aren't you?"

No point in lying about it, so I didn't. "Yes."

"You told me that you and Emmett weren't close...like that." A dull flush settled over his cheeks, and I couldn't help but laugh.

Leaning back against the counter, I jammed my hands into the pockets of my robe. My belly had already calmed down. If I waited a few more minutes, I might even be able to eat. "It's not his baby."

"All right." Aeric pushed off the wall and came closer. "Who is the father?"

"You don't need to worry about that."

He narrowed his eyes.

I stared him down. "I'll be raising the baby on my own, Aeric."

"So, you ended up sleeping with a deadbeat." He heaved out a breath and looked away. "Sorry, that came out wrong. We all end up meeting people we really wish we hadn't let into our life."

Words burned in my throat, things I wanted to say, but couldn't. I swallowed them down and stared at the middle of his chest.

"Is this why my aunt and uncle have been giving you so much trouble?"

I gave a stiff nod. I'd confided in him in several texts, but I also knew my mother had talked to my aunt on several occasions, bitching about me, no doubt.

"They'll start up again when you go back home."

Home. New York. Even the thought of going back there made me want to dive back into bed.

"You can stay here—"

"No." I cut him off and eased past him, heading into the bedroom. I had a set of clothes left in the closet, and I checked to make sure everything else, save for my underwear and bag, was packed. "Besides, I've already decided I'm not going to stay in New York. I want something different for my child. I grew up surrounded by my parents' expectations, and it made me miserable. My baby is going to have better than that."

"If you're not going home, then why not stay here?" Aeric laid a hand on my shoulder.

I shrugged it off, giving him a dark look. Aeric had all but invited me to stay in the henhouse as the fox partied.

That look gave away too much, though.

"Who is the father?" he asked softly.

"Don't worry about it."

But when I went to shut the door, he stopped me, wedging his frame in and simply muscling his way inside. The look on his face was intense, practically skewering me.

"You're hiding something."

"I'm not *hiding*," I said, but the words came out too quick and rushed, and I couldn't even look him in the eye. "I'm trying to get moving so I don't miss my flight, Aeric. There's a difference."

"If you weren't hiding, you wouldn't keep avoiding my eyes."

With an exasperated sigh, I looked at him. "Happy?"

He took a step forward and leaned in, peering into my eyes. "You don't want me to know who the father is, do you, Stacia?"

"Don't be so dramatic." I huffed out a breath and pushed my hair back.

"Can't you give me a *yes* or *no*?"

"Yes, I can."

"All right, then tell me...do you want to tell me who the father is? Yes or no?"

He was being insanely obstinate.

And we both knew why. The more I resisted, the more obvious it was that it was exactly what I was doing.

Sighing, I turned away from Aeric and moved to the bed, sitting on the edge. I hugged my clothes to my chest and looked at him. "You're not going to like it."

"The way you're sidestepping already told me as much." He slid his hands into his pockets and leaned back against the door. "It's one of the men on my security team, isn't it?"

I opened my mouth, then closed it with an audible click. A giggle escaped, and I passed a hand over my face. "No. If only it was that simple."

"I'm so glad I amused you," he said sardonically. "Now, who is the father?"

I swallowed hard and told him.

His brows dropped low, face going dark.

"Have you told him?" Aeric asked neutrally.

To my horror, tears filled my eyes.

Horror filled his as he realized I was about to start crying.

Before the tears even fell, I was caught up in his arms.

THIRTY

LUKA

It was nearly noon when I dragged myself out of bed. My head pounded, and there was a thick, nasty coating on my tongue. I could blame the bottle still sitting on the nightstand for my problems, but I was the one who'd opened the damned thing, hoping to drown out the memory of her face, the catch in her voice right before she left the room.

You're wrong, though. The baby isn't Emmett's. You're the only man I've ever been with.

I hadn't had much success. I hadn't exactly slept so much as passed out, and I still felt as exhausted as I'd been when I collapsed face down on the bed.

The sheets still smelled like her. Like us. Like sex and the erotic, intoxicating scent of her body. That scent was the reason I climbed out of bed, the reason I stumbled into the bathroom and into the shower, turning the heat up, hoping to steam away the headache and the misery, the scent of her that had settled into my pores.

It helped marginally.

A sports drink in the hotel refrigerator helped a little more while a cup of coffee and some painkillers offered a little more respite, but I still felt like shit.

The pounding on the door immediately made the brutal throb inside my head increase, and I got up only because I knew I had to make whoever in the hell was knocking *stop* it.

I had to know the person on the other side of the door. Otherwise, the hotel desk wouldn't have given the visitor my information, and that cut the list down to only a handful of options.

I could easily nudge most of them right back to the elevator, leaving me free to drop back down on the bed and wait for the painkillers to kick in.

Already focused on the idea of stretching back out on the bed with the lights off, I opened the door.

"Aeric." I frowned at him, vaguely surprised—and uneasy —at the sight of him, although he had been one of the few on the list who could have gotten my information. If the Hereditary Prince of Monaco couldn't find the hotel room of a guest in the hotel so close to his own palace, who could?

He didn't say anything, just shoved past me while my security team looked at me with varying degrees of confusion and apology. I waved them back and shut the door.

No sooner had I turned to face the other man than I found myself slammed up against that door, his hands fisted in the open lapels of my shirt.

"What the fu—"

He shoved his forearm against my neck.

I was hungover, and truth be told, still a bit drunk and not at my best, so he took me by surprise. I couldn't precisely gape at him. He was using enough pressure to make it damn uncomfortable, and behind me, I could hear my men banging on the door, their concern apparent.

Aeric let up on the pressure at my throat. "Tell them to shut the fuck up."

Pride had me wanting to tell him to fuck off, but at the same time, if I didn't, my men would find a way into the room, and that wouldn't be good for any of us.

"Would you calm down?" I bellowed through the door. "I'm fine."

The pounding ceased immediately.

I grasped Aeric's arm and shoved, but he didn't move. The man was a veritable giant, towering over me by a good five inches, and I had no leverage. "Back the fuck off, Aeric, or I'm going to forget we're friends."

"I've already forgotten." He pressed hard again for a count of ten then shoved away from me and paced farther into the room before spinning back to glare at me. "What the fuck is wrong with you?"

"Me?" Pushing away from the door, I glared at him. His shout had my head ringing, but I wasn't about to tell him to keep his voice down. "You're the fuck who barged into my hotel room and proceeded to get into my face. What the fuck is wrong with *you*?"

He prowled closer and pointed at me. "You're going to stay the hell away from Stacia. You understand me?"

Fuck. Well, hell. *Now,* I understood. I was surprised she'd gone weeping to him, to be honest. Didn't she think I'd push to see what she'd told him?

"What did she tell you?" Lies, no doubt, but I didn't say that to him.

"What did she tell me?" He snorted, a look of sardonic, bitter amusement twisting his features. "She *told* me that she's pregnant, that you two fucked when she was here last, and when she told you she was pregnant, you assumed the baby belonged to Emmett Finch, then you kicked her out of your hotel room, but only *after* accusing her of trying to trick you into marriage or conning you for money." He paused, cocking his head. "Did she miss something?"

I opened my mouth, then shut it. Apparently, she'd told him just about everything.

"Nothing to say now, Luka?" The humorless smile on his face took on a mean slant, and he shook his head. "Oddly enough, I'm not surprised."

I still couldn't find the words and stood there mutely as he cut around me.

"You think she needs money. But crazier still is that you think she's the kind who'd *lie* and *use* somebody like that. It's weird. I never would have taken you for being stupid." He glanced back at me, expression cold, mouth tight. "I meant what I said. Stay away from her."

THIRTY-ONE

STACIA

"Enjoying this heat?"

The soft voice, thick with a southern accent, roused me, and I looked up to see Ellen Finch, Emmett's mom, pause on the steps of the shaded gazebo where I'd been sitting, taking in the view. Well, I *had* been taking in the view. Then I'd fallen asleep.

"I'm sorry, honey." She winced. "I woke you, didn't I?"

"It's fine." I waved for her to join me. "I don't need to be sleeping anyway."

"Honey, you're pregnant." She put a tray down on the table between us. "If you're sleeping, it's because your body is telling you that you need sleep."

I grimaced. "But then I won't sleep tonight. I can't get my body on any kind of regular schedule these days."

"Hormones and pregnancy can do that." She looked like she wanted to say something else but gestured to the tray instead. "I thought you might be hungry and thirsty."

"I wasn't, but I am now."

She smiled at me, and before I could, poured us both some of the water from the pitcher. It was one of those designed to be an infuser, and I could see strawberries, kiwis, and other assorted fruit floating around inside. There was also a plate filled with more fruit, plus cheese and veggies.

"This looks delicious. You ought to be catering parties or something."

She beamed. "You're so sweet. I do love throwing a party. Never used to have the time or the money for it, but then... well. Emmett and all his races. He's telling me he's going to turn my backyard into some sort of mini waterpark oasis. I told him I didn't need all of that. I'd be happy with a nice little pool and a jacuzzi I can use in the winter. But that boy doesn't listen."

"He loves you," I told her.

Her face softened. "I know."

"He's told me a lot about how much you all sacrificed for him so he could chase his dreams." Picking up a piece of cheddar, I took a bite, looking out over the water. "He wants to pay you back."

"Silly boy." She sighed, but the pride in her voice was obvious. "It's not really a sacrifice, or it doesn't feel like it at the time when it's your child. You want the best for them, you know? I'm sure your parents did the same for you. Oh, there's that son of mine now."

Her distraction made it easier for me to compose my face at the mention of my parents.

No, they hadn't been big on sacrifice.

Since I'd left New York City, neither of them had tried to reach me. Well, if they had, they hadn't tried hard. I'd turned my phone off after texting Emmett to let him know the plane had landed in Lexington, and I hadn't turned it on since.

But they had my email.

Neither of them had reached out.

Plenty of other people had—people who were acting under the guise of friendship, although we rarely spoke unless it was at a gathering orchestrated by my parents, or friends of theirs.

And that was why I was hearing from the people contacting me.

They were either younger acquaintances or the sons and daughters of people my mom or dad knew.

Subtle but friendly probes...

HEY, I haven't seen you around lately. Want to get together for lunch?

I WAS THINKING about hitting a play this weekend. Why don't you give me a call?

People who never spoke to me now suddenly reached out, and it was all orchestrated by my parents—specifically, my mother. I knew it as surely as I knew my own name.

The sound of a booted foot hitting wood had me looking up.

"What are my two best girls doing hiding out here?"

I rolled my eyes as Emmett came over and sat by me. He snatched a square of cheddar from the tray.

"You came out here because you smelled food," I told him.

"Well, there's that, but I could have eaten the plate Mom left inside on the counter." He slung a friendly arm around my shoulders and kissed my forehead. "I preferred to come out and enjoy your company."

"You preferred to come out and steal our food. I think you think it tastes better that way." I poked him in his hard, lean abdomen.

He yelped, curling in protectively. As he gave me a baleful look, Ellen chuckled. "She's already got your number, Emmett, doesn't she?"

"Mean woman." He sighed and took an apple slice. "Mom talk to you about the plans I've got for her backyard?"

"For heaven's sake." Ellen rolled her eyes and stood up. "I don't want to listen to this crazy talk again, young man."

She was still shaking her head as she walked off.

Emmett frowned, watching her go.

"I don't think she wants some mini waterpark, sweetie," I told him, leaning over to bump his shoulder with mine. "Why don't you watch one of those backyard renovation shows, see if you can't find something more her speed? She's more interested in a nice pool, a jacuzzi."

"I just want them to have something nice." He scowled, sulking a little.

"I understand. But it seems kind of impractical." Hitching up a shoulder in a shrug, I looked around. "Just... scale down a little. You could do something with the area under the second level deck. Maybe an outdoor kitchen. Your dad loves to grill, right? A seating area with a firepit that led up to a jacuzzi, then the pool...something like that. It would be nice, yes, but more their speed."

He considered it and started to nod slowly. "Maybe."

"I think you wanted the water park option for you."

"That's playing dirty."

"The truth hurts," I said with a laugh.

We lapsed into silence, munching on the food from the plate in front of us, enjoying the light breeze that kicked up over the small lake.

I lost track of how long we sat there, the peace lulling me into complacency.

"How are you doing, Stacia?" Emmett asked softly.

"I'm fine." Keeping my gaze on the lake, I added, "You probably noticed I'm sleeping all the time, but the OB/GYN your mom recommended tells me that's not unusual. At least I'm not losing my cookies every night now. Especially considering I'm talking literal cookies...your mom makes some of the best white chocolate macadamia nut ones I've ever had."

"You know that's not what I'm talking about." He stroked a hand down my back and gave my braid a tug.

Slumping back against the seat, I closed my eyes. Tears wanted to come, and I decided to blame it on the hormones. It wasn't just the *hurt* that made me weepy all the time, either. I was *angry*. But I hadn't ever been one to angry-cry. Or even one to weepy-cry. I *rarely* cried.

Before this, I'd rarely cried. But in the past month? I'd turned into a leaky faucet, and I couldn't seem to find the right valve to shut off the waterworks.

"You can talk to me, you know."

I gave him a sideways look. "I have talked to you."

Emmett knew about the baby, about Luka. I hadn't told him everything. I didn't want to cause problems with their friendship or make Emmett feel like he had to pick sides.

I'd just told him that Luka hadn't handled it well and had assumed the baby was Emmett's, then had been angry when he thought I was trying to play him by making him think the baby was actually his.

"But it is Luka's baby, right?" He'd been baffled as he asked it, confused by how Luka had acted. Then pissed.

Before I'd even relented and told him, I'd made him promise he wouldn't do anything, that he couldn't tell anybody or go yell at anybody or hit anybody, so even as angry as he was, he'd been trapped.

He'd sulked and tried to talk me into just letting him *give Luka a talking to.*

I told him if he said *anything* to Luka, I'd punch him.

I'd never hit anybody in my life, and I didn't even know if I could follow through. But at the time, I'd meant it.

He'd looked at me like he didn't know whether to laugh or shake his head.

In the end, he'd just asked, "Why?"

"I'm not begging somebody to believe me, Emmett," I'd told him. "Not even by proxy."

"You used to laugh and smile more than this," he told me softly, pulling me back to the present. "I'm worried, Stacia. That's all."

"Actually, I only laughed and smiled because you were around." Shrugging, I shifted position on the padded bench to avoid the sun's changing angle and met his gaze. "My parents weren't the kind to foster a happy home life, Emmett.

Trust me...I've been through worse than this, and I had to do it alone."

"You didn't go through it *pregnant* and alone."

"True." Feeling drained already, I shrugged. I couldn't let him see that though. He was so sweet, and he already worried too much. I gave him a wide smile and said, "Besides, Emmett. I'm not alone. I've got you, don't I?"

"Yeah." He grabbed my legs and pulled them over his lap so he could slide closer, giving me a friendly hug. After dropping a kiss on my forehead, he added, "I'm here for you, as much as you need me to be, Stacia. I want you to know that."

Hearing the *but* hanging off his words, I met his eyes.

The rich, deep blue was full of compassion, but at the same time, stark in all its honesty. "You and me both know, it's not the same thing, is it?"

THIRTY-TWO

LUKA

Her picture flashed across the screen again.

For the past twenty minutes, I'd done little more than channel surf, jumping from one American news channel to the next, trying to find information on the story that had caught my eye earlier.

American Heiress, Stacia Harden, Missing

Harden.

I hadn't known a fucking thing about her, not really. Yes, I'd seen her last name in the *New York Times*, but I hadn't ever thought to look up anything more about her.

That had changed exactly twenty minutes ago.

American Heiress, Stacia Harden, Missing

A fucking heiress.

No wonder Aeric had called me an idiot.

I *was* an idiot.

The Harden family of New York wouldn't surpass the

Hahns as far as fortunes went, but there weren't many in the world who could compete with a family as old and as monied as mine.

However, Stacia wasn't a pauper either.

She could have laughed in my face when I'd suggested she'd been out to get money from me.

Instead, she'd just looked...wounded.

Pushing the memory from my mind, I leaned forward and focused on the pretty black woman on the screen. That hurt too. She had a hand resting on the ripe swell of her belly as she gestured to a media screen featuring a picture of Stacia, one that had clearly been taken at some sort of charity ball. The woman's pregnant belly made me think of Stacia's words.

I'm pregnant.

You're the only man I've ever been with.

The memories were like acid, and every day, the misery got worse instead of better.

Now, listening to the reporter on air talk, I thought I might be sick.

"Sources close to the family report having corresponded with her via email, but nobody has talked to her or received so much as a text or phone call in two weeks, Matthew. Many of them are very worried, and nobody is sure where she's gone or if she's even safe."

Matthew, a blue-eyed brunet with a too-white smile that looked out of place as he nodded at the other woman, responded, *"Erica, their concerns are quite understandable. We've contacted the NYPD, of course, and they tell us there's no cause for concern, but clearly, there is, wouldn't you think?"*

"According to one source I spoke with, Ms. Harden simply doesn't want to talk to anybody." Erica's hand shifted slightly, and I found myself staring at her belly yet again, entranced.

Was Stacia starting to show?

Was she safe?

What if something had happened? Nobody would even know—

"Are you going to stop staring at the fucking TV and do something?"

The sound of Geraint's voice jerked me out of a hypnotic daze so complete, I hadn't even realized he was in the room. Swinging my head around to look at him, I spotted him in the chair sitting at an angle to mine, just over a meter away. He held a glass of wine in one hand, and it was down to the last few sips. There was a bottle on the table between us, and a glass, untouched, sat next to it.

Trying to ignore his comment, I asked, "Is that for me?"

"Yes. As I said to you nearly thirty minutes ago, how about we watch something bloody and stupid and relax?" He sipped his wine, eyes narrowed on my face. "You grunted at me and just kept staring at the television. Clearly, you didn't even hear me."

"My mind is elsewhere." I grabbed the wine and tossed it back.

"I noticed." He swirled the rest of the wine in his glass before draining it and reaching for the bottle. After pouring more, he leaned back and studied me. "Let me guess...it's somewhere in America, am I right?"

I glared at him, not realizing until it was too late that I'd given away more than I'd prefer.

Geraint saw my reaction and scoffed. "No point in hiding it, Luka. I've been sitting here all this time watching you bite your nails to keep from trying to call her." He looked pointedly at the phone I'd left on the arm of the chair.

I'd lost track of how many times I'd reached for it.

Geraint arched his brows. "I had a bet with myself. I lost, but you could still call her."

"I don't know what you're talking about." I finished the wine, but instead of pouring more, I rose and went to the sidebar, searching out a bottle of brandy.

I splashed into the wine glass, much to Geraint's horror.

He shuddered as I turned to him and tossed back a healthy swallow. "That's barbaric."

It was. I didn't care. I needed something stronger than red wine.

"You are out of your mind over her," he mused. "I thought I saw something between you two at Aeric's birthday party, but I wasn't certain. Now? Oh, I'm quite certain."

The expression in his eyes had me fighting the urge to look away. I didn't allow myself to do so, but it didn't help.

Geraint rose, putting his wine down. I tensed as he crossed the room to me, stopping just an arm's length away.

"You need to stop fooling yourself and go after her, Luka."

"We *can't*—"

"Oh, fuck the *can'ts*." He shook his head. "We're not living a hundred years ago. Things *are* different. People are different. And our parents love us enough to want us to be happy. *Go after her*."

I stared at him for a long moment, not even daring to breathe.

"Go." This time, he shook me a little.

Tossing back the brandy, I went.

THIRTY-THREE
STACIA

A COLD FRONT HAD MOVED IN OVERNIGHT, AND THE SKY overhead was leaden, low-hanging clouds heavy with the promise of more rain. It was an ugly, windy day and it reflected my mood perfectly. I'd woken up with a headache, likely due to the rapid change in weather, and dreams had haunted me throughout the night, making sound sleep impossible.

My mood was too sour for me to handle being around Emmett or his family, so I was grateful when they announced they were going into Lexington.

An hour after I climbed out of bed, I walked with them to the front door where Emmett caught my hand and squeezed. "You sure you don't want to come? You've spent the past few weeks trapped up in here."

"I *like* being trapped up in here," I said, forcing a light tone I didn't feel. "I've spent most of my life trapped in New York. The peace and quiet here is surreal. I love it."

"Okay." He tugged my braid and smiled. "I gave that

realtor a call. She's supposed to get back with me later about times. Unless you want to turn your phone on so I can text her your number?"

I grimaced. "No."

"You can't hide from them forever."

Behind him, his mother called. He looked back and waved. "In a minute, Mom!" When he swung back to me, there was understanding and compassion in his gaze, and it made me want to weep. "No matter how long you keep that phone off, they'll still be waiting around, and you'll have to figure out how to handle this."

"They aren't *waiting* around." Temper snapped in my voice, and I tried to bank it because it wasn't his fault my parents were judgmental pricks. "They made it clear that it was *unacceptable* for me to be *pregnant and single*. I told them it wasn't their call and left. I'm not playing their game." Covering the hard, firm plane of my belly, I added fiercely, "*This* isn't a game."

"No." He nodded at my stomach. "That's their grand-child. They're still looking for you. You know that. They're worried, Stacia."

"No, they aren't."

He looked like he wanted to argue, but he just sighed and shook his head. "All right. If Melinda calls about the house, how about we go see it at seven tonight?"

"Sounds great." I forced a toothy smile, relieved he'd decided to let it go, then hugged him. From the doorway, I watched them all pile into the big SUV and pull out of the circular driveway before locking the door.

They'd be gone for hours, and I had no idea what I wanted to do with my time.

NOTHING SOOTHED the ragged edges of my mood. I tried binging on my favorite Netflix show, but the gory zombie action seemed pointless. My second favorite, a sitcom, came off as flat, and the guy's endless pining for a girlfriend and a connection filled me with melancholy.

After striking out on even *Black Panther*, I gave up and turned the TV off, heading into the library Emmett had built for his parents with the money from a win a year earlier.

Searching the books on his mother's side, I waffled between romance and urban fantasy, unable to find anything that really caught my eye. I finally settled on a well-loved favorite, a romantic suspense author I'd read so many times I could quote some passages by memory. Even having read her so many times, the book still enthralled me, and I managed to lose myself for almost an hour.

A blast of thunder shook the house just as the killer was looking for the heroine, though, and the unexpected sound scared the crap out of me, and I shrieked, dropping the book in alarm.

The lights flickered, and I rose to go look out the window.

Rain started to lash the glass, and I found myself smiling.

At least the weather understood me today.

I put the book on the table next to where I'd been sitting and headed to the kitchen, slipping out the double french doors to the covered back porch. The fresh, clean scent of the air filled my head, and I crossed over to stand by the railing. The wind had the rain blowing at an angle away from me, but still, a few raindrops hit.

I didn't care.

Lightning split the sky, and the scent of ozone filled the air.

An afterimage of the jagged streak left an imprint on my eyelids even after the bolt had disappeared. Had it hit something, I wondered? Destroyed it?

Implacably, I thought of Luka.

He was lightning. He'd struck me, right in the heart and destroyed me.

I shoved the thought aside immediately, pissed off by the idea. No, he hadn't destroyed me, and I wouldn't *let* him. He might have left me feeling scorched and burned, but that stuff could heal. Covering my belly protectively, I said, "It's going to be all right, tidbit. You and I can do this."

I didn't need anybody else.

There was another blast of lightning, and the wind kicked up, shifting and sending a wall of rain at me.

It was cold and bracing, and I jumped back, gasping.

From the corner of my eye, I saw a shadow and whirled, panic lurching into my throat as I caught sight of the tall, looming form at the far edge of the deck.

Amber eyes connected with mine, and the strength drained out of me until I had to slap a hand against the column near me just to stay upright. I locked my knees for good measure.

He took a step toward me, and I shook my head, blinking

the water out of my eyes. I had to be imagining things. Had to.

But Luka kept coming.

When he was five feet away, the weird paralysis snapped, and I backed up.

He froze.

Throat tight and scratchy, I said, "What are you doing here?"

"Looking for you." His eyes roamed all over me, searching my face then moving lower.

It wasn't a sexual look, but it was intimate, and I crossed my arms protectively over my chest.

"Why?" I asked sourly. "Are you here to slap legal papers at me, threatening to sue me if I say a fucking thing about you or your family? If I come near you in public? Relax. That will *not* be an issue. I don't even plan on stepping foot in Europe any time in the foreseeable future. I'll just Skype with Aeric and the rest of my family, or they can visit me here."

His mouth spasmed as he looked away.

If I didn't know better, I'd think he was embarrassed.

I didn't care.

I wanted him *out* of there.

"Come on, give me whatever it is you want me to sign." I snapped my fingers impatiently. "Although, why *you* brought them, I don't know. Surely you have an assistant who would have been happy to spare you the indignity of dealing with a barracuda like me."

"Stop it," Luka said, looking back at me, hollow-eyed.

"Stop what?" I gave him an innocent look. "I'm just

trying to expedite things. I'm *tired*, I have a headache, and I want to go lay down."

Instantly, his expression changed, eyes widening in alarm. "Are you well?" His eyes dropped to my belly, and his mouth parted slightly.

My cheeks flushed as he stared at me. Turning away, I marched back over to the waist-high railing and stared back over the lake. *Get home, Emmett.* I didn't know how to deal with this.

Why in the *hell* hadn't I gone with them to Lexington?

"Is everything all right with you and..." He hesitated, not continuing for so long, I couldn't tell if he was going to say anything else or not.

"I didn't get rid of it, if that's what you're asking," I said sharply. "But you don't need to concern yourself. This baby is *no* concern of yours. She's *mine*. Nobody else's."

"She." His voice was soft and full of something I couldn't pinpoint. I didn't want to look at him, but I couldn't *not* do it either. He was watching me again, staring at my face with avid interest, as if he'd been aching to see me again.

A knot lodged in my throat, and I swallowed around it, looking away once more. I couldn't stand there and see that expression, that look he'd once given me, like I *mattered*.

"It's a girl, then?"

His question splintered my thoughts and my attempt to ground myself. Flinching, I hunched in on myself and stared at the surface of the lake so hard, it should have started to boil. "I don't know. It's too early."

"Oh. I guess it was just a slip of the tongue."

"What the *fuck* do you care?" I snapped in *another*

apparent slip of the tongue. I rarely cursed, but nerves and need and misery churned in me, spiking my anxiety and my need and my hurt. I shot him a dark look. "It's not like the baby is *any* of your concern, right? I was either trying to trick you into marriage or a payout, and clearly, I won't get either. Shouldn't you be taking care of whatever paperwork you need me to sign so I don't try to entrap you again?"

"Stop!"

Thunder cracked just as he spoke, making his voice nearly indistinguishable, but I heard him all the same.

He came for me, and once more, I backed up, the remembered shame and pain twisting in my belly like an unseen knife. Luka's face contorted, like *he* was the one hurting, and fury ripped through me. *He* had the nerve to look hurt? *He* had the nerve to look like he was suffering?

"What do you want?" I shouted, wrapping my arms around my middle and glaring at him while the rain pelted us.

He was soaked to the skin, the white shirt he wore plastered to his muscles, his hair slicked tight to his skull. It left his strong, proud face unframed, making his eyes look more intense, even a little wild.

He didn't speak, and I wanted to swing out and hit him, hard. Hard enough to hurt, so that he had some idea of how *I* hurt.

"Answer me," I said, forcing the words out from between clenched teeth. "What in the hell do you *want*?"

"You."

The word, spoken so simply, left me speechless. But not for long.

I snickered. It turned into a giggle, then an outright guffaw. Hand pressed to my mouth, I wheeled away and blinked back the hysterical tears burning my eyes.

"You don't want *me*, Luka," I said bitterly even as the jagged, unhinged laughter continued to choke its way past my lips. "You might want to *fuck* me, but that's not the same as *wanting* me. Trust me. I know."

"You're wrong." His voice was a rasp, and too close. He spoke directly in my ear, and I jolted in shock, tried not to melt in surrender when he pressed his face into my hair with a groan. "Fuck, Stacia..."

I felt the weight of his cock against my butt, an answering heat flickering to life inside me, and some part of me whispered, *Do it. You want him. He wants you. What else matters?*

My *pride* seemed stupid and paltry in comparison, paling next to the need and love warring inside me, but *pride* was all that had held me together when I left Monaco, as I faced my parents, as I came to Kentucky and asked Emmett if he'd meant it when he invited me to come visit.

He nuzzled me and lazy, sweet need, like honeyed fire, rolled through my veins. I had to tense every muscle to keep from leaning against him, and when he brought both hands to my hips, the only thing that kept me from moaning was the simple act of biting my lower lip hard.

I waited for him to do something else.

But all he did was knead my hips restlessly and nuzzle me through the fall of my hair. The warmth of his breath teased my neck, making goose bumps form while my blood turned into molten lava. The wind slammed into me at the same time, along with a fresh deluge of rain.

Luka reacted deftly, lifting me and spinning around, putting me down even as I wiped the water out of my face. I pulled free. His hands lingered just a fraction of a second before he let go, and I heard a soft sigh escape him as I hurried to put room between us.

"Why are you here?" I asked him again. I was cold now, and I desperately wanted to be warm, but I felt trapped here on this big, open porch with him. "Emmett isn't here—"

"I'm not here for Emmett." He took two big steps, closing the distance between us once again. "I've told you."

I froze as he reached out and cupped my face.

"I'm here for you," he said softly.

The ache that had lived inside me ever since I all but ran from his room expanded, threatening to split me in two. "You've already humiliated me, threatened me. What in the hell was so important that you had to come across the damn ocean for?"

"I..." His lids drooped briefly, then he met my eyes once more. "To apologize."

I jerked back. "No."

I moved away so fast, I nearly tripped, would have if he hadn't steadied me, but I'd have rather gone down on my ass, hard, than have him touch me. I wrenched away and kept backing up.

"Go away," I said, shaking my head. "I don't want to hear this. Understand? I don't want to *hear* it!"

"Stacia—"

"Shut *up!*" The word ripped out of me in a broken plea. "You don't get to do this. You don't get to humiliate me, throw me out of your bed minutes after you got done fucking me, accuse me of *lying* to you, of *using you* for money, trying to trick you into marrying me, then show up weeks later and think you can say *I'm sorry* and all's good and well."

Luka stared at me from under his lashes for a long, tense moment.

"I didn't come to *say* I'm sorry, Stacia," he finally said.

I stiffened, and once more, that familiar humiliation washed over me.

But I had no real chance to process it, or anything else because Luka went to his knees in front of me.

"I'm here to *beg* your forgiveness."

One of the cracks in my heart widened, and something seeped out. Pressing my lips together, I shifted my attention back to the lake and crossed my arms over my chest.

"I was wrong," Luka said, apparently determined to continue this farce whether I looked at him or not. "I was so wrong. I reacted out of fear and instinct...and want. Want, misery, and frustration."

My stunned gaze whipped around to meet his. He remained where he'd been, kneeling in front of me, head bowed, voice rough. But, as if sensing my gaze, he lifted his head, and the seductive amber of his eyes met mine. "I *wanted* to believe you. Some part of me even did, but I crushed it, smothered it, and buried it. It was too risky, me falling in love with you. I...well...I've been groomed from childhood knowing I'd be looking for a bride with specific ties, connections to the aristocracy." A dull red washed over his cheeks, and he looked away. "Freedom to marry whomever I wished was never encourage. I was expected to find a wife, one somehow connected to one of the royal families, or who at least had ties to the aristocracy. It's just how things are done."

"Yes, I heard you when you told me about the rules about *marrying well*," I said, the knot in my throat so big I could barely speak around it. "But I don't recall *asking* if we could get married. I certainly never told you I wanted that, so I don't know where you're going with this."

"*I* wanted it." His gaze roamed over my face as I struggled not to react to what he'd just said. "Everything in my life was drifting by just fine. Then came you. Everything I never realized I wanted."

"Stop." Holding up a hand, I backed away. *I wanted it.* I wanted to clap my hands over my ears and block those words out. But it was too late.

He started to rise, and I spun away.

I reached the door, but not in time.

"Listen, Stacia...please." He caught up with me before I could twist the knob and duck inside, his body crowding into mine, one hand gripping my hip while the other held the door closed. "Please...just hear me out."

I don't want to.

I kept the words clenched behind my teeth through sheer will. Pressing my forehead to the glass in front of me, I focused on the cool, smooth surface and how it felt against my skin.

Taking my silence as acquiescence, Luka started talking once more. "Even from the first night, things were different. I didn't want to think about how different, but I felt it even then." His thumb swept across my hip and the top I wore, not quite long enough to reach the waistband of my skirt, slid up so that the calloused surface brushed against skin.

I squeezed my eyes shut.

No, no, no...

"Every time I thought I wouldn't see you again, you turned back up, making it that much harder to put you out of my head, but I kept telling myself it really *would* be the last time. You'd return to New York, and I'd stay in Luxembourg City, and that would be that. That's how everything was supposed to turn out."

His voice had dropped down, rough and low, making things inside me feel weak and needy, but I clenched my knees and jaw, refusing to give in.

"That *is* how it turned out." Opening my eyes, I stared through the glass into the brightly lit, cheery kitchen where I'd shared breakfast with Emmett and his parents. "Go back to Luxembourg, Luka. Leave me alone. I won't be going back there, and I promise never to bother *you* again."

"You *bother* me every minute of every day. You have from the first time we spoke." He gathered my hair into his fist and pulled it aside, bearing my neck. "I close my eyes, and I see your smile. I sleep, and you're there with me. I wake up, and you're gone...because of me."

He kissed me then, and my knees quivered. Stupid knees. Even locking them wasn't helping, and I didn't know if I could keep from wilting against him.

In desperation, I summoned up a memory of that last night. He'd said so many hurtful things, there was a plethora of painful options. But there had been one comment he'd made over and over that had eaten me like acid.

Stacia, darling, you're good in bed, but nobody is that good, and you're far from the first to try and pull this sort of scheme.

A scheme.

The first lover I'd ever had, and he thought everything that happened between us had been a scheme.

The heat flickering to life in my belly died an abrupt, cold death.

The flush suffusing my body disappeared as if it hadn't existed. In the wake of the frenzied, heated lust, I felt chilled.

Luka sensed the change and lifted his head. When I pulled away, he didn't resist. I half-stumbled until we had a few feet between us, then I wrapped my arms around myself, shaking.

"I don't see what the problem is, Luka. After all, I might be good in bed, but nobody is *that* good."

He flinched, his mouth spasming.

Why did that make *me* feel guilty?

"I'm sorry," he said roughly. "I'm sorrier than you'll ever know. For every word I said that hurt you, for treating you like that. Stacia...I'm sorry."

"Fine." Huddling in on myself, I looked away. "You're sorry. I forgive you. Is that what you need to hear? I'll say it again. I forgive you. You can leave now."

One of the wooden boards creaked under his weight as he took a step toward me.

"So, it's over then?" he asked raggedly. "Have I truly destroyed everything?"

"There was nothing to *destroy*," I lied. The words wavered and wobbled, but I met his eyes squarely as I said it. "We had a fling, Luka. It's over."

Jaw going tight, he crossed to me and caught my arms, moving too quickly for me to avoid him. "It was more than that. I know it. You know it. You felt it, too. I can see it in your eyes, just like I saw it every time we touched, every time you made me laugh and every time I made you laugh."

"We had fun together!" I fought the urge to wrench away. I wanted to run and hide and pretend he'd never come here. I wanted the day to start over again so I could make another decision—go with Emmett and have him as a buffer when Luka showed up.

But I didn't have any of that. I didn't even have time to pretend to compose myself, and I was desperate not to let him see how much he'd hurt me.

"We had sex, we had some laughs, and I gave you a ride to Montreal. *That is it*," I told him. "There's nothing else between us."

He let go of my upper left arm, and I thought, *Finally*. But then, before I could so much as move, he cupped the slight swell of my belly.

"There's this."

Tears sprang up. "Don't." The words were like glass coming from my throat.

"She's mine, isn't she?"

"Don't," I said again, shaking my head. "You don't get to *do* that. Not after what you said, what you did."

He brushed the material of my shirt away, then nudged the waistband of my skirt down just enough so he could place the flat of his hand completely against my skin. The contact was shocking. After so much time away from him, after finally convincing myself that I wouldn't see him again or touch him again and that was just *fine* with me, having his hand on my bare skin was almost too much.

I wanted to punch him.

I wanted to yell at him.

I wanted to scratch and bite and hurt...

I wanted to melt.

I wanted to breathe him in.

I wanted to sink against his chest and just *feel* him again.

Only my pride kept me from doing so. Generally, I was of a mind that pride could be a stupid motivator at best, but it had kept me going the past few weeks, and I wasn't going to kick it to the curb *now*.

"Stacia?"

"Why are you doing this to me?" My voice broke.

So much for pride.

Glaring up at him, tears burning my eyes, I half-yelled and half-sobbed. "*Why?* Don't you think you've humiliated me enough? Slammed me hard enough? I wasn't *asking* anything from you. But you kept pushing me to drink the damn champagne, and I couldn't and..." My voice hitched, then broke and what little strength remained in my legs drained away. Although having him touch me practically hurt, I couldn't help but be a little grateful because if he hadn't caught me, I would have collapsed at his feet. And wouldn't *that* just top off my humiliation nicely?

Still, as he swept me up into his arms, I shoved against him. I wanted to be away from him, from this, from here, all of it.

But he held me close and against my hair, he whispered, "I'm sorry, Stacia. I'm so sorry."

All the tears I'd been hiding from Emmett, pain from Luka's rejection, from my parents, the fear, everything poured out.

Vaguely, I was aware he'd sat down on one of the padded outdoor chairs, and I could hear the gusting wind and rain, but over all of that, I heard his soft, endless murmurs. My name, apologies, pleas.

Eventually, the tears passed, and I sat there, too drained and too embarrassed to move.

But then he started talking, and I went to bolt.

His arms tightened. "I don't have any right to ask," he said, the words spilling out. "But please listen."

He didn't loosen his hold either, talking at such a rapid-fire pace, I couldn't get a word in edgewise unless I interrupted—and yelled.

"I'm sorry. I hated myself from the second I made you leave, but I was confused and angry and...fuck me, I was jealous, Stacia, understand? I'd spent weeks seeing pictures of you and Emmett together online, and even though I had no right to be, I was eaten up inside with jealousy. *He* could have you, I thought. He wasn't chained to a country, culture, to a life that had been set before he'd even been born. That wasn't me, and part of me even hated him a little for that, because he could have you. Then you showed up at Aeric's party, and he wasn't there, and I thought maybe I'd misunderstood, maybe you were only friends. When you told me about the baby, I...fuck, Stacia. I just didn't think. Please, please, *please* understand, I'm *sorry*. I didn't think, and I was stupid and selfish, and part of me lashed out because I was hurting. But another part of me that I couldn't even acknowledge until just the other day...that part of me *wanted* that baby, wanted to believe she was mine, that *maybe* you could be mine except I am who I am and it would get in the way, and I was fucking pissed off that what I wanted more than anything couldn't happen."

Another one of those cracks in my heart split open, weeping bitterly.

He stroked a hand down my hair, and I could sense the weight of his gaze on me, all but hear his silent urging.

Look at me...

I didn't dare.

"Is it too late?" he whispered.

"What?" I said sourly. "Too late for what? For another couple of quick twists in the sheets? For—"

He swiveled me around until I was straddling him, moving so quickly it knocked the breath out of me.

"For *us*," he snarled. He shoved his hands into my hair, a half-wild look on his face. "*For us*. You want to know why I'm here, Stacia? That's it. I'm *here* for *us*. Is it too late for that?"

I gaped at him.

He continued to stare at me, his jaw set so tight, the bones stood out in stark relief.

"There can't *be* an us." I shoved against his chest, angry and hurt and furious...and hopeful. "You just raged on about it. Don't you remember? *You* are expected to *marry well*, as you so clearly pointed out."

His face softened. "I couldn't possibly marry better than you."

I was still gaping at him when he yanked me closer and slammed his mouth down on mine, his tongue thrusting in deep, stealing my breath. Still, I tried to breathe in, but all that did was draw him deeper. He slid an arm around my lower back and pulled me more firmly against him...and his kiss softened.

"Tell me I haven't ruined this," he pleaded against my lips. "Tell me I haven't ruined us."

I couldn't even speak.

He kissed me again, gently now, both hands cradling my face. A whimper escaped me.

"I love you, Stacia," he whispered as he pressed a soft kiss to the corner of my mouth. "I don't know when it started, or how, but I know I love you, and I can't bear to think of a life without you or this baby."

My head spun as he rose, then shifted, put me down crosswise on the long, expansive open-sided couch. My legs dangled off the side, and he went to his knees in front of me.

I tensed as he pushed my shirt up then bent over me, pressing his mouth to my belly.

"Tell me I can make this right." He kissed me, lips to my navel, then lower, along the stretchy waistband before drifting higher as if he had to touch every inch of my abdomen. "Tell me I can fix it."

Tears burned paths out from under my closed lids, and I didn't know what to say, didn't know how to answer.

I didn't even know how to *hope* right then.

"Stacia..."

He levered up over me, one hand by my head to support his weight as he stared at me, eyes haunted, hungry...and he looked every bit as scared as I felt.

"You hurt me," I whispered.

"I know. I'm sorry." He lowered himself, but still kept his weight away from me as he rubbed his lips against mine. "Please forgive me, baby. Please."

I reached up and curled my hands into the damp material of his shirt first.

I was such an idiot.

"I forgive you."

His eyes widened. "Really?"

I nodded jerkily, not even certain what was next, although part of me hoped it had to do with the heavy weight of his cock pressing into my thigh. *That* was easy. *That* I understood.

But Luka caught my hands and pulled me into a sitting position while he still knelt in front of me.

"Do you love me?" he asked with a vulnerability I'd never thought to see from him.

"I...yes." I didn't know how it changed anything, but...

He withdrew something from his pocket.

A velvet box.

My heart stuttered to a stop.

"What..." I licked my lips and tried again.

"I meant it when I said I couldn't marry any better than you. Because you make me want to *be* better, Stacia Harden. You chase away the parts of me that are rigid and hard and formal. You make me feel like a man, not some automaton, crafted from birth to be a leader. You make me feel like *me*. I know I still have work to do, and I know I've made mistakes. But I want you to be my wife. I want to be a father to our daughter. Will you have me?"

THIRTY-FOUR

LUKA

I half-expected her to grab the ring from the box and hurl it into the rain, although I hoped with every cell of my being that she wouldn't.

It had been in the family for a century and a half, and if it was lost, I'd have a hard time explaining it to my father.

But she didn't touch the ring. After a quick, darting glance, she didn't even look at it. Her eyes bounced off the sparkling, square-cut diamond, then she quickly covered her face with her hands and shuddered out a breath. "I can get over you," she said, her voice muffled.

My heart sank. "I know you can."

"I can get over you and raise this baby and be just *fine.*" The words came out with a bit of a snarl, full of a hot, angry pride that made me smile a bit even as they crushed me.

"I know that, too." I doubted I'd get over her, but I kept that quiet. I'd done enough damage, and this wasn't about me. It couldn't be.

She lowered her hands, staring at me with troubled, turbulent eyes.

"But none of that is what I want," she whispered, her voice catching.

I didn't dare breathe.

Her lashes swept down, and she dropped her head forward until it fell onto my shoulder. Afraid to touch her, but desperate to do so, I curved my hand around the back of her neck and cradled her close. She shuddered, and I squeezed my eyes closed, terrified she'd cry again but swearing mentally I'd take it. I hated her tears, but I was the reason for them.

"Damn you, Luka." A ragged breath slid from her as she turned her face into my neck. "Why couldn't you just stay away?"

"Is that what you want? Should I leave?"

"I should say *yes*." She looked at me finally, and her soft blue eyes glittered with tears. "I should say yes and run away from here, far enough away you'd never find me."

I'll always find you. But I didn't say it. I could find her, wherever she went.

But if she turned away from me, that was it. I didn't even deserve this chance.

"Are you telling me to leave, then?" I tightened my hand on the ring box.

"No." She closed her eyes and sank against me, her body practically melting against mine. "No, I'm not. Damn it, I love you too much."

Reflexively, I clutched her against me, arm tight around her waist. "Stacia?"

"Shut up," she mumbled, her face pressed to my neck.

I shut up.

Seconds ticked by. Slowly, her arms came around, and the tension that held her so tight drained away. "You were supposed to beg."

"Please." Turning my face into her hair, I said it again, "Please, Stacia. Forgive me. I was stupid and cruel and prideful and scared...a complete idiot, and I'm sorry. I'll crawl if you want me to. Just say the word."

She eased away and looked at me, her eyes somber. Instead of saying the word, or anything else, she leaned in and pressed her lips to mine. The kiss was meant to be quick and light, and even though need tore into me like a ravenous monster, I held it back.

She sucked in a breath as she tipped her head back, staring into my eyes.

I groaned as she kissed me again, this time not so hesitant or shy. I slid my hand to the cushion, gripping the edge of it before I lost control and gripped *her*. Her mouth slid over mine, her tongue darting out to tease at my lips, and I opened, starving for her but locked in place, afraid to do anything.

She knew something was wrong and pulled back, brow furrowing.

"Luka?"

"Does this mean you'll give us another chance?"

She cupped my face in her hands, a faint smile curving her lips. "I was lost pretty much from the moment you said you couldn't imagine living a life without the baby. I just kept trying to talk myself out of it."

"Are you done doing that now?"

She nodded.

"And you'll marry me?"

"I..." She hesitated and glanced down, looking at the ring. "Your parents, Luka. Your country. It's so complicated."

"It's not. Just answer...do you *want* to be married to me?"

She blinked and nodded. "Yes. I do."

"Then say *yes*...and trust me."

A tear slid down her cheek. "Yes."

Relief unlike anything I'd known crashed through me, and I caught her in my arms, hauling her against me. I kissed her roughly, need clawing, but before it took over, I pulled back and tugged the ring from the box. "Here. I want you wearing this. I want the world to know."

Her hand shook as I slid the ring into place.

"It fits," she murmured.

"Yes." Dropping the box, I pulled her against me and took her mouth again. "Let me have you, Stacia. For fuck's sake. Let me have you."

She didn't answer out loud.

But when I pushed her skirt up, she didn't resist, her thighs parting for me as I skimmed my fingers along her soft skin. The skirt was long and full, reaching the ground, and I was impatient, working the excess material upward until it was in a tangle around her waist. "Lay down for me," I said. "I want to taste you."

A whimper escaped her, and she sagged backward onto her elbows, watching me.

That just made the need more intense. Mouth watering, I stripped her panties away and shoved them into my pocket.

Holding her gaze, I lowered my head and pressed my mouth to her cunt.

She jolted, then cried out, head falling back so that the long, supple line of her throat was exposed.

I licked her, opening her from bottom to top, then flicked my tongue against her clit. It was already engorged, so swollen she jerked at that light touch. I wanted more —needed it.

Shifting slightly, I maneuvered so I could push two fingers into her pussy, curling them.

She moaned and fell back completely onto the padded cushions beneath her.

Devouring her, I worked her to the edge, but just as she was ready to come, I stopped.

She groaned, staring at me, but the noise was trapped in her throat part way as I stood and dragged my zipper down, watching her. "I don't have any condoms."

Stacia licked her lips. "Okay."

"I don't want one."

When I grinned, her breath shuddered out of her, and it made her whole body tremble. Under the tank she wore, her nipples were tight and hard, and they looked larger too. I couldn't wait to push her top up, see them, touch them, bite them.

"I want to feel you wet and naked around my cock. Can I?"

"You're awfully big on asking permission today." She lay a hand over her belly, watching me with a direct stare that somehow still held so much vulnerability. The ring on her left hand caught my attention, the sight of it filling me with possessive pride.

Mine. She said she'd be *mine.*

"Does that mean yes?"

She licked her lips, then nodded.

Holding her eyes, I freed myself and palmed my cock, stroking up, then down before going to my knees in front of her.

I caught her butt and pulled her to the edge of the chaise, positioning her just where I wanted her. Still watching her, I fit the head to her wet, slick folds and slowly filled her.

A sweat broke out before she'd taken all of me, and I shuddered like I had a fever. "Fuck, that's sweet," I whispered. As much as I wanted to rear back, then do it all over again, over and over, I didn't, because this was too good to rush. "You're so soft, so wet."

She whimpered, gripping the cushion beneath and rocking her hips upward.

I went to catch her butt to lift her up, but even as I did so, I felt the hard press of her belly and stopped. She convulsed around me, the milking contractions of her pussy more intense, the silken walls sweeter.

She reached for me and moved lower, but she continued to tug. "Come here."

"I don't..." I glanced at her belly. "I don't want to crush her."

A laugh snickered out of her. "She's barely two inches long. I think she'll be fine. Come here." She didn't wait for me to respond, rearing up and curling her hand around my neck and pulling me down.

Our mouths were already fused together before she hit the padded cushion, tongues rubbing in welcome. The soft, full weight of her breasts pillowed my chest, and she whimpered when I thrust deeper, harder. "More," she moaned.

"I won't hurt you?"

"You're hurting me *now*." She bit my lower lip and urged me on. "Please Luka..."

I couldn't deny her anything then. Gathering her up, I thrust harder, filling her and reveling in the warm, wet feel of her, of each moan, the bite of her nails through my shirt...in *her*. An ache spread through my chest, but this time, it didn't bother me.

It was because of her, and she was here, and it all made sense now.

She wailed under me, rocking against me madly, and I grabbed her hips, lifting her up.

She came, and I didn't even bother trying to hold back anymore.

"WE SHOULD GET up and get dressed."

I smoothed a hand down her back. "I'm quite content like this."

"Emmett and his parents will be back eventually. We can't *stay* like this."

"I don't see why—"

The sound of an engine broke over the rain.

Stacia jolted upright, staring at me in wide-eyed surprise for a few seconds before fumbling free of my arms. I wasn't entirely happy with the situation, but it was probably wise, so I didn't stop her.

She smoothed her top down, then her skirt, looking around frantically.

"What's wrong?"

"I don't know where my panties are!"

I hitched up my pants and fastened them then checked my pocket. I smiled at her. "They're in my pocket."

"Oh." She blew out a breath and pushed her hands through her hair.

I smoothed my shirt down, listening to the sound of the engine as it drew near.

Stacia grabbed my hand. "We need to get inside."

Amused at her embarrassed expression, I said, "Does it look more compromising for us to be standing out here?"

She glared at me.

I stepped up to her and smoothed my hands down her arms. "Relax. They won't be able to tell."

She blew a breath and pressed her palms to her flushed cheeks. "I hope not. Besides, it's too late now."

I turned just in time to see the big black truck Emmett loved to brag about as it pulled into its space behind the house. Emmett jumped out and all but ran up the stairs. He had an annoyed expression on his face as he looked from Stacia to me. His gaze lingered on her for a long moment, and something about the protectiveness on his face put every possessive instinct I had on red alert.

I shut those urges down and reminded myself that she was wearing my ring, that she had chosen me. I half expected him to confront me, but he focused all of his attention on her as she came to stand by my side.

"Stacia." He moved to stand in front of her, curving his hands over her shoulders. "Do you want him here? Because if you don't, I'll haul his uptight ass away."

"The two of you are friends," Stacia said.

"Yes, and we can be friends even if I haul his uptight ass away."

Stacia reached up and patted one of his hands, then kissed his cheek. "It's okay. I've got this handled, but you're a sweetie to be concerned."

I scowled at the exchange between them but managed to clear my expression before either of them could look at me.

Emmett finally switched his attention to me, but when he spoke, his words were clearly still directed at Stacia.

"Has he upset you at all?"

Stacia huffed out a sigh. "No, Emmett. He hasn't."

"I'm standing right here," I pointed out. "You could talk to me."

Emmet gave a slow blink, his expression settling into that lazy, disinterested one he used when he played slow for the people who expected little more from him. That usually lasted for all of thirty seconds before he jerked the rug out from under them—or he just verbally eviscerated them.

It didn't bode well for me. Wary, I watched him.

Emmett smiled. "Yes, you are standing right there. Never mind the fact Stacia has been here several weeks, and you could have shown up at any time to apologize...you're here now." He cocked his head. "Did you apologize?"

Stacia cut me off before I could respond.

She stepped between us, nudging us farther apart. "Yes, Emmett. As a matter of fact, he did."

She gave me a *be quiet* look that chafed, but I felt I really had no business doing anything but honoring her wish. Then she turned her expression toward Emmett.

To my disgust, she gave him a smile. "You've been a doll helping me out and taking care of me, but it's okay. And, to answer your question, he actually did come here to apologize." She shot me an impish grin before looking back at Emmett. "Actually, his exact words were *to beg*. It's all okay."

I half expected Emmett to offer another argument, and I reminded myself with gritted teeth that I would handle it calmly.

But a broad grin broke out over my best friend's face, and he smacked his hands together. "Well, all right then. I'm—"

He broke off mid-sentence and eyed Stacia with a bemused look of shock. Then he started to laugh, deep and loud before catching her around the waist, sweeping her up and spinning her in a circle. "I don't believe it."

Stacia shrieked and smacked at his shoulders. "Put me down, you goofball."

After another circle, he did. Catching her face in his hands, he smiled down at her. "Do you have something to tell us?"

She glanced over at me with flushed cheeks. "Maybe?"

Emmett's parents, Dale and Ellen, had finally joined us, although if they'd been lingering in the truck because of the rain or to give us privacy, I had no idea. Now they stood near the steps watching everything with a mix of amusement and curiosity.

I nodded at them, although I had a fair amount of apprehension. I had no idea how much Stacia had shared about what had happened between us, and I couldn't blame her if she had told them everything. Especially Ellen. She was the sort of person you just wanted to share things with.

As much as I had hurt Stacia, she probably had needed somebody to confide in. My own shame kept me from being able to squarely meet either of the elder Finchs's gaze.

Dale was the first to speak, his deep voice filling the air. "How about somebody fill us in?"

Emmett went to speak, but Stacia smacked her hand over his mouth. "I think that's *our* news to announce, Emmett."

She looked at me, and I moved to stand next to her, taking her hand.

"Do you want to?" she asked, her nerves apparent.

I took her hand and rubbed my thumb over the ring before nodding. "Stacia and I are going to be married."

Emmett looked at me and slung an arm around my neck as his parents broke into laughter. "I knew that idiot pride of yours couldn't be that massive." Then he smacked a loud kiss on my cheek before looking at his parents. "It's not too early in the day to crack open a bottle of wine since there's an engagement to celebrate, right?"

TWO HOURS LATER, Emmett walked with me to my rental. He had his hands in his pockets, his vivid red hair still mussed and tangled from his dash through the rain earlier. His face was relaxed and happy, which made me feel better.

331

The one thing I had worried about over all of this was that however things ended or settled with Stacia, I hadn't wanted to ruin my friendship with Emmett. Clearly, that wasn't the case.

Stacia still stood on the porch, talking with Ellen, and I leaned against the rental car to look at her.

"You know you'll have to bring her back here on a fairly regular basis. I think my mom is about ready to adopt her." Emmett's mouth twisted in a sneer. "It's not like she doesn't need it. That mother of hers is a piece of work. Her dad isn't much better. Have you met them?"

"No." Troubled, I glanced back at Stacia before meeting his eyes. "We're going to New York before flying back to Luxemburg."

"You wouldn't be missing much if you just skipped that stop altogether, but I imagine Stacia has things she wants to take back with her if she's ready to move over there entirely." He grimaced and added, "Besides, as much as I've told her to settle things with them, I don't see her disappearing from the country without at least letting them know where she's going. They'll try to work their way back inside her shield and hurt her again, especially that mom of hers. She's a leech if ever there was one."

"She won't deal with them alone. And if she doesn't want to deal with them at all?" I shrugged. "I can have Stuart tend to the matter. She does want to take care of things there, though. She's going to try and convince her driver to come with her. And she wants to see about getting her home packed up, plus there's paperwork since she'll be emigrating to Luxembourg. I'll have the embassy handle most of it, but there are matters to be dealt with aside from her parents."

I scratched my chin and decided I should get the subject out in the open so it didn't fester. "You know, I worried I would show up here and have to win her back from you."

Emmett looked at me with a blank expression. After several long moments, he started to laugh. Finally, hand pressed to his side, he muttered, "It's not good for me to laugh like that. My missing spleen hurts."

"It's *missing*," I pointed out, irritated. "What's so funny?"

"Shit, man." He grinned at me and punched me in the shoulder. "I know I'm good at keeping secrets, but I would have thought *you* would have figured it out by now."

"What?" Confused, I just stared at him. "What secrets?"

Emmett, still grinning, just shook his head. "Stacia figured it out pretty fast. I mean, you've known me how many years now?"

Staring at him blankly, I said, "I have no idea what you're talking about."

"Clearly not." He punched me again. "Luka, I'm gay."

I gaped at him.

He almost bent over laughing. "That expression on your face. Man, I'm gonna remember that for a long time."

"You...*you're* serious?"

"Serious as I know how to be." The amusement on his face faded, although a faint smile remained. He shrugged and glanced toward the porch where his mother and Stacia still talked. "I never set out to keep it a secret like this. My parents know, and they're good with it, but this area? Hell, it's touch and go, and that's putting it mildly. There's some shit I'd put up with in the circuit, yeah, but I'm more worried about the crap my parents might have to put up with."

"They wouldn't care, Emmett."

"*I* care," he said in a flat voice. "A few other friends have figured it out. I'm not kidding. I'm surprised you haven't. But there are people here who'd give my parents grief over it. Between that and the headache I'd get from the circuit...?"

"You shouldn't have to hide who you are."

"I'm not hiding. I'm just not putting myself out there for the world to judge me. I'll tell people when *I* decide to." He glanced back at the porch, then at me. "And I don't want my parents knowing how much they factor into the equation."

"Fuck." I blew out a breath. "It's not like I'm going to tell them."

A heavy silence fell, and I tried to wrap my head around what he'd just confided.

After a few seconds, he crossed his arms over his chest. "Did I break your brain, Duke?"

I scowled. "No." Mentally, I was more honest with myself. *Yes*, but not for the reasons he might think. I didn't give a damn who he was attracted to—although I was glad it wasn't Stacia. I just didn't like how he felt he had to hide it. Yet a part of me understood his reasoning, at least as best I could with the life experience I had. Emmett loved his parents more than anything, and I knew he would do anything to protect them.

At the same time, I hurt for him.

"Are you happy?" I asked.

The scowl on his face softened, replaced by a smile.

"Yeah. Yeah, I'm happy. I've got the life I've always

wanted, and I can give my parents everything they sacrificed so I could have this life, and then some. I've got great friends, I drive kick-ass cars...and when I want to hook up..." He winked. "Well, I'm never alone unless I want to be. Look, Luka, I'm not doing this because I'm forced to. It's my choice. And when the time's right, I'll let people know. But again, that's going to be my choice."

Not knowing what else to say, I hugged him. "I guess that's all that matters then. If you're happy with your life, that's what matters to me most."

He hugged me back, and as I pulled away, I said, "And thank you."

"Why?" Emmett cocked a brow.

Stacia moved to join us at just that moment, and I glanced at her, too much emotion spilling free inside in that moment. It took another moment for me to steady myself, then I looked back at Emmett.

"For being willing to kick my ass if need be."

"Oh, that?" He rolled his eyes. "Don't mention it."

THIRTY-FIVE

STACIA

"I can't believe I let you talk me into this."

Luka collapsed face down on the plush mattress, groaning. I sat in a chair, grinning at him and telling myself I was *not* smirking over his misery. I was sore, too. I hadn't ridden a horse in years. But Luka had bragged, or at least *confidently stated his experience* with horses, and the tour guide had taken him at his word.

My horse had been placid and calm, while Luka's seemed to come straight out of an old country-western, one of those horses called Diablo or Hellfire or something. It spent the first part of the trip trying to throw my husband, and the rest of it giving Luka the roughest ride imaginable because he hadn't succeeded in the throwing.

"Tell me there are no more horses or camels or..." He suddenly jerked up his head and glared at me. "You said something about elephants. Stacia, I'm *not* riding an elephant."

"That's good to know because I wasn't planning on it

either. No, we're just going on a photo safari, and we'll be some distance away. They try to respect the animals' natural habitats with this company." I sipped the glass of wine, savoring the treat while I could. After tomorrow night, I'd be back to no alcohol since I'd be back home feeding the baby. For now, I was pumping and dumping every few hours so my milk production didn't dry up.

Luka and I had been married for six months, but this was the first trip we'd actually been able to take for ourselves, just the two of us. We'd had a private ceremony not long after arriving in Luxembourg but had elected to hold a more public one after the baby was born.

That had been just days ago, and we were enjoying a quick honeymoon in Africa. Luka had just gaped at me when I told him I wanted to do one of the luxury safaris I'd read about, complete with tents.

He'd tried to talk me out of it, but the deal had been if we went on a honeymoon without Ella Rose, then *I* got to pick where we went and what we did. And it could only be for five days. She was close to three months old, and although the doctor had told me she'd be fine with Willa and the nanny we'd hired, I still felt odd leaving her, even for just a few days.

We were on the third day of our trip. I'd always wanted to see Africa, especially Kenya, but it wasn't a trip I'd wanted to take alone. Something this memorable needed to be shared —and who better to share it with than my husband?

Even as I thought that, he flopped onto his back and threw an arm over his eyes. "The point of a honeymoon is for me to fuck my wife senseless, and you bring me on this torture trip where I'm so sore half the time, I can't even *think* about sex."

"Really?" I finished my wine and rose from the chair, walking over to him.

He must have heard something in my voice because he lowered his arm and cracked one eye, then the other, open.

"You can't even *think* about sex?" I stood in front of him, slowing unbuttoning the nightshirt I'd pulled on after my shower. This luxury expedition came with *everything*.

"Well." He let his gaze slide lower as I finished with the buttons. "Maybe I can think. If you do all the work, I might even be able to do more than think."

"I guess I can work with that." I shrugged out of the shirt and let it fall to the floor. Bracing one knee on the edge of the bed, I unzipped the khaki-colored, lightweight pants he'd tugged on after his shower, then worked them down and off. I bent to kiss the head of his cock, but before he caught hold of my head, I pulled back, moving to straddle him. "You're probably too tired for the whole nine yards, Your Highness."

"I'm actually feeling quite a bit better, My Duchess."

"Hmm...well, I'm the one in control tonight." I slid back and forth over him, enjoying the thick heat.

He shifted beneath me, going to angle his hips, but when he would have gone to push inside, I pulled away. "No, no, no...I'm doing the work, remember?"

"Stacia..." He gave me a pained look.

"Shhh..." I pressed a finger to his lips, then reached down and held his cock, watching him as I slowly sank down on him. "There..." My breath caught as he jerked inside me. "Isn't that nice?"

He gripped my thighs. "It'll be better when you move, darling."

"Be patient...all things in good time." I swayed forward and braced my hands by his head, watching him with a grin. "Now...you just lie there and think of Luxembourg while I take care of all this."

A shout of laughter escaped him as his hands slid to my ass. "Oh, Duchess...that's the last thing I'm thinking of."

I started to move, shuddering at the feel of him, the game falling by the wayside all ready.

"Don't you want to know, Stacia?"

His voice teased a response from me, and I focused on him, moving faster, curling my hands into the sheets.

"Know what?" I whispered.

He moved then, flipped us over with a speed and dexterity that made his claims about being *too sore* seem like little more than fluff. He filled me, deep and hard and fast, "What I think of. Do you want to know what I think of, Duchess mine?"

"What?"

He kissed me, soft and slow, a contrast to the rough possession of my body.

"You, Stacia...always you. I love you."

"And I love you." Curling my arms around his neck, I gave in to the hunger, the need...and the love.

Always the love.

THE END

ALSO BY M. S. PARKER

The Perfect Guy (Filthy Rich Royals)

His Obsession

His Control

His Hunger

His Secret

Sex Coach

Big O's (Sex Coach 2)

Pleasure Island (Sex Coach 3)

Rescued by the Woodsman

The Billionaire's Muse

Bound

One Night Only

Damage Control

Take Me, Sir

Make Me Yours

The Billionaire's Sub

The Billionaire's Mistress

Con Man Box Set

HERO Box Set

A Legal Affair Box Set

The Client

Indecent Encounter

Dom X Box Set

Unlawful Attraction Box Set

Chasing Perfection Box Set

Blindfold Box Set

Club Prive Box Set

The Pleasure Series Box Set

Exotic Desires Box Set

Casual Encounter Box Set

Sinful Desires Box Set

Twisted Affair Box Set

Serving HIM Box Set

Pure Lust Box Set

ABOUT THE AUTHOR

M. S. Parker is a USA Today Bestselling author and the author of over fifty spicy romance series and novels.

Living part-time in Las Vegas, part-time on Maui, she enjoys sitting by the pool with her laptop writing her next spicy romance.

Growing up all she wanted to be was a dancer, actor and author. So far only the latter has come true but M. S. Parker hasn't retired her dancing shoes just yet. She is still waiting for the call to appear on Dancing With The Stars.

When M. S. isn't writing, she can usually be found reading— oops, scratch that! She is always writing.

For more information:
www.msparker.com
msparkerbooks@gmail.com

Made in the USA
Middletown, DE
05 November 2019